OUT ON A LIMB (VIGILANTE JUSTICE SERIES)

Erin Hart Book One

V F STREETS

Page Turner Books

For my kids.
Even though I won't let you read my books yet, you are always
super excited when I publish.

———————————

Chapter 1

———————————

YELLOW LIGHTS COATED the upmarket strip in a garish luster that rivaled the daylight. Not all city streets matched this one in fluorescent pageantry. Only those with lavish jewelry stores and high-end fashion boutiques warranted the extra security against would-be thieves at this hour of the early morning, and it was the only time such glamorous wares would dare be warmed by its vulgar glow.

For the most part, it worked.

But there was a lone woman who cut a small figure, striding down the sidewalk. Her fashionable flats and designer jacket spoke to her kinship with daytime customers of the nearby stores. Her brother always taught her to be prepared for everything, so she made sure she fit in with her surroundings, even after 2 a.m., when most people on the street were drunken passengers of passing cabs.

Slowing her pace as another taxi went by, she

approached a gap only a few feet wide between two buildings. When the street emptied briefly, she slipped into the small space, snugging into the shadows where she felt most at ease.

Resting her head against the cool wall, she closed her eyes and took in a slow, deep breath, unsure if she was imagining the smell of Lake Michigan that was only a few blocks away, or if it could carry this far into the city, penetrating through the tang of asphalt and concrete.

Erin had spent her whole life in Chicago, and there was nothing she loved more than quiet city streets and warm autumn nights. Tonight, she got them both.

Her body vibrated to the rumble of the nearby El as she leaned forward to take one last look up and down the road, and she watched as a stray plastic bag tumble-weeded down the street. If it didn't make its way to a less desirable area in the city, it would end up in the garbage. Refuse didn't last long in this part of town.

The closest traffic light clicked through its cycle as the face of a building to Erin's left lit up with headlights. She ducked back into her refuge and pulled a hood out of the back of her jacket, slipping it over her head to conceal her light-pink hair tied up in a loose ponytail.

She kept her face pointed to the ground until the car passed, then reached up a slender hand and ran it along the smooth marble of the wall in front of her. She felt no flaws indicating a change in the block until she stretched her fingers well above her head.

A smile edged up her face.

She appreciated craftsmanship, and Lindom & Co.

was a superior building with its black-and-white marble facade. But what she approved of more than the quality of the construction was its stature. It was many stories shorter than the surrounding establishments, making it an easy target.

She slipped off her flats and tucked them into her pocket. Climbing shoes would have worked for tonight's job, but when it was warm enough, she preferred the feel of cold stone on her skin.

Cupping her hands, she spit into her palms and rubbed them together, then ran a clammy hand across the soles of her feet.

After wiping her hands clean, she pulled on a pair of gloves and pressed them on the marble in front of her before anchoring one foot up on the wall behind her. Then, she lifted herself off the ground and secured her other foot below her hands.

It was a slow climb this way, but Lindom didn't offer another option. With only four stories, it wouldn't take long.

As she climbed, she kept her attention on the placement of each limb, but when she neared the top, her focus shifted to the lip of the roof, just feet above her head.

Lifting her back foot for its next placement, she didn't see the thin pipe that was camouflaged against the wall. Her foot failed to grip properly and slipped, dropping her backward. A short, sharp breath was the only indication that she was about to plummet to the concrete slab below.

Using her backward momentum, she pushed one arm across the chasm, stopping her fall, while thrusting her foot back in place. She allowed herself a moment to firm up her resolve before she finished the ascent and pulled herself onto the ledge.

Now seated safely on cement with her legs dangling over the side, she breathed her body into stillness, allowing the adrenaline time to run its course. She'd need to take a few minutes to recover and clear her head. She couldn't afford to take the same chances she used to, not with her brother in prison. Just the thought of getting caught had her checking over her shoulder.

She took another deep breath, pushing the image of her brother's arrest out of her mind. Now wasn't the time to reflect on past mistakes.

A BMW went by on the street below as she prodded the sore ligaments in her shoulder and elbow. She didn't slip often, but past injuries flared up quickly. She'd need to give her arm time to recover after tonight.

Luckily, the rest of the evening's tasks were easy ones. Lindom & Co. wasn't new to her, something else she learned from her brother. He taught her that if you balanced it right, you could enjoy the luxury of hitting the same place more than once. By settling for a smaller haul that didn't warrant too much attention, you gained valuable experience.

Now, having let Lindom settle back into its normal routine after hitting it nearly a year ago, she knew exactly what to do and how to do it, not to mention the rope hiding in the ceiling where she had left it last time. It was a risk that paid off tonight.

She touched a hand to her throat as she pictured the necklace she had chosen when she visited the store earlier in the week. It was priced low enough to keep it out of the vault at night — vaults were her brother's domain — but high enough that she could take only that one item, and she'd have enough. She already expected the news reports of the theft, if there were any, would presume it was an inside job. It might be vain, but she enjoyed being an enigma. No one ever guessed her strategy for breaking in. It would seem impossible to most.

She took one more slow breath then rolled her head and stretched before swinging her legs onto the roof. After slipping her shoes back on, she stood and tugged a small metal box out of her pocket. Running her fingers over its smooth edges, she puzzled over it as she walked to the far side of the roof. She'd used it many times before but never got over how stunning it was in its simplicity. It gave nothing away.

When she reached the electrical lines, she attached the small box to the same place she had a year ago, then checked the switch in her pocket. It would cut the power long enough for her to get the job done. She would have between ten and fifteen minutes before the backup generator kicked in and the security came back online. If they had the same generator as last time, it would be closer to fifteen.

Once the technology was in place, she moved to the air duct, shoving her hand in her pocket as she went and fingering the other device that she now carried on most jobs. It was a marble-sized ball. The flashy older brother to the cherry bomb. She'd only ever used it in practice, and she carried it mainly because it made her feel safer. But having the capability of causing a mini explosion might be useful one day.

She pulled her hand from her pocket when she reached the air duct that would bring her back down to the ground floor showroom. Last time she was here, she hadn't bothered to screw the metal cover back on so only had to guide it off, sending a scraping echo down through the tunnel.

There weren't many people who could fit through the opening. At five-foot-six, she wasn't overly short, but her delicate, waif-like frame bent whatever way she needed it to. It's what got her involved with her brother's heists in the first place. He was an expert safe cracker who excelled at puzzling things out and finding solutions. Ten years ago, when she was fourteen, she became one of his solutions. An opportunity to help the big brother she idolized was one she couldn't pass up.

After squeezing through the opening, she manipulated herself through the first several feet. That was the easy part. But a tapered section at the second floor had to be carefully maneuvered. She wrenched her shoulders closer to her body, sending a searing pain down her injured arm, but she ignored it as she continued to wriggle her way through the maze she had memorized, until she reached the entry point. The extra space there made prepping and dropping the thick rope from the ceiling a quick task. After moving the ceiling tile out of the way, she prepared the rope, then dusted herself off as best she could, making sure the bottoms of her shoes were clean. Then she hooked the rope behind her knee and pressed the button to cut the power before falling into the room with only the wisp of a sound.

Chapter 2

NICK FOLDED his arms across his chest. The aban-
doned warehouse was cold and damp despite the unusu-
ally warm breeze in the night outside. He observed the
scrape of a man tied to the rusty metal chair and felt a
little sorry for the guy, but Nick had a job to do.

"Come on, Bobby, you're going to have to give me
something."

"I swear — "

Nick didn't let him finish. His fist shot out with a
speed that any boxer would relish, but he reserved some
strength. He didn't want to break anything yet.

Bobby spit blood on the ground and whimpered.
"Please, Nick. Don't make me say. You know what
they'll do to me. I have to stay neutral. That's my job.
You can't expect me to say anything about anybody."

"If you wanted to stay neutral, you should have
stayed out of it."

"I did."

"You arranged the meeting."

"How'd you know that?"

Nick sighed and pulled his cap down lower over his face, then crossed his arms again. He let Bobby stew for a minute as he walked a slow path around the back of the chair. Bobby tried to twist and keep him in sight, but Nick stopped out of view. "You put me in a really hard position," Nick said, more annoyed than angry.

Bobby twisted one way "Nick, I" — then the other — "I'm sorry."

"Do you understand what will happen if I let you live but get nothing from you?" He circled his way back in front of the chair.

"Hammer," Bobby almost shouted. "I can give you Hammer."

"Hammer did it?"

"Nonono, I can give you information about him. A job he's doing next week."

Nick closed his eyes and dipped his head. "Bobby — "

"I got a kid, Nick. Did I tell you that?"

Nick pressed a hand to his face and let it drop until his fingers were on his chin. "You have a girl to go with this kid?"

"Yeah, yeah, Krista. She's real pretty and nice. You've never met a nicer girl than Krista."

Nick sucked in air through his teeth. "Why'd you go and do a thing like that, Bobby, eh? A girl and a kid?" He dropped his hands onto his hips and looked up at the ceiling, pushing his frustration out with a hard breath. "All right." Nick paused, shook his head, and squatted down in front of Bobby so he could look him in the eyes. "You give me the name I need — "

"No, I — "

"Eh." Nick put a hand up to stop Bobby interrupting. "And I'll make sure no one knows it was you who gave it to me. I'll tell my boss that you gave me a lead that led to me finding out who did it. And that way my boss is happy, and you don't end up dead. But I need to know who the idiot was who shot Monkey. Kennedy loves him like a son, and he will not let up until he knows. If I don't bring him a name, there's is no telling what he'll do." Nick shrugged. "Otherwise I gotta kill ya."

Nick was sure that Monkey meant little to Kennedy, who wasn't the type to be sentimental. Kennedy liked to pretend that he cared. Monkey's injury, although somewhat minor, gave Kennedy an excuse to go after his competitors with abandon, citing fatherly love as his motivation. But Monkey had nothing to offer the man besides adoration, and Nick didn't think there was much of that going on. He was just a thirteen-year-old kid, all arms and legs, who hung around a lot because he was nearly homeless, with a mom who was addicted to drugs. Nick didn't even know his real name, and he assumed Kennedy didn't either since Kennedy had a thing for proper names but never called Monkey anything else.

Bobby licked his bloody lip. "You swear? You swear no one will know it was me?"

"On my mother's grave."

"Your mom's dead? I — I'm sorry."

Nick dropped his arms to his side and stepped back, huffing. The sincere concern on Bobby's bloody face as he strained forward against his restraints almost made Nick laugh. "God, Bobby, you're an idiot. Of course my mom's not dead. Just give me the goddamn name."

"Okay, okay." Bobby cleared his throat. "It was Brayson."

Nick pursed his lips. "That's what I thought. All right, Bobby. Thanks for the info. Now, which finger will it be?"

"What?"

"Which finger? I'm gonna have to tell my boss you gave me something, otherwise he'll expect you to be dead. But you didn't give me a name, remember? So he's going to want extra payment from you."

Bobby paled. "But you said — "

"Yeah, that I wouldn't say where I got the name and I wouldn't kill ya, but if I don't get a finger, then Kennedy will just send someone else. Someone like Stanley."

"No, not Stanley." Bobby choked on the words. "Don't let Stanley near me."

"Oh, you don't have to worry about him sending Stanley to you. No, he'll send him to that nice girl and kid of yours."

Bobby started crying. "My little finger." He sucked in a rattly breath. "Take my little finger. Left hand." He finished with a sob.

Nick put a hand on Bobby's shoulder. "You're right-handed. Taking your left-hand pinky won't be good enough, I'm afraid."

"Oh god, oh god." Bobby moaned. His head lolled back and forth.

How a guy like this had survived so long in this business was impossible to guess.

Bobby's body was shaking now. He was going into shock and losing a finger wouldn't help.

Nick cursed under his breath. He wasn't real keen on taking the finger either, so decided to get it over with.

Bobby's scream rang through the empty warehouse, echoing off the filthy walls. Nick slipped the severed index finger into a plastic bag in his pocket. He ran his tongue over his teeth. It had taken him almost a year to earn enough trust from Kennedy to be sent on a job like this. It meant he was moving up in standing, and it was the only way to rise in the ranks. But his sights were set on a loftier prize than being Kennedy's muscle.

The only positive outcome from tonight was that Nick was the one who got to decide to let Bobby live. None of the other guys would have. Bobby might not realize it, but he got lucky tonight.

Nick ripped a piece of Bobby's shirt off him and wrapped it around the bleeding stump. "Hold that tight. Someone will be by soon to get you help." He turned to go but then stopped. "A word of advice. Don't mention the girl and the kid to anyone ever again. Or better yet, get rid of them. They'll be better off without you."

Bobby's whimpering was the last thing Nick heard as he walked outside and made a quick call to a neutral party. Someone would be by soon to cut Bobby loose.

ERIN DANGLED for a moment in the air, scanning the room before dropping to the ground. It was a back showroom of some sort, with thick carpet and plush couches. But she didn't have time to waste on enjoying these luxuries. Instead she relished in the cushiony feel under her feet as she eased down the hall and onto the more sensible but chic tiled floor of the showroom, where she ducked behind a cabinet to keep out of sight from anyone who might pass outside.

The gems twinkled in the greasy light that seeped through the windows from the street as Erin ran a gloved hand along the glass, heading for her quarry.

She paused at a necklace with a slim gold chain and square diamond she guessed to be about three carats. If she could pick anything out of the store for herself, it would be that one, but that wasn't why she was there. The necklace she was after wasn't for her and was worth a lot more money.

Advancing from that cabinet, she slunk around to

the next where she found what she was looking for: a mixed diamond cluster necklace with yellows and oranges. Erin's face twisted in revulsion. It was one of the ugliest necklaces she'd come across, but with just over seven carats of good quality diamonds, she'd get close to twenty thousand dollars for it. Less than what it was worth, but you always had to take a cut when you were selling on the black market.

She pulled back her sleeve to check the time as she got into position at the sliding glass panel. She was cutting it close, but not too close.

With the lock picks in hand, she set to work. Her brother would have had the lock open faster than she could blink, but he'd taught her well, and she had been practicing.

When she felt the lock give, she sighed in satisfaction, but then had to brace herself. The next part always made her jittery. She knew the power was out, but her heart still hitched as she slid the panel across. She'd been jumpy since her brother went to prison. She couldn't afford to have that happen to her. There was too much at stake.

With the cabinet open, she breathed again and reached in and pulled out the gaudy necklace, clipping it around her neck.

"Freeze." A man's voice came from behind her. "I'm a security guard for Lindom, and I need you to put your hands in the air and stand up slowly."

She turned enough to see the guard with his arms out straight, two hands clasping a gun that was pointed at her. She could make out the stitching for the letter S on a fold on the front of his jacket. She pinched her lips together and angled her head away so her face remained covered by the hood. They'd never had a security guard before. She should have checked. *Dammit.*

"I said, put your hands in the air and stand up slowly."

The glass doors of the shop were in front of her, on the other side of the counter. She reached into her pocket with the arm the guard couldn't see and lifted the other in the air.

She felt the marble shape between her fingers. It slipped smoothly from her pocket, and as she lifted her hand, she tossed it at the front door. It made contact and flashed before the glass exploded. The guard lifted his arms to protect his face from the blast and Erin jumped up, flipped over the counter, and raced out the door.

Nick had his cap pulled low over his eyes as he walked along the city streets, moving from the less desirable part of town and into a higher-end business section. He liked walking the streets at night, even in the more dangerous areas. He was confident in his ability to defend himself. The feel of that confidence was like a warm coat, one that he'd worn for many years. It was in those moments that he could forget about what was out of his control and focus on what he could do.

When he turned the corner, a man in a gray wide-brimmed hat and a trench coat was leaning against a streetlight, smoking. Nick felt as though he had stepped into an old private detective movie.

The tip of the man's cigarette was glowing, but as Nick approached, the man dropped it on the ground and twisted a foot on top of it, then flicked his hand in a lazy greeting. "You get a name?"

"Hello to you too, Murphy. You're looking very *noir* this evening."

"If a long-legged blonde bombshell wants my help, I'm open for business. But did you get a name?" At the repeat of the question, Murphy's face folded up like a bassett hound's.

Nick had known him less than a year and always got the feeling the sixty-something-year-old didn't give a damn about much and was always irritated that he had a job to do.

Nick put his hands in his jacket pockets, felt the bag with the finger, and switched to his jeans pockets. "I did get a name. It's who we thought."

"When are you going to tell Kennedy?"

Nick looked at his watch. It was almost three in the morning. "I'll leave it for today."

"All of today?"

"I've got to wait for at least twenty-four hours."

"Why's that?"

"Make it look like Bobby only gave me a lead instead of a name. I need today to make it look like I'm following that lead."

Murphy grunted, then pulled out another cigarette. "Not worried that you're making things complicated just to save some junkie?"

"Maybe, but Kennedy doesn't need a name right this second. He's left it with me to sort out. Monkey'll be in the hospital for a couple more days. I've got it under control."

Murphy lit his cigarette and took a long drag. "You do much damage to Bobby?"

Nick's hand, closest to the finger, flinched. "You really want an answer to that question?"

"Okay then, how about this one? Will Kennedy be satisfied?" He sucked in another lungful of nicotine.

"I told you, I've got it under control."

Murphy nodded and blew out, blinking through the smoke, then hitched his thumb down the road. "You parked in the usual place?"

"It's twenty questions with you tonight."

"I'm in a hurry tonight," he said, picking something off his tongue.

"Looks like it. Well, I'm certainly not going to park it in the type of place I just came from. Besides, I like the fresh air."

Murphy exhaled more smoke, tipped his hat, and pushed off the light post. "Give me a call if you need me."

Murphy gave Nick a lazy pat on the back as he passed to walk in the direction Nick had just come from.

Nick watched him until he went around the corner. He was having trouble working Murphy out. He was an old dog coming close to retirement. Nick couldn't tell if he was bored, disinterested, or both.

He set off again for his car, a pristine black 1969 Yenko Camaro. He wouldn't normally go for something so flashy, but he didn't have a choice. It was an unexpected gift and the only thing Nick had of his dead brother. He would only park it in a part of the city where he knew it would be safe.

Erin risked a look behind her as she bolted down the sidewalk. She was a fast sprinter, but her short legs didn't take her as far as she would like. The security guard was no slouch, and while she had a bit of distance on him, it wasn't enough that she could sustain a lead for long. And she would need more space if she expected to scale a building without him seeing. She had to lose him fast.

The road she was on was too wide. She quickly scanned the buildings ahead and couldn't see the indicators of an alley, so when she reached a smaller side street, she grabbed the side of the building to slingshot herself into it and didn't discern fast enough that there was a man in her path.

Nick heard the running steps coming from around the corner and instinctively braced himself when a woman swung around and crashed into him. He was pushed back a few steps, but she fell to the ground, knocking her hood off to expose pink hair and a pretty face.

"Are you okay? Are you hurt?" He reached down to help her up but couldn't quite judge the look on her face.

She looked pissed, but then she jumped up and grabbed onto him, her blue eyes wide with fear. "A guy is chasing me. He tried to jump me." She was frantic.

Nick stood up a little straighter and pulled his gun from the holster at his back. "It's okay." He could hear the guy coming now. "Just stay behind me. I'll make sure you're safe."

She spun around to his back and he could feel her hand grabbing hold of his jacket as he stepped back so he had room when the guy turned the corner.

When the security guard rounded the corner into Nick's path, it took him only a moment to register the gun. He stopped dead and quickly scooted backward, throwing his hands in the air. "Don't shoot. Just take it." His eyes snapped behind Nick, then back at the gun.

Nick lowered his gun a fraction. "What?" He reached a hand behind him to reassure the woman but felt only air.

The guard shook his head. "They don't pay me enough to take a bullet." Then he sucked in a sharp breath and averted his eyes to the ground. "I haven't seen your face, I swear."

Nick snorted. "Are you kidding me?" He pivoted to check with the mystery woman, but she was gone. He turned back and observed the security emblem on the guard's jacket. He let the gun drop a little more. "Who are you?"

"I — I'm just the security guard."

"Security guard from where?"

The guard risked a quick, confused look up at Nick. "Lindom & Co."

"The jewelry store?"

The guard nodded.

"Why were you after the woman?" He had his gun completely lowered now, and his voice was thick with disdain. He didn't know which was more irritating, that she lied to him or that he believed her.

"Uh, you don't know?" Nick raised his gun again. "Okay, okay, she stole some jewelry. Not to mention destroying property."

Nick nodded when he heard the sirens. "Sounds like the cops are on their way."

"So wait, you're not going to shoot me?"

"She just ran into me on the street, just then. Said you were after her. I thought I was protecting her."

"Hang on." The guard straightened as a bit of confidence returned. "If you weren't assisting in her theft, I'll need you to come give a statement to the police."

"I'm not giving a statement to the police. I've got somewhere I need to be."

"But you have to. It's your fault she got away."

"Okay, I'll make sure to tell the police that you told me I could take the jewelry."

"But you were threatening me with a gun."

Nick raised his gun again to make his point. "You didn't stop to wonder why I'm packing heat in the first place?"

"This is America." Nick stepped forward aggressively. "Okay, fine, whatever." The guard turned and slipped back around the corner. "I don't get paid enough for this shit," he said under his breath as he turned the corner.

Nick spun around and hurried back the way he came, looking down an alley and around a corner, but knew she'd be long gone by now.

"Damn." He returned the gun to its holster and headed for his car, avoiding the commotion at Lindom. He should know better than to be suckered by a pretty face.

The sky held the first hint of daylight when Erin arrived home. She pulled open the gate and winced at the squeak. She kept forgetting to oil the hinges.

The grass that needed to be mowed tickled her ankle as she walked up the path. Its overgrown state matched the ivy that plagued the front of the house, nearly covering the brick.

At the door, she dug around in her bag for the key and slipped it into the lock but paused for a moment before unlocking the door. She had messed up. Her hand trembled slightly as it turned the key. That guy she ran into turned out to be a godsend. Once he was on her side, it had been easy to slip into the nearby alley and get onto the roof. She could have gotten away across the rooftops, but she waited. She wanted to see how things transpired between the guy and the guard. It was amusing to say the least, but she could tell the guy wasn't happy about her ruse. She had watched him look for her and only came down once he was definitely gone.

Inside, she flicked on the light and attempted to reassure herself that it would all be okay. It had to be.

She pulled off the tacky necklace and rubbed at her neck where her skin had been irritated by her temporary accessory. She propped it up in her hand and shook her head. "Still ugly." She put it in a locked drawer in the hall, then dragged herself into the living room over to her favorite old beat-up couch. Kicking her legs up, she dropped onto it and stared up at the yellow globe light, full of bugs. She should clean that. She hated cleaning.

Grabbing her phone, she let it drop onto her chest before blowing out a slow breath up toward the ceiling. She lifted the phone again, but then dropped it and chewed a nail before finally picking it up and sending off a text:

Can you come by in the morning?

Then she let the phone slide to the floor before she propped her arm across her eyes and fell asleep.

Chapter 4

ERIN JUMPED awake and winced at the searing daylight shining through the window directly onto her face.

The hollow thunk of someone knocking at the door sounded. Probably what woke her.

She swiped strands of hair from her forehead and grunted as she pushed off the couch. Staggering toward the window, she flicked the curtain aside. The man at the door wore an expensive suit and ran his hand through his dark hair before lifting his other hand to knock again. She groaned and shuffled to the door, briefly resting her forehead on the frame before unlocking it and pulling it open.

"Come in," she said without looking at him and headed back to the living room.

"You look like hell," he said as he entered, but his heavy green eyes examined her appreciatively.

Erin dropped onto the couch and threw her head

back to settle the pounding. "Always the gentleman, eh, Ryan?"

"I happen to think very highly of hell."

Ryan and her brother were in the same class in high school, and they quickly discovered their mutual love for things outside the law. For Peter, it had stemmed partly from wanting things he couldn't afford and being able to use his skills to get what he wanted. For Ryan, it was different. He came from a rich family. She could never quite figure out what stealing did for him besides maybe give him a rush. But whatever his reasons, he and Peter had worked together on most jobs. Ryan had connections that meant he could supply technology that aided in their robberies. Technology that came in handy for her now that she was working on her own.

Ryan took off his coat and dropped it on the back of a rocking chair her mom used to sit in to knit, then he settled into an old La-Z-Boy and pinched closed a hole in the arm that was oozing fluff. "When you texted, 'come in the morning,' did you really mean afternoon?"

"No," she groaned and lifted her head to look at him.

He was the epitome of tall, dark, and handsome with his wavy hair and emerald eyes. The problem was, he knew it. He was a playboy in the full sense of the word.

When she was fourteen and had joined her brother for her first job, she acquired an unfortunate crush on him. Lucky for her, she was too much of a kid at the time for him to notice her. Eventually, she recognized that he wasn't her type.

"I messed up," she finally said.

"This wouldn't have anything to do with Lindom & Co., would it?"

Her body jerked. "How'd you know that?"

"I was up early enough to catch the morning news."

"Damn. It wasn't supposed to make the news."

"Where'd you get a gun?"

"What gun?" she mumbled, pressing a finger against her throbbing temple.

"The security guard said you threatened him with a gun."

"You know I don't carry a gun." She perked up. "I did, however, use one of those bomb things you gave me, to escape. It was pretty awesome, actually."

"You know, I think you might be a touch bipolar."

"What's that supposed to mean?"

"Never mind. They did mention there was damage."

She dropped her head back onto the couch. "At least I got away. Oh, shit!" She sat up again. "The gun. Did the news mention anyone besides the guard? Any other witnesses?"

"No. The guard said you fled the scene, and when he chased you around the corner, you threatened him with a gun. You didn't let him see your face, did you?"

Erin moaned as her head collapsed into her hand.

"Erin, you know that's the number one — "

"No, not him. I didn't have a gun. I crashed into this guy when I was running away. He's the one who had a gun. I told him the guard was some guy after me. He pulled a gun out, ready to defend me." She started to laugh. "It was pretty clever, I thought. He fell for it easy."

"A pretty girl like you? I'm not surprised. I'm sure most guys would have been happy to defend you."

She scrunched up her face and shook her head. "Anyway, when he turned his back, I snuck into a nearby alley and scaled up to the roof."

"But he saw your face."

"I couldn't help it. I slammed into him when I sprinted around a corner and my hood fell off. But it's fine." She looked down at her hands. "He obviously didn't stick around to chat to the police," she said, mostly to herself.

"What if he changes his mind?"

"He didn't seem the type."

Ryan cleared his throat. "What type did he seem?"

"The kind that carries a concealed weapon at three in the morning. That type doesn't usually want to chat up the police."

"You got lucky."

"Yeah, well … " Erin scratched the side of her neck. "I've got more bad news."

"Jesus." Ryan looked up to the ceiling. "What else happened?"

"I lost your power thingy. I mean. I'm pretty sure I did. The cops would have been able to follow my trail to the roof because I wasn't able to conceal it like last time. And if they've got any brains at all, they would have found it."

Ryan stood, took a deep breath, then went over and sat down next to Erin. He put an arm around behind her and studied her for a moment. "As long as you're safe. We can replace the other stuff, but we can't replace you. And there is no way they can track the 'power thingy' back to me."

"I'll pay you back." Erin shifted uncomfortably.

Ryan touched a thumb to her arm and looked at her under his dark lashes. "Don't worry about it. I owe you and your brother. You're like family to me. We all make mistakes. Besides, you need the money."

Erin stared at her chewed nail and rubbed at it with her finger. "Thanks."

"And like I've offered before. I've got money you can use if you ever get stuck."

Erin nodded but kept staring at her hand. "Thanks, I appreciate it, but I don't like owing people stuff."

"You know it wouldn't be like that." He put his hand under her chin and lifted her face to meet his. "You can count on me."

Erin pinched her lips together. Her stomach was squirming. The last thing she wanted was to become one of Ryan Thomson's accessories, so she stood and went to the hall drawer and pulled out the necklace. She held it up to change the subject. "Ever seen anything uglier than this?"

"Yikes. You think you can sell that thing?"

"I've already got someone lined up. I'm going to get rid of it today. Then tomorrow I'll visit Peter."

"How's he doing? Good?"

Erin scowled. "Good? Nobody's good in prison. You should visit him."

Ryan puffed out a sarcastic laugh. "I don't think that's a good idea."

"What happened between you two? I don't get it. I mean, Peter's not the type to hold a grudge, and I can't understand why he'd be pissed at you because you got sick that day. It's not like you could help it."

"I hate to say it, but I think he wishes it were me in jail and not him. I can't say I blame him either."

"But that's crazy. If you had been there that day, then you'd both be in prison." Erin shook her head. "I just think you should go see him. Try to clear things up. He needs all the friends he can get right now."

"Listen." Ryan stood and walked to her, lifting the necklace and smirking. He shook his head and moved his hand to her shoulder. "I understand you want to be a peacemaker here, but you have to trust me on this. Peter doesn't want to see me, and you're probably better off not mentioning that we catch up now and then."

Erin bit her bottom lip. "To be honest, I didn't expect to see you again after Peter went to prison."

"I told you, you're like family to me. I know things aren't great between me and Peter, but that doesn't mean I skip out on people I care about."

"Well, I appreciate it. And I appreciate you allowing me to use your gear, even when I lose it."

"What's mine is yours. And it's what Peter would expect. Or at least, it's what I would expect if I were Peter. How's your mom, by the way?" Ryan asked, changing the subject as he walked over to the fireplace to lean on the mantle.

Erin stayed where she was. "We're supposed to get some test results back soon. I'll know more then."

Ryan nodded. "You want me to come with you?"

"No. I like it to be just me and her. But I appreciate the offer."

"Don't mention it."

Erin put the necklace away, then paused before saying, "I don't mean to kick you out, but I've gotta get ready for the day. You said yourself I look like hell." She smiled faintly.

"Of course." He grabbed his coat and headed for the door. He opened his mouth like he was about to say something, but then turned and pulled the door open. "Call me if you need anything," he said as he leaned over and kissed her cheek.

"I will. And sorry again about the" — She flicked her hand in the air — "doohicky."

"Let me know if you need another. It's easy to get."

Erin smiled with only half her mouth when she said goodbye and locked the door.

She wondered how Peter would react if he knew Ryan was hanging around. Peter had always treated him like a brother and trusted him with his life, but neither one of them would come clean about why they weren't speaking. Not only that, but since Ryan started turning up again, he was acting like he was looking for something more from her. Something she wasn't willing to give. She was walking a fine line. She needed Ryan's help, but how far was she willing to go to get it?

Nick buffed the smooth line of the hood of his car with a soft cloth, something he'd seen his brother do most days while he was alive. Nick had always given him a hard time about it, saying his brother loved that car more than his girl. But only because he had been jealous of his brother, who not only had a really cool car but also a great relationship with Sasha. It wasn't that Nick had any trouble getting a date, but Brian and Sasha had something he hadn't seen before, even in his parents' relationship. Not that they were such a great example. They may still be married, but only by definition. He didn't think his dad sitting on his ass all day drinking beer and watching ESPN while his mom cooked and cleaned up after him constituted a proper marriage. But Brian and Sasha genuinely cared for each other and were willing to sacrifice anything for one another. That's what did his brother in, in the end.

Sasha's older brother was involved in a gang that thought she should date a gang member. Brian did his best to stand up for their relationship, but his fatal flaw was that he was too trusting. Brian had divulged one day to Nick that he and Sasha were making a plan to elope and move away, somewhere they could be free of her family. But then Sasha's brother appeared to be extending an olive branch by inviting Brian to come out with a bunch of them for a night on the town. They ended up in a gunfight.

Nick had been in New York at the time and got a call from his mom. All she could do was sob on the phone while Nick tried to pick out pieces of information from among her keening. He finally gave up and spent several minutes trying to get her to put his dad on the line so he could find out what had happened and even then, his dad said only about two words.

Sasha attended the funeral, but she was escorted by her brother. It was all Nick could do to not smash his face in.

Brian must have known his life was in some amount of danger because he had a will that left Nick his car and a stash of money for Sasha. His dad was incredulous but couldn't expect much from a son he gave no time to except to criticize.

Now the car was all he had left of his brother and a constant reminder of the consequences of life choices and falling in love.

He used his time polishing to remind him of that while he paid homage to his brother.

Chapter 5

ERIN STOOD STILL with her hands clasped in front of her, waiting. When a familiar buzz filled the cool, still air, she lifted her eyes to the door. A loud clang followed the buzz before a prison guard pulled open the door. She smiled at him but wedged herself against the cold steel of the doorframe to give him as wide a berth as possible. She didn't like the way he looked at her but didn't want to make trouble for her brother, so she took the passive aggressive route and hoped the guard didn't notice.

The room was half empty, and after a quick scan, she could see her brother wasn't there yet. She headed for an empty table in the middle of the room, passing a kid, about ten, who sat with his mom on one side of the table, with what she supposed was the kid's father on the other. She watched covertly as the boy looked to his mom for how to act. Erin wondered if this was their first visit. Both mother and son sat up straight with their hands in their laps. Dad's hands were on the table, pushed forward like he was hoping for some sort of contact.

The first time Erin had visited Peter, a cold void had crept farther into her with each step she took inside the walls. She wasn't sure it had ever really left.

No one smiled, or if they did, it was a sympathetic grimace. One time while she was there, someone had laughed, a genuine joyful belly laugh. It had an odd effect on the place, like something bad must follow something good.

An irrational fear always plagued her when she visited Peter. A fear that at any moment, they'd realize she should be in there too, and they wouldn't let her out. She wouldn't come here if it were anyone but her brother.

Her fingernails drummed a beat into the now-familiar table full of scratches and dents. Leaning back, she ran her thumb along the edge where the initials T.R. were etched.

When the door buzzed to open again, Erin dropped her hands into her lap like the mother and son. It was a safe position in here, as though it could keep the feel of the place from getting to you. It didn't work, but she had to try something.

Peter came through the door and spotted her straight away. He had their father's build, tall and lanky but wide in the shoulders. He had a big brain, but he was also strong and capable, not the kind of guy you'd want to get in a fight with. She was proud of how handsome he was. They shared their mother's eyes, although Peter's were lighter blue than Erin's. He hadn't lost any weight, which was reassuring, but his shoulders stooped and that bothered her. He had always had good posture.

She waited till he reached her before standing and giving him a quick hug, then they both sat down, silent for a moment while Peter looked her over.

He lifted his hands to rest clasped on the table.

She reached up and rested her tiny hand on his large one and cleared her throat. "How are you?"

He nodded. "Fine. How's Mom?"

"Good." She nodded, then stopped when she realized she was parroting him. She dropped her eyes to the table before continuing. "We get the latest test results back today. I'm headed there next, but she's looking good. Better than she has in a long time."

"Good." Peter frowned. "You, uh. You do any work recently?"

She shrunk back slightly. "Yeah, yesterday. Early."

"How'd that go?"

"Fine," she said cautiously.

Peter nodded. "I saw the news." Erin closed her eyes for a second then thudded back in the chair and dropped her hands back into her lap. Peter leaned forward. "I thought there was no way it was you. Couldn't be. You don't make such a big mess."

"It's fine. I lost some tech, but — "

"Tech?"

"Uh, yeah. It's nothing. I got away clear. I got — "

"I didn't think we had any tech. I thought Ryan had it all."

"He, uh, does. I actually had to dodge this guy on

the street. Got away by pretending I was a damsel in dis
— ”

"You've seen Ryan?"

Erin let out a puff of air. "Yeah. I have. And he's happy to help. He offered, but, I mean, it's just tech."

"Erin, I don't want you involved with him."

"We're not involved. He's just helping me out."

"Doesn't sound like his stuff helped you out."

"It wasn't his stuff that was the problem. In fact, it's what saved me. Things just didn't go to plan. Nothing to do with him." She leaned toward him, close. "Listen, you two gotta get over whatever's wrong. I know Ryan bailed on you on that job, but just think, if he were there, he would have been arrested too."

Peter's jaw clenched, and he glanced up at the guard, who was scanning the room. "I told you. It has nothing to do with that. You don't need Ryan's help. There's got to be a better way."

"Well, there isn't. I'd have to take smaller jobs, which means more of them. It's better this way."

"No, it's not." Peter rested his face in his hands. "No way is better, and it's all my fault. I never should have gotten you involved."

"Peter." She dropped her voice and reached for his hand. "If you hadn't taught me how to do what I do, Mom would be … " She couldn't bring herself to say it.

"I don't know how you can think that. If I would have gotten a regular job in the first place, I'd be at that job right now providing for you and Mom. You could have finished college."

"Stop it. There's no point talking like this. Things

are what they are. You shouldn't even be in here in the first place."

"You don't think so? Even though they caught me red-handed?"

"But you didn't take the diamonds."

He would have thrown his hands in the air if it wouldn't have drawn attention. "You think I wouldn't have taken them if I could have?"

"It's still not fair. It's not your fault the rocks disappeared."

"I've made peace with this. I'll serve my time."

"It's too much. Thirty years? God, you'll be an old man when you get out. That's your whole life."

"Nah, it's a breeze."

"Stop trying to make light of this. I'm pissed."

"You gonna stay pissed for thirty years?"

"I sure am."

Peter smiled and squeezed her hand. She hated him because she couldn't keep a smile off her own face. She wiped at it, but it was no use.

The door buzzed again and Erin looked up long enough to note a bag of bones walking in, but she turned back to Peter as he squeezed her hand again to get her attention. "I want you to promise me something, okay?"

"Why do I have the feeling I'm not going to like this?"

The new inmate walked behind Peter and pivoted at the last second. He looked like he hadn't eaten in weeks, his bones pushing ridges into his prison clothes. His close-cropped hair and goatee accentuated the sharp angles in his face.

"Pete, my man. Who's the dish?" he said, winking at Erin.

She rolled her eyes.

"James, that's my sister. You wink at her again, I'll break all your fingers."

James put his hands up. "Sorry man, my bad." His face paled a little. "I just thought I was admiring your girl."

"And you think I'd react differently if she *were* my girl?"

"No, I … "

Erin held back a laugh that ended in a snort. "Ignore my brother, James. Just don't do it again."

The guy nodded politely and walked to a table to visit with someone who was definitely a brother. The bony build must have been hereditary.

"Sorry about that. James just came in. He's trying too hard to make friends."

"Poor guy. Look at the size of him. He does need friends in here. Go easy on him. We can't all be social geniuses like you. Besides, his effort was mildly amusing."

Peter shrugged. "It's painful to watch."

Erin glanced up at the clock on the wall. "I should get going. Mom's got some other tests today. I want to see her before she goes in."

"It's good to see you. Always cheers me up. And hey, that thing I want you to promise me."

Erin pinched her lips together. "I had hoped you forgot."

"When Mom's better — "

"Hang on." Erin put two hands up to stop him. "We don't know yet if she's going to get better."

"When Mom's better, I want you to give this up. Go back to school or something."

Erin's leg jiggled under the table. She didn't like making promises. If you make promises to people, they have expectations about you. "I'll think about it."

"Erin. I'm going to be stuck in here for the next thirty years. It will be easier for me if I know you're in a safe profession."

Erin's hand went to her sore arm. "Do I have to promise?"

He gave her a playful glare. "Yes." He nodded his head toward her arm. "Somethin' wrong there?"

She looked at her hand and dropped it. "No, it's fine."

"Did you hurt it while you were working?"

"What, are you my occupational safety officer now?" She smiled to hide her fear that she was going to make things more difficult for herself. "I gotta get going," she said, standing.

"You haven't promised me yet."

Erin grunted in annoyance. "Fine. Once Mom is completely better and no longer needs medication, I will get a new job."

"Why do I have the feeling you won't hesitate to twist those words around if necessary?"

She put a hand on Peter's head and scrubbed up his

hair before he stood to give her a hug goodbye. "We both do what's necessary. We always have."

Peter wrapped her up in a big, quick hug before she left.

It was drizzling as she walked to her car, creating a miserable film on everything. Erin pulled her jacket more tightly around herself. If only she could find those diamonds. Or better yet, prove someone else took them. She shook the idea from her head. She'd spent the first six months of Peter's imprisonment trying to figure out what happened, but it was just clutching at straws.

She got in her car, took a deep breath, and slapped her cheeks a couple of times. Time to put on a happy face for Mom.

Chapter 6

NICK WATCHED from the doorway of the hospital room as Kennedy talked quietly to Monkey, who was sitting up in bed but, judging by the droop in one eye, was probably drugged up with painkillers.

Kennedy might have a shady interest in Monkey, but Nick suspected that Monkey's feelings weren't straightforward either. Nick liked the kid and was probably a little overprotective of him, but there was something elusive about him. Monkey was a part of the group before Nick turned up on the scene, but while he acted like he wanted to be part of the gang, he always appeared to be scoping out another angle. Nick spotted him more than once listening in on conversations he wasn't invited to.

Kennedy stood close to the bed, playing his part as the doting fatherly figure so he could go after Monkey's shooter with a vengeance and say he had every right.

In the corner of the room stood Paddy with his bare

arms crossed. He was only there because it was expected of him.

Nick had never seen Paddy in anything but sleeveless shirts, even in the middle of winter. The ex-champion boxer stood several inches taller than Nick at six-foot-five. Of all the guys on Kennedy's team, Nick liked Paddy the most. He talked straight and did what he was told without asking questions. He said little, and despite his willingness to smash someone into a pulp on command, for Paddy, killing and maiming was just part of the job, like taking out the trash. No offense.

Stanley, on the other hand, who was now staring at Nick with his beady eyes, had a taste for blood. Nick could never tell what Stanley was thinking, but he was sure it was bad. The man's jaw stuck out to one side on his thin face, probably because at some point it was broken but ignored until it set sideways. He had tats covering his sinewy neck and gold rings on his fingers. Kennedy kept him on a leash most of the time because Stanley was somewhat psychotic, but the leash stretched farther than it should. Kennedy kept him around to do what no one else would.

Stanley's specialty was messing people up, but not like Paddy did. Messing them up inside and out. If Kennedy wanted to really scare someone, he'd send Stanley.

When Nick had told Bobby that Stanley would come after his girl and his kid, the threat was real. Stanley wouldn't hesitate to break them in the worst way possible, and Nick prayed to God that it never came to that. No one deserved Stanley's brutality.

Nick folded his arms and leaned against the door, ignoring Stanley's menacing gaze until Kennedy spotted him and waved him in.

"Hey Boss." Nick nodded and strolled in.

"Nicholas." Kennedy's penchant for always using a full name if he knew it grated on Nick. It felt condescending and probably was. "You get me what I need?"

"Bobby didn't know, but he gave me a lead that I followed yesterday and found out it was Brayson."

Kennedy studied him for a minute. "Did you show Bobby what happens to worthless creeps?"

"Well, the lead checked out, so I only took a finger. You'll find it in the freezer back at Messina's."

Kennedy grimaced. "God, Nicholas. You put human flesh in my restaurant's kitchen freezer?" He wagged his finger. "You are one sick son of a bitch."

"I thought you'd prefer to confirm it rather than take my word."

A flicker of a grin appeared on Kennedy's face, then was gone. "Patrick," Kennedy said, still looking at Nick, but he turned to Paddy when the man stepped forward in response. "Check out the finger, then dispose of it properly please." He turned back to Nick. "Which one'd you take."

"Index, right hand."

"Excellent choice."

"How's Monkey doing?" Nick asked as Paddy slipped by him and out the door.

"He'll live." Kennedy turned to the bed. "Won't you, Monkey? But you gave us quite a scare."

Nick took a couple steps toward the bed, uncomfortably aware that Stanley was watching him. The two men had already made it apparent that they had no liking for each other.

Monkey waved at Nick with a sluggish finger. "They're givin' me the good stuff. Better than I ever got on the streets," Monkey said through thick lips. Nick knew for a fact that Monkey didn't take drugs, but he liked to talk big.

"Hey kiddo." Kennedy said, leaning forward slightly. "We've got the guy who shot you, and we're going to make him pay."

Monkey shrugged and leaned his head back on the pillow, closing his eyes. "Let me know when the nurse brings me some Jell-O. I hope it's purple today. The green tastes like feet."

"Do me a favor," Kennedy said, placing a hand on Nick's shoulder and leading him away from the bed. "Stay with him for me while I get some business sorted out. I don't like leaving a young kid like this all alone."

"It's okay." Monkey said. "Nurse Powell will be here soon."

"Nurse Powell, eh?" Nick turned and winked then smiled as a flush reddened Monkey's neck.

Kennedy moved closer to Nick and dropped his voice. "Just stay with him for a bit. I want to make sure he doesn't say anything he shouldn't while he's high on these drugs they're pumping him full of."

"Sure. I'll just go grab a coffee and come back."

Stanley was still watching him as he left the room. Nick really wanted to punch that guy in the face every time he saw him.

Nick's shoes squeaked as he walked down the antiseptic halls, headed for the food court. He knew where to get the best coffee in the hospital. For a place that must go through gallons of the stuff a day, you'd expect them to be well practiced in the art of coffee making, but there was only one place here he knew of where it was drinkable.

He pulled out his phone to check his messages as he got in line at the café, then he lifted his head to observe the other patrons. His eyes stopped on one in particular as he swore under his breath.

A young woman sat at a nearby table with her chin in her hand. She was reading a book. Her pink hair was pulled up into a tight bun.

"Well, I'll be damned." Nick said to himself as he shuffled forward in the line. The woman in front of him turned.

"Sorry?"

"Oh no, not you, sorry. Talking to myself." He smiled politely, but the woman frowned and turned back to give her order as they moved forward again.

Nick watched the girl with the pink hair turn the page, oblivious to the room. Her makeup was smoky around the eyes, just like when he had first seen her, but it wasn't gaudy. She was dressed with sophistication, and the makeup added to her put-together look. It gave the stark room a glamour that it wouldn't have had without her presence.

He could tell she took pride in the way she looked. The confidence was alluring, but he wasn't stupid.

"Ahem." The annoyed cough pulled him from his observation, and he turned to see the employee waiting to take his order. "What can I get you?" Her fingers were poised over the register, waiting to input the order. "Just a regular black coffee, thanks."

He paid, then moved to the side to wait and took the opportunity to watch the woman again. He'd go talk to her. He couldn't give up an opportunity like this. Especially when he was still a little cut that she'd gotten one by him. It didn't matter that, if the tables were turned, he'd have done the same.

"One black coffee," the attendant called out. Nick reached out to take his order in response. Then he made a beeline for her table.

He paused briefly on the opposite side to allow her time to notice him, but she kept reading. "Must be a good book," he said as he put his hand on the back of the chair to pull it out.

"That seat's taken," she said without looking up.

He paused, amused, then went to the next table, grabbed a chair and twirled it around. It spun better than he expected, so he glanced at her, hoping she had seen it. She still wasn't looking.

As he sat down in the chair, she said, "That seat's taken, too." Then she folded the corner of the page over and finally looked up at him, her lips lightly pursed. She wasn't impressed.

He grinned and tipped his head sideways. "You've forgotten me already?"

She squinted at him then looked him up and down. "Trying to pick a girl up at the hospital? That's just poor form."

He kept the grin on his face, but it fell out of his eyes. "You have forgotten." He clicked his tongue and crossed his arms.

She let out a heavy breath. "I'm sorry, but I think you have me confused with someone else."

"I don't know, Pinky. I don't forget a pretty face that quickly. It was only yesterday, after all."

She blinked a couple of times. "I didn't go anywhere yesterday."

Nick leaned forward and rested his arms on the table. "It was the early hours of the morning." He feigned offense. "I can't believe you've forgotten. I practically saved your life. But I didn't get your name. Mine's Nick."

He held his hand out to her. She looked at it, and her face squashed up in confusion, until the truth lit her eyes, and her expression slackened, dropping her mouth open. "No," she whispered.

Her eyes flicked to the exit over his shoulder. She couldn't make it out past him. She was trapped, and Nick could see she knew it.

He watched in fascination as her demeanor changed instantly. The fear was swept away into a confident pose. She leaned back, deceptively relaxed. "Nick, eh?"

"So you do remember. It was a pity I didn't have the opportunity to introduce myself properly after I saved you, but you disappeared so quickly."

"I had things to do. I'm a busy girl."

"Must be. Sorry, I didn't catch you name?"

"You a cop?"

"Nope. Just an innocent bystander."

She laughed easily. "With a gun."

He shrugged. "Worked in your favor though, didn't it?"

"Sure. You were a big help. Thanks," she said, dryly.

Nick pinched his chin, considering his next move. She was wily, this pink-haired waif. "Well, my feelings were a little hurt when I got to be all heroic and went through the trouble of threatening that guy with my gun and then come to find out, you weren't exactly who you said you were."

"Sure I was. That guy was after me, just like I said."

It was Nick's turn to laugh. "I guess he was. Look, I'm not here to give you trouble."

"Liar." Her eyes narrowed. "Just tell me what you want."

He licked his lips but couldn't keep the grin off his face. "I'm curious to know what you're going to spend the money on. Manicure?"

She looked at her chewed fingernails as her phone dinged. He couldn't read the message from where he was, but he saw dread pass across her face. She covered it quickly and looked back at him. "What difference does it make to you?"

"I'd like to know how frivolous you are before I make my decision." He had no intention of turning her in, but he wanted to make her squirm. She deserved at least that much.

"And what if I am spending it on a manicure?"

He sucked in a sarcastic breath. "Tough call, this one."

Erin shifted in her seat when her phone dinged again. "Okay, listen. I'm not the begging type, but please, can you let it go? If it's money you want, just tell me how much so we can get this over and done with. I've got things I need to do."

He chewed on the inside of his cheek. "All right. I'll let it go if you do one thing for me."

Her leg was bouncing under the table. He could feel the quiver in the tabletop. He had her cornered. "What?" Her temper was getting close to the surface.

"I don't want your money, but I want you to give all the money you got on that job to charity."

The shaking stopped. "That's a very noble notion."

"I thought so."

"What if I told you it's already going to a charity of sorts?"

"You're joking, right?"

"I don't joke about money."

"What charity?"

She drummed her fingers on the table and glanced down at her phone again. "If I show you, will you let this drop?"

"Show me?"

"Yes."

She looked nervous, and that made him curious enough to concede. "Okay. Deal."

She jumped up from the table before she could change her mind. "Follow me."

―――――――――――――

Chapter 7

―――――――――――――

ERIN SPED DOWN THE HALL. Every time she turned a corner, she glanced over her shoulder to make sure he was still there. Or maybe she was trying to lose him. She couldn't decide.

She turned again as she slipped around several doctors huddled around a chart. Nick had to stop to avoid crashing into one who had taken a step back.

She kept going, but felt her muscles tighten as she slowed her pace so he could catch up.

He jogged up next to her when the hall cleared. "You know, you're pretty fast for such a small person." He had a stupid grin on his face, which only deepened her scowl.

"That's why I was able to stay ahead of the security guard the other night."

"It's also why you hit me so hard when you came screaming around the corner. If you had slowed down, you might not have blown your cover, and we wouldn't be here right now."

"If I had slowed down, I would have gotten caught." She stopped when they reached her mom's room and put a hand up to keep him from going any further. "So far, I prefer this option, but promise me I won't regret it."

"I'm not prepared to make you any promises," he said with the same stupid grin.

She glared at him, then leaned into the room, hoping her mom was sleeping. Unfortunately, she was sitting up, sipping on a straw and looking at a magazine. Erin's chest tightened at the sight of her mom looking so well. Not that long ago she had looked like only a shell of herself.

Erin leaned back out again. She took a deep breath. "Can you at least promise to be polite?" She lifted her eyebrows. "Please? This is my mom."

"Your mom?" That was not what he expected.

"Yeah."

The smile slid off his face and was replaced by a grim frown. "Then yes, I promise."

Erin felt a small weight lift as his change in countenance suggested he was now taking her seriously.

She turned away from him and forced a smile onto her face, stepping stiffly into the room. "Hey, Mom."

"Erin," she said, flipping the magazine closed. "There you are. Thank goodness. You saved me from a story about a woman who was murdered then brought back to life to help save the person who killed her. I don't know where they get these magazines from."

Erin laughed nervously. "You're looking good."

"I'm feeling good. Best I've felt in a while." Her eyes

twitched over Erin's shoulder, and she jutted out her chin, suppressing a smile. "Who's your friend?"

"Uh, that's just Nick. We were having a coffee, and I was telling him how wonderful you are, and he said he'd like to meet the amazing woman I was describing." She turned to him and gave him a murderous look that told him he had better watch himself. "Nick, this is my mom, Jodie. She's got cancer."

Jodie laughed. "Erin's never been one for subtlety. It's nice to meet you, Nick." She held her hand out, waiting for him to make his way over and take it.

Nick wrapped his fingers gently around hers and kissed her hand. "It is a pleasure to meet such an amazing woman."

"My aren't we trying hard?" She dropped her voice. "You must really like my daughter."

Nick turned and looked at Erin. "She's surprising, I'll give her that." He winked at Erin then turned back to Jodie. "But how could she not be with a mother like you?"

"You're putting it on a bit thick now, but I assure you, I'm not as incredible as what Erin might have suggested."

"I doubt that. You've already proven yourself to be quick-witted. I can tell by the sparkle in your eye there is a lot going on there."

"Hah! If you'd have been here last week, there was no sparkle. I'm doing much better this week."

"You mind if I ask what kind of cancer you have?"

"Oh, it's one of those tricky ones I can't be bothered trying to pronounce. It has as many letters in the name as zeroes on the medical bills. But I'm lucky. My daughter has a job with health insurance to cover it. Can you believe it? A company that's willing to look after their employee's mother, for goodness' sake."

Erin piped up. "Yes, I told Nick about the company I work for."

"Yeah, she did. Businesses try hard these days to keep good employees. It appears to have worked well for your circumstances."

Jodie laughed. "Yeah, I'd be a goner otherwise."

Erin seized. "Mom. Don't say things like that."

"Why not? You don't have to be so serious all the time. You're going to have to learn to lighten up."

"Yeah, Erin." Nick smacked her lightly on the arm. "Lighten up a little."

Erin pressed her hands together. "Well," she said through gritted teeth. "Nick's gotta go." She grabbed his arm and pulled him toward the door. "I'll see him out and be back in a sec."

Erin pushed Nick out into the hall and didn't stop until they were well clear of the room. "There, happy?"

"That's very Robin Hood of you. Robbing the rich to pay for your mom's health care?"

"Shh," she said, pushing him further away from the room. "Now you know, and you can leave me alone." She looked back, scanning the people in the hall.

Nick crossed his arms. "Do I make you uncomfortable?"

"Yes."

"That's too bad. I'm actually a nice guy."

Erin choked out a laugh. "Uh-huh. I've gotta get back to my mom, okay? Will you please go?"

"Okay." He put his hands up in surrender. "I'll go."

She waved him off as though she were shooing a fly, then turned.

"Goodbye, Pinky. It was nice knowing you," he called after her, watching her rush back to her mom's room.

He put a fist on his hip. Few people surprised him, but this girl with the pink hair seemed to have gotten under his skin a little. Good idea to get out now. He slapped his hands together as though brushing off dirt and tucked them in his pockets as he headed back to see Monkey, ignoring the pang of disappointment that he'd never see her again.

Erin sat down in the chair next to the bed. "Have they given you the results yet?"

"You're flustered."

Erin put a hand on her cheek and felt the heat. "No, I'm not."

"You going to tell me who the guy is, really?"

"He's no one."

"Erin, I'm your mother. I changed your diapers and kissed your scrapes. And I knew every time you snuck out of the house."

Erin looked into her lap. Her mom might have known when she snuck out as a teenager, but she didn't know why. She didn't even know Peter was a thief until he was arrested. Erin could still remember the look on her face when she found out the truth after he was arrested, moving from disbelief to anger to grief. Erin and Peter had agreed never to let her know Erin was involved, and she'd keep it that way.

Jodie reached out a hand. Erin looked at it, then took it. "He really is no one that matters."

"Why don't I believe you?"

"That's a good question."

They stared each other down playfully until her mom broke into a smirk. "He's cute."

Erin felt the red creep into her face, so she blew out a breath and turned her face away for a second. "He's just … someone from work who was giving me a hard time about leaving work to come to the hospital. He didn't believe me. Thought I was lying."

"I thought you said you told him about your business and how great it was. Now you're saying he works there?"

Erin puffed out her cheeks. "There was a time when your memory wasn't so good. I miss those days. Please don't worry about it."

"I'm your mother. It's my job to worry."

Erin rolled her eyes. "Mom, stop. I'm a grown woman. Now, I'm done talking about Nick. Tell me what you've heard from the doctors."

"Not much. They'll be in shortly to talk specifics. That's why I texted you. But they did say that I'm responding very well to the treatment. And I'm feeling fantastic. A bit tired, but not as sick."

"You're looking better too. I stopped by to see Peter this morning. He's doing well."

Jodie frowned. "Poor Peter." She looked pained. "I sometimes wonder if your father hadn't died … if Peter would have made different choices."

"Mom, things are the way they are and there's nothing we can do about it." She hated the words as they came out of her mouth.

"You got your practicality from your father, not from me. Peter's more sensitive. He was just so overwhelmed when your dad died, and then they didn't give us the payout we expected." She frowned. "He was so angry." She paused for a moment, then the shadow on her face passed. "I'm just glad you've found yourself a great job. I was afraid you'd regret not finishing college when Peter went to prison."

"No regrets, Mom," she said and kissed her mom's forehead. "Peter said he's made peace with how things are and so have I."

Nick stepped into Monkey's room and stopped. Monkey's favorite nurse was there. She was young and pretty. No wonder he liked her.

Nick cleared his throat, and she looked up. "You can come in. I'm almost done." Her voice was higher pitched than he expected.

She ripped open the velcro cuff she had around Monkey's arm. "Your blood pressure is running a bit high. How are you feeling?" She tipped her head sideways in concern, and Nick could see Monkey's neck redden again.

"Nurse Powell, is it?" he asked, coming to the rescue. "I think he's getting a bit stressed staying in the hospital so long. He just wants to go home. Isn't that right, kid?"

Monkey nodded but didn't speak.

"I'm sure it's nothing, but he could probably use a rest."

"I'll be back later for another checkup." She smiled at Monkey, then collected her things and left.

"Aw, Nick. I didn't want her to leave."

"Sorry bud, it was the best I could do on short notice. At least she left your blood pressure issues alone. Next time, try closing your eyes and thinking of something peaceful."

"I'd rather close my eyes and think of her."

"You want to be stuck here forever? They'd never let you out if your blood pressure skyrocketed. What about home?"

"Home's not peaceful." He rubbed his face with his hand. "I kinda hate these drugs. I can't think. I don't like not being able to think."

"Better than being in pain though, right?"

Monkey shrugged. "My mom came in this morning."

"Oh yeah?" Nick said, pulling a chair over. "How'd that go?"

Monkey shrugged again. "Hospital expects her to visit, I think. I don't know. I told her she didn't care about me and should never come back."

Monkey had never said much about his mom.

Kennedy might be right to keep an eye on him so he doesn't say the wrong thing to the wrong person. He was being liberal with the truth at the moment. "At least you've got Kennedy to visit. He cares."

Monkey snorted. "Yeah right." He wiggled his finger at Nick to bring him closer. "Between you and me? I think he's using me as much as I'm using him."

Nick was experienced enough to keep the surprise off his face, but his own blood pressure would have risen. "Yeah?"

"That guy who shot me? He thought I was settin' him up. I just wanted to give him … somethin' … " Monkey dropped off and his eyes went vacant for a moment. "What was I sayin'?"

Nick turned to make sure no one was at the door. "You were telling me about your favorite flavor of Jell-O."

Monkey blew a raspberry, and Nick backed up to avoid a spray. "It's nice having you here, Nick. You're a nice guy."

"That's what I keep telling people, but I don't know if they believe me."

"Well, I believe you." Monkey took a deep breath and settled back on his pillow. "They letting me out of here soon? I got places I need to be."

"Should be only another couple of days."

"Good. Peter's going to kill me."

"Who's Peter?"

Monkey looked at Nick, startled, but then settled again into the haze of drugs. "He's stuck in prison. I told him I'd keep an eye on his sister, but I've been stuck in here."

"I'm sure he'll forgive you. She cute?"

"Oh yeah. Not a chance for me, though. Older woman."

"Like the nurse?"

"Probably."

"You're doomed."

Monkey closed his eyes, and Nick let him rest. If Monkey was trying to pass information to Kennedy's competitors, he'd be dead if he were ever found out. Nick wondered if this Peter guy was connected. He didn't know anyone with that name that he could think of but didn't want to push Monkey for further information. Better to let it sink down into the fog in his mind, never to surface again.

Chapter 8

NICK APPROACHED MESSINA'S, an award-winning
Italian restaurant in the city known for its authentic
cuisine, and not its crime connections. They had a signa-
ture dish of homemade gnocchi that Nick had become
very familiar with. One of the perks of the job.

It was Friday night and, despite the restaurant
having only just opened, it was already packed. Nick
weaved around the crowd waiting out the front to get in
and jogged up the alley to the back door.

Even through the closed door he could hear the
hectic buzz of the kitchen, and when he pushed the
door open, he was met by the heavenly aromas he had
come to expect. His mouth watered in anticipation.

He squeezed past a waitress and zigzagged through
the kitchen, sampling as he went.

Approaching the head chef, a sixty-year-old widow
with curly hair and a strong Italian accent, he snatched
a piece of salami off the cutting-board as she sliced up
the rest of the meat.

"Che palle!" she bellowed and smacked him on the wrist with the flat of the knife. "You are lucky I didn't cut off a finger."

He grimaced at the reminder of his own deed but then leaned in and kissed her on the cheek while making a grab for more food.

"Enough," she said with a scowl, pushing him toward the back of the kitchen. "I thought I might see you tonight." She sucked in a breath to squeeze her bountiful torso between two counters. "I already put something aside." She slid a plate toward him.

He wrinkled his nose. "That's a salad."

She pinched his arm. "You don't think I can look after you? It's full of all the good stuff. Salami, bacon, croutons, and a hefty serving of creamy dressing. Eat."

"I was kind of in the mood for gnocchi tonight."

"You are always in the mood for gnocchi. Later. Eat." She pointed at him, squinted ominously, then went back to her work, pressing back through the crowd of staff and appliances.

He took the plate and found a fork, taking an over-sized bite. "Buonissimo," he called out to her through a mouthful as he headed for the office. He smirked at his good luck in attaching himself to such a generous woman who had a matronly crush on him.

Kennedy's office door was open. He had a job for Nick to do tonight, but Nick stopped when he saw a guy around his own age with wavy hair and a fancy suit sitting in Kennedy's chair, swiveling back and forth like he owned the place.

Nick couldn't remember his name but had seen

him around before. The guy never spoke to anyone but Kennedy as far as Nick knew. Whatever business he had there, Nick had never been involved, but Kennedy always seemed nervous when he was around. That made Nick suspicious enough to nose around now.

"How's it goin'?" Nick asked after swallowing another bite.

The guy nodded. "Sampling the goods?" He was smiling, but it was clear he was sizing Nick up.

"Can't recommend something you've never tried." Nick took another casual bite but was sizing the guy up right back. "You hungry? Sofia makes a mean gnocchi." The guy looked at Nick's plate skeptically. Nick shrugged. "I tried for the pasta. She's making me eat my greens first. The price you pay."

Nick set the fork on the plate and wiped his hand on his pants, then held it out. "Nick. Sorry, I forgot your name."

The guy leaned forward and shook hands. "Don't think I ever gave it to you." His voice was flat.

"It's a secret then?"

A cocky smile crinkled the side of his mouth. "Ryan."

"Ryan. Nice to meet you." He picked up his fork and took another bite.

"Yeah."

"So what's happening tonight?" Nick mumbled through his food.

Ryan pushed the smile across his face. "I don't believe that's any of your business."

"Whoa." Nick laughed. "Not trying to step on any toes. Just making small talk."

"Sure you are."

"Gentlemen." Kennedy said from the door.

"Hey boss," Nick said and moved out of the way so Kennedy could enter his office. The fact that Kennedy didn't seem to mind Ryan sitting in his chair spoke volumes. "You said you had something for me?" Nick focused on the two men, trying to read their reaction to one another.

"You'll have to come back later. I have a prior engagement." Kennedy eyed Nick's plate but didn't comment.

Nick smiled. "She's making me eat it."

Kennedy always made a smart comment when he caught Nick feasting, but whoever this Ryan guy was, he had Kennedy second guessing everything before it came out of his mouth. There weren't many people who did that. Whoever this guy was, he needed to find out. He'd have to do some digging on his own to find Ryan's connection.

Nick made no move to leave but watched as Kennedy and Ryan made eye contact. Ryan leaned back in the chair easing the tension, then the stiffness in Kennedy's face left and he turned toward Nick. "Can't blame you for coming in to see Sofia for a meal," Kennedy said, patting his stomach. "You hungry, Ryan?"

"No." Ryan remained casual, but Nick had the suspicion it was all on his account. Then Ryan crossed his arms and stared at Nick, making it clear he was now an uninvited guest in the room.

"Well," Kennedy said, gesturing toward the door. "If you'll excuse us. I just need to have a word with Ryan here. You can shut the door on your way out."

"Yes, sir." Nick glanced at Ryan as he pulled the door shut.

He took a few steps down the hall, but then turned back to the door and leaned against the wall like he was going to relax there to finish his meal but didn't take a bite. Instead, he tipped his head toward the door and focused on the murmuring, but it was useless. He couldn't decipher anything that was being said.

He scraped up what was left on his plate then shoveled it into his mouth before sucking dressing from his lip.

As Nick headed back to the kitchen to dispose of his dishes, he noticed a squealing, gargling sound coming from out back. He spun toward the door and threw it open. Stanley looked up from where he was sitting on a box. He had his foot on the tail of a cat he had been messing with.

"What the hell are you doing?" Nick almost yelled, disgusted.

"Don't think it's any of your business," Stanley said smoothly.

The cat was half dead. Nick wasn't much of a cat person, but torturing animals was something else. He shoved Stanley aside and put the cat out of its misery.

Stanley jumped up, stepping up to Nick. "The cat's

been into the garbage. I was taking care of it. You need to learn to mind your own business," Stanley snarled.

"You think the boss would be okay with your doing stuff like that at his back door?"

"He lets me do what I want. Besides ... " Stanley spit at Nick's feet then he sucked in his cheeks, making his face look skeletal. "I was bored. And when I'm bored, I do what I want. And there's nothing you can do about it, unless you want to end up like that cat."

Nick saw the flex in Stanley's jaw and knew he was about to make a move.

Nick swung his arm around Stanley's, dislodging the knife that he had flicked into his hand, about to strike. Stanley gave up on the knife and twisted his own arm, pinning Nick against himself. He swung Nick around against the wall and pushed his forearm against Nick's throat, constricting his breath.

Nick reached around with his free arm and grabbed Stanley around the neck, pulling him down. The two men wrestled, throwing punches where they could until Paddy found them and pulled them apart.

"You guys got a screw loose or somethin'?" Paddy said, pushing Nick toward the door with one thick arm. He hadn't lost any of his boxing physique and would probably still be a contender if he hadn't been caught throwing matches. "Nick, you better go cool down."

Stanley dropped his head slightly, looking at Nick under hooded eyes. Nick saw murder there. "One of these days, Nick."

Nick took a step closer to Stanley, pressing against Paddy's outstretched arm. "Kennedy might let you get away with that stuff, but I won't. You step across too many boundaries. And one of these days, Stanley … you're going to find yourself at the wrong end of your sadism."

Stanley laughed, exposing blood smeared across his teeth. "You better watch your back, pretty boy, because I'm gonna take you apart piece by piece and I'm going to enjoy it."

Nick shook his head and turned his back on Stanley to prove a point. But if Paddy hadn't been there, he never would have done it. He knew Stanley wasn't lying. But if Nick ever got the opportunity to do the same to Stanley, he wouldn't hesitate either. He would have smashed Stanley's face in if he could have, but they couldn't touch each other here. Not really.

Paddy grabbed Nick by the arm and pulled him inside, leaving Stanley to whatever sick thing he'd find to do next.

"You are an idiot, Nick. You should know better than to mess with him. He's crazy."

"Kennedy shouldn't keep him around. He's messed up in the head and it's going to cost Kennedy one day."

"Let *him* worry about that. You just keep away from Stanley."

"Not making any promises," Nick said, shaking off Paddy and heading out of the building through the front door. He didn't consider how the diners might react to the blood on his face. Some looked startled, but he didn't care enough to notice.

———————————

Chapter 9

———————————

ERIN STOOD in front of the foggy bathroom mirror, breathing in the steaming air. She had just received word that her mom was responding exceptionally well to treatment, and if she continued progressing, there was hope that she might return home and continue treatment there, maybe even before Christmas.

Erin found it hard living in the old house alone. Maybe having her mom back would be the motivation she needed to clean the place up. And if she kept her promise to her brother, she would get a regular job when her mom was better and maybe even make some friends. Perhaps one day she'd feel normal.

She dragged her finger across the mirror, writing the word *normal*. The older she got, the more she felt that being normal was overrated. She wanted her family back together, sure, but she didn't know that she'd handle normal well. She was too used to the odd pattern of her life, not following the rules.

She pushed her towel along the mirror to clear it,

then leaned in close, running her fingers along the dark circles under her eyes. She had been having a lot of bad dreams lately, which meant she was only getting a few hours of sleep a night before she gave up on it. The money from the necklace was nearly depleted, and even though the couple weeks' break had given her arm time to recover, almost getting caught had spooked her. She got lucky in so many ways on that job. She couldn't afford to risk letting luck carry her through again. The next job she was planning was a quick, easy one. It wouldn't bring in as much money, but it was lower risk, which was what she needed.

She thought a lot about Nick's ambush at the hospital and his response to her and to meeting her mom. She should be angry, but the way he handled the situation was off-putting in all the wrong ways. Or maybe all the right ways.

When she had visited her mom most recently, she caught herself looking for him, which wasn't so unusual. It could be expected that she would look for him out of fear, but fear wasn't her motivation. It was a hope that he would turn up again. And that was irritating.

She drew the familiar dark lines around her eyes, then switched to brushes to achieve the smoky look she was used to. Some people might call it a mask, but it gave her confidence.

She pulled her hair into a tidy bun on top of her head, letting the shorter bits of hair fall around her face. Looking put together helped her feel put together, even if sometimes she felt anything but.

After getting ready, she headed out the door on the

way to visit her brother. She could have told him about their mom over the phone, but she wanted to see his face. She needed that little bit of joy. The idea of being able to bring him good news gave her a skip in her step. They had so little to smile about these days. Good news was always welcome, and this time it was the best they had gotten in a long time.

As Erin locked the front door, she heard a strange bird song. One she hadn't heard in a while. She smiled and turned, spotting the singer. A boy, about thirteen, leaned on the fence. He was all arms and legs these days. He'd grown a lot over the last year. When she made eye contact, he dropped his head.

Several years ago, Peter had volunteered with a big brother program. Tommy was his kid. As they got to know each other, Peter discovered Tommy was an expert pickpocket and found jobs for him. Peter didn't make such a great big brother for the program, but he loved Tommy like a brother and Tommy loved him, which meant that to Erin, he was like her little brother as well. She didn't know much about his home life, but she knew it wasn't good. If things had been different, she would have kept him with her.

She skipped down the steps and hurried out to him. "Tommy! Haven't seen you in a while. I've missed you. How've you been?"

He still wouldn't make eye contact. "I'm awright. You okay?"

"I'm fine. Tommy, what's wrong?"

Tommy bunched his shoulders up to his ears, holding them there for a second before dropping them. "I was supposed to keep an eye on you."

"Is that so?" He nodded. "And?"

"And I haven't. Peter made me promise. I screwed up."

Erin hitched her bag higher onto her shoulder and reached out to lift Tommy's chin to look her in the eyes. "Tommy. I don't know if you realize this, but I'm old enough to look after myself."

"But I promised," he whined.

"Well, what were you doing instead?"

"I got shot."

"Oh my god!" Erin dropped her bag to the ground and reached for him, but was afraid to touch him, afraid she'd hurt him. "Where? What happened?"

Tommy grabbed at his arm. "Here. It hurt, but I'm okay."

Erin slammed her hands onto her hips. "What were you doing that you got shot?"

His eyes dropped to the ground again. "Nothin'."

Erin took a deep, disapproving breath and let it out before she continued. "I know Peter got you mixed up in some stuff, but you are a great kid with huge potential. I'd hate to see you end up in prison or worse," she said, nodding toward his arm.

He shrugged again. "I told Peter I'd look after you."

"Yeah? And how is getting shot helping?"

"It's not. It wasn't supposed to happen."

"What *was* supposed to happen?"

Tommy threw his arms out and winced, pulling his

left back in. "It's … Other stuff. It doesn't matter. Trust me, okay? I'm just here to make sure you're doing okay."

She softened. The poor kid was trying his best. "Listen, I'm headed to see Peter right now. I'll let him know I saw you." Tommy started to protest, but Erin put a hand up to stop him. "I'll make it sound like you have been keeping a regular eye on me."

"Really? Thanks."

"No problem. You eating?"

"Some."

"If I give you some cash, will you promise me you'll spend it on food?" He tried to growl, but the sound came out mewling. "I take that as a yes?"

"Fine."

She held out fifty dollars to him but didn't let go straight away when he grabbed it. "No video games. Promise?"

"Yes, ma'am."

"And no girls."

His face reddened. She laughed then finally let go, scruffing up his hair. "I guess I'll be seeing you around?"

"As long as I don't get shot again."

"Tommy," she scolded.

"Yes, ma'am." This time Tommy was a little mocking.

"Can I give you a lift somewhere?"

"No thanks."

Knowing that Tommy was keeping an eye on her warmed her heart. She couldn't wait to tell Peter about that, too. Despite everything, today was going to be a good day. Maybe she'd sleep well tonight.

Nick waved away the smoke that blew into his face when Murphy exhaled. "Remind me to stand upwind from you next time," Nick said, leaning further over the railing of the bridge to find some fresh air.

Murphy started to laugh, but it ended in a hacking cough. "I'd give them up, but then what would I do with my hands?"

Nick opened his mouth but then closed it. The crass comment he was about to make was a little below him. "It's a real conundrum, isn't it?"

"Brayson is out of the picture."

"You get anything from him?"

"Some, not much. He said something about some kid setting him up. He's full of bullshit. But he's small fry anyway."

"I might have something else. There's a guy that turns up now and then. I haven't been able to get a last name. First name is Ryan. Can you see if you've got anything on him?"

"Tall guy about your age but better looking?"

Nick shook his head and smirked. "Yeah."

"We've got our radar on him. Name's Ryan Thomson. Don't know much about him and not sure what his connection is with Kennedy. He moves in different circles. He's loaded and we think he's connected to some crimes, but it's all circumstantial. He's got friends in high places so we can't do anything to him unless we catch him with a smoking gun. Maybe your guys know more."

"He makes Kennedy nervous."

"He should."

"That bad, eh?"

"Let's just say, he's a man who's used to getting what he wants."

"I'll see what I can find out."

"Nah. Don't waste your time. I told you we've got guys on it."

"Whatever you say."

―――――――――

Chapter 10

―――――――――

ERIN CHEWED her thumbnail as she waited for Peter. It was taking longer than normal for him to come through, and she was eager to share her news. She dropped her hand into her lap and started jiggling her leg under the table.

The door buzzed, and she sat up straight, but slouched again when she saw it was the bony guy, James, from the other day. He looked depressed, and before she could avert her eyes, he made eye contact. His eyes bulged, and he headed her way.

"Great," she mumbled. She couldn't help shrinking back when he slid into a chair next to her.

She glanced at the door, praying it would buzz her brother in. Alerting the guard was an option if she needed it, but she'd rather not make trouble if she could help it. Her eyes passed by James to his brother, who was focused on a spot on the wall and hadn't noticed James had come in. Or didn't care.

James's eyes flicked around the room then settled on

her wiggling leg. She stopped it dead and decided to put some distance between them. "You better watch what you say, or you'll end up making an enemy out of my brother, and he's not the kind of guy you want for an enemy." She had felt bad for him when her brother was around, but him coming to her like this was not okay.

He startled, then smiled. "Hey, I come in peace." He was wringing his hands, belying his grin. He looked around the room again, then leaned toward her. "I'm only tryin' ta help." His eyes were fidgeting worse than his hands.

Erin crossed her arms to maintain some distance. "Yeah, sure."

"It's about the diamonds."

She waited a beat, feigning disinterest, but her heart sped. "What about them?"

He nodded then rubbed a hand across his mouth. "I know who took 'um. I'm just trying to help."

"Why?"

"I help Peter. He helps me."

"Then why don't you tell him?"

"I tried. He didn't want to know about it."

"If my brother's not interested, then he must have a good reason. Why do you think you'll get a better response from me?"

James sucked air through the side of his mouth, making it squeak. "He just doesn't want to make more trouble. But you seem like a good sister. You don't want him in here, right?"

Peter put a heavy hand on James's shoulder. Erin

hadn't even noticed him come in. "What are you doing with my sister?"

"Nothin', man, nothin'. Just keepin' her company while she waited for you."

Peter pushed him up out of the seat. "Your brother is waiting, go keep him company."

James mumbled something as he went.

Peter sat heavily in the chair. "What was that all about? Is he trying to come on to you?" He huffed out a breath. "I think he's got a death wish."

Erin leaned forward and stared her brother down. "He said he knows who's got the diamonds."

"Yeah, right."

"Peter, shouldn't you be taking this seriously?"

Peter smacked his hand down on the table. A guard turned their way and Peter lifted his hand into the air in a light wave and smiled innocently. But when he looked back at Erin, his smile was gone. "Stay out of it, Erin. It's got nothing to do with you."

"Like hell it doesn't," she hissed. "Mom and I are struggling out there without you. If you have a chance to get out, you need to take it."

Peter leaned back casually. "He's just talkin'. Trying to get on my good side."

"That's not what it sounded like to me."

"Forget about it, Erin. It's nothing."

If there weren't any guards in the room, she would have slapped him. "It's not nothing. I don't believe you. If you don't tell me what's going on, I'm going after this thing. Whatever it is."

Peter shot forward and grabbed her hands. "Erin,

please. You need to let this go. These are dangerous people."

"So James does know what he's talking about then. He knows who has the diamonds. Did he tell you?"

Peter pushed his index finger into the table to make his point. "Whether they took them or not, my family is not getting mixed up in it."

"But — "

"No, Erin. Stay out of it."

She sulked for a minute but didn't even know what could be done. She couldn't do anything anyway. She could break into a place and steal merchandise, but beyond that, she had no experience.

She changed the subject. She wasn't there to fight. It was time to improve Peter's mood. Maybe soften him up a bit. "Mom's gotten more good reports. The doctor said she might even come home soon."

Peter's face was a mix of relief and elation. Erin couldn't decide if it was because she had changed subjects or because of her news. Probably both.

"That is really great news."

"That means she might be able to come visit you." A black look crossed Peter's face. "Come on, Peter. She misses you so much."

"I know. I just hate the idea of her seeing me in here."

"It's not like she doesn't know what you've done."

"That's not the point. I've disappointed her, and I can't face that look again."

"She's not disappointed in you. She's just sad not to have you around."

"Right. You believe what you have to."

Erin decided not to push it. "Well, at least you have some time to get used to the idea. She's not coming home just yet."

Peter scraped at his nails and stayed focused on his hands. "You've done a great job, Erin. With everything. I'm really proud of you."

She grinned. "Does that mean you approve of my employment?"

He shook his head and laughed. "I'm happy to know if Mom can get to where she doesn't need any more treatment, you can find other employment. I won't ever let that go."

"How am I supposed to find a satisfying job after all the experiences I've had?"

"I'd think by now you'd be happy to settle down."

"What? I'm only twenty-four, I've got a lot more adventure left."

"Adventure, sure. But what you do isn't adventure."

"No? What would you call it?"

"A hazardous stunt."

"I'm pretty sure that's what you said when I started that kids circus training, but it worked out for you in the end, didn't it?"

"Yeah, sure. Rub my face in it." Erin watched James shuffle out. He didn't look at them. When she turned back to Peter. He was frowning. "I told you to let it go."

"What'd I do? Oh, I almost forgot to tell you. I saw Tommy."

"Oh great. How's he doing?"

"Well, he came to check on me like he promised you he would."

"I love that kid."

"Yeah, but he's gone and gotten himself shot."

"What? How?" The shocked concern on his face reminded her of her own when she found out.

"Don't know. He wouldn't tell me."

"Damn. You have to find out for me. Tell him I don't want him mixed up in anything. He needs to stay out of trouble."

"This coming from you?" She smirked. "I tried to tell him that. He wouldn't listen."

"Then tell him I'm telling him."

She shrugged. "I'll try, but you know Tommy. That kid's got a mind of his own."

"Erin, I'm serious. You have to get him uninvolved with whatever it is he's involved with that got him shot."

"I told you, I tried. He doesn't belong to me. I can't *make* him do anything he doesn't want to."

"Doesn't it bother you that he's in danger?"

"Who said he's *in* danger. He was probably in the wrong place at the wrong time. He does spend a lot of time on the street."

Peter was distracted after that, and the rest of their conversation was small talk.

Erin found she was distracted as well. She needed to get out of there and think through some stuff. "Well, I guess I should get going."

"Thanks for visiting. Your news really cheered me up." He didn't look cheered.

"It made my day to bring it to you." Erin's voice was strained.

They stood and hugged. Erin grunted when Peter gave her a tighter squeeze than usual. "Careful or you'll squash me. I'll let you know if anything changes with Mom."

He put a hand on her shoulder when she turned to go. "I love you, sis."

"I know you do. You too."

She walked out into the parking lot, sure she was going to lose even more sleep after what James had said. She was confused and frustrated and wondered if there was a way to orchestrate another meeting with him.

She slapped a hand on the roof of her car when she reached it. She had worked hard to put away any notion of getting Peter out of prison, and now her mind was racing with impossible scenarios.

"Hey, hold on," someone called out from behind.

She turned to see James's brother jogging toward her with an unlit cigarette hanging out of his mouth. She had to hold her breath to keep from reacting. He squinted at her against the sun, then lifted a hand to his forehead to block it. "James wanted me to give you a message."

"Yeah?"

"He wanted me to tell you he used to do some work driving for a guy called Mr. Kennedy. Apparently, he works out of that Italian restaurant in the city, Messina's."

Erin scoffed. "An Italian restaurant? I thought that was just in the movies. Mobster stuff."

"I'm just telling you what he said. Take it or leave it." He lit his cigarette and waited for her to indicate she wanted him to continue.

She sighed. "Fine, please go on."

"He said someone knew your brother was doing that job with the diamonds, and Kennedy arranged to have him caught as a distraction so they could steal the rocks and your brother would take the fall."

Erin bit her tongue to keep from reacting. It took her a couple seconds before she could find her voice. She coughed into her hand to stall. "And what am I supposed to do with this information?"

"I don't care. I'm just passing on the message. Do what you like. But James is sticking his neck out here. All he asks is that you put in a good word for him with your brother. Look — " He moved in closer. "My brother is a shrimp. He's always tried too hard to be way tougher than he is, but he knows he needs people on the inside or else he's screwed. Just let your brother know he's worth looking after."

Erin nodded. "I appreciate his offer of information, but I don't think there's much I can do with it," she lied. "And I can't promise anything with my brother. But I'll ask."

"That's all he wants."

He turned and walked toward the bus stop. Erin watched him go, and she was still sitting in the car when the bus left. This was the opportunity she had been hoping for since the beginning, but all it did was reveal the very real chasm between wanting to do something and actually doing it. If she could prove Kennedy took the diamonds, that would change everything. But the enormity of what that would require sent a ripple of panic through her body.

"Not now." She pressed her fingers into her closed eyes as she breathed in and out deeply.

All she wanted to do was help, but how was she going to find the courage to face a crime boss, or whatever he was, and get to the truth, when all she had ever done in the past, when it really mattered, was freeze?

———————

Chapter 11

———————

ERIN HAD a jewelry store lined up to rob that night. She had scoped it out the day before, and it was a good night for it. She had even gotten dressed and ready to go because the truth was, the last thing she wanted to do was go after this guy named Mr. Kennedy. But the fear that ate away at her was making her agitated. Too many times in the past she had stood by and done nothing, letting those she loved suffer. First when her dad died, then when her brother was arrested, and now finally she had the information she needed to help Peter and she was pushing it aside to stick with what she knew. What, in her mind, was safe.

She stood at the threshold of her bedroom, her insides churning. She was desperate to turn her back on the new information she was given. After all, it was what Peter wanted.

It's what Peter wanted. But she knew that her desire to stay away from the truth about the diamonds had nothing to do with Peter and what was best for him. It was all down to fear, and she was tired of being afraid to act.

She rubbed her hands down her scrunched-up face and blew out an explosive breath when she finally made her decision. She wouldn't run away from the hard stuff anymore. She couldn't let her brother down. Not again.

She grabbed her laptop and lay down on her bed to do her research. She attempted to access floor plans for Messina's but, on such short notice, that idea was a write-off, so she looked up their opening hours instead.

The reviews were good and said it was a place the locals loved, which was usually a marketing gimmick. It also mentioned excellent service, great food, and a reasonably priced menu. She clicked through pictures showing checkerboard tablecloths, dim lighting, and somehow tasteful wallpaper covered in grapes.

It wasn't what she expected, although she wasn't sure what she had thought it would look like. Maybe pictures of people passing money under the table or something? But this looked like a regular restaurant with regular people. She breathed out some of the haunted feeling that cooled the inside of her bones and told herself it was no big deal. Breaking into a restaurant would be way easier than breaking into a jewelry store. And, assuming James was correct, there might even be diamonds in there, if she got really, really lucky.

Also, there was no way she could confirm the information without checking for herself. All she had to do tonight was check.

Easy.

She grabbed her phone and started typing a text to

Ryan to see if he could help, but then stopped. If it somehow got back to her brother that she was not only pursuing the matter but doing it with Ryan, he'd explode, and she was already pushing enough boundaries with him as it was. Besides, tonight was just an information gathering exercise. Whatever she found out, it would be a low-risk job. If she discovered something promising, she might even be able to get some help from Peter. He knew people. If a safe needed cracking, he'd be able to give her a contact. If she could convince him it was a slam dunk, he would get on board. He had to.

She clicked on a map and switched to street view. There was an alley to the side of the building, which meant there was a strong possibility of an entry point at the back that would be easy to reach. Simple.

"You just keep telling yourself that," she said as she closed her laptop.

It was 1:30 in the morning when Erin turned up outside of Messina's. According to the website, they had closed at 10 p.m., but with several bars nearby, the street was lively. The activity would help her blend in on the street but would make it harder to slip into the building unobserved if the alley didn't pan out.

Erin walked past the restaurant without giving it any attention except what she could see in her peripheral vision. It was dark inside, and chairs were upturned onto tables.

She went into a hole-in-the-wall bar a block away

just to show her face and give her a reason for being there, in case questions were asked. In all the years she'd been doing this, she'd never needed it, but despite her anxiety and her desire to get the job over with, she couldn't afford to cut corners. She would do this like any other job. She'd break in and if, by some miracle, she found diamonds, she'd take them just like she would anywhere else. Just because she'd never stolen from criminals before didn't mean it wasn't a valid opportunity like every other one.

This was the commentary she had running through her head so she didn't lose her nerve.

The bar she entered had low lights and loud music, and the floor was sticky under her feet. She ordered a whiskey sour and turned around, leaning her elbows on the counter, also slightly sticky, while she let her eyes progress across the room. People were crowded around tables and in various groups, yelling over the music to make themselves heard. A few were dancing on the small dance floor.

A guy with bleach-tipped hair caught her eye. He would do perfectly.

He stood around a table with a couple of other guys. Raking their eyes up and down every girl who got too close, they were obviously on the prowl, but because they looked like a bunch of jackasses, they weren't having much luck.

When her drink arrived, she held it inches from her lips and watched him. He was laughing with his friends. Possibly a dirty joke or offhand comment about one of the girls who had turned him down. But his eyes were never far from scoping out the room for his next prey. It wasn't long before he locked eyes with her. That's when she took a sip and kept her eyes on him. The side of his mouth curled up slyly as he rose from his seat and elbowed the friend closest to him. He headed her way.

Perfect. If anyone asked, he'd remember the pink-haired girl who was drinking at the bar, and if anyone found her in the alley behind the restaurant, all she had to do was act drunk and confused.

"Hey there," he yelled over the din.

"What?" She pretended not to hear.

He leaned closer. "I said, hey there."

"Oh, hey."

"Have I seen you in here before?"

"Yeah, sure. I've been in here a bunch of times."

"Can't believe I missed you."

"What?"

"I said you're beautiful."

She smiled shyly. "Thanks."

"Can I buy you a drink after that one?"

She spent the next half hour pretending to get tipsy. It was hard to keep his mouth off her, but pretending to be drunk allowed her to purposely misunderstand what he was trying to do. Several times she laughed at something he said and pushed him away in jest, keeping a hand firmly on his chest.

After she decided she had had enough, she gripped his arm and opened her eyes wide. He was trying to kiss and grope her again, so she slipped her hand up and pressed it against her mouth and said, "I think I'm gonna be sick," then took off through the crowd.

The bathroom was at the back of the room and around a corner where he would lose sight of her. She stopped when she reached the bathroom door. There was the possibility he'd come looking for her, so she'd need to slip out in case he decided to take the risk of seeing her vomit.

She waited only a minute before moving stealthily back into the main room. A man, who she assumed played football judging by his size, stood just in front of her. The perfect cover.

She peeked around the wall and could see White-tips still sitting at the counter. He hadn't stopped checking out the room. He turned her way, and she sucked in behind the big guy, holding herself straight, then leaned over like she wasn't feeling well, just in case.

He wouldn't wait long before either coming to find her or moving on. Most likely moving on. What guy who wants to get laid waits to deal with puke?

When she ducked outside, it was drizzling, and a cold, miserable haze had settled on the street. The perfect reason to pull her hood up and cover her pink hair.

She kept her face toward the ground and slowed her walk like she often did to try to time her exit into the alley for the best chance of remaining unobserved. She glanced around her at the people on the street who were mostly concerned with themselves. She staggered a bit. A drunk girl heading wherever the night took her. She kept up the act until she made it into the shadows of the alley, then slipped around the corner and out of sight of the street.

The air was thick and felt sticky, even though it was cold. A dim red light lit a small patch around the back door. The wet air gave it a halo effect.

Street sounds were muffled, but a clattering bottle hitting the ground from somewhere nearby sent her sprinting for cover behind a trash bin. She took a shallow breath to avoid inhaling the stench of the garbage before venturing out into the open to have a quick peek around the corner and out onto the street. It was empty.

After confirming her safety, she turned her attention back to the dim red light. The door looked heavy, which made no difference to her. Doors were not an entryway for her most of the time.

Her gaze shifted to a barred window to the left. Bars were good footholds. Directly above that window, one floor up, was a smaller one that looked like it belonged to a loft storage area. It had no bars because it was too high and too small for anyone to squeeze through. Anyone but her.

She went back one more time to check around the corner and reminded herself, once again, that this was just another job. But she couldn't ease the pressure in her chest.

Before climbing up to the window, she pressed an ear to the door to listen. There was no noise and no light coming through anywhere. She rubbed her hands together as she stepped back and created a mental path, marking in her mind each place she intended to use.

She swung her arms to loosen them up, then twisted at the waist to stretch her back. If this were really like every other job, she would have been up there by now. She could feel her resolve waning, so took a deep breath and, without any more thought, stepped forward and planted her foot on the lower window ledge, standing to rise above it, then she wedged her hand into an inch-wide crevice between bricks. Her other foot poked under a piece of metal that held a pole in place and from there it was all easy grabs to the top.

When she reached the window, she anchored herself in place by pushing her foot hard against a pipe and anchoring her arm in a little nook. The window was grimy so she couldn't get much of a look inside, but it looked safe enough to keep going.

Jiggling the window, she found it unlocked but stuck. She gave it a bump with her fist in a few places on the rotting frame and wiggled it open. She tucked her arms in first, then her head. Using her elbows as leverage, she pulled herself the rest of the way through.

Inside, she dropped her hood back and allowed her eyes to adjust. Judging by the dust, it was a space that hadn't been used in a long time. This room, at least, was safe.

There were bits of old broken restaurant furniture including tables and chairs and some boxes of who knows what, covered in dust and cobwebs. The smell of mildew had her rubbing at her nose.

Using a small penlight, she scanned the floor for the way out and found a folded ladder door. She unhitched it and lowered it an inch. Dim light flooded through the opening, startling her enough that she nearly dropped the ladder. It seemed bright to her dark-adjusted eyes, and being moderately terrified about what she was doing was making her jumpy. She waited and listened, breathing steadily through her mouth. When she was confident it was safe, she lowered the ladder fully, then slipped down into a room full of supplies. The door was open, and she could confirm that the light came from the hallway security lighting. She listened carefully again before checking the hall.

Double doors to the right suggested the entry into the dining room so she turned left. She checked rooms until she found one that was locked. She tapped it lightly with her finger in triumph before pulling out her lock picks. Her hope rose as she fiddled with the lock and allowed herself to imagine finding the diamonds inside, even though she knew it was an impossible scenario. If the diamonds were still around, they'd be in a safe of some kind.

With a satisfying click, the lock disengaged. The door swung open easily as she turned the knob, but it squeaked when she pushed it open fully and sent a prickle down her back.

It was dark in the room, but there were no windows, so she could have a good look around.

She checked her watch. 2:30 a.m. The hard part was over, so she stopped to have the luxury of a few deep breaths to clear her mind and get ready for the search.

Her pen light made a thin stream into the room. She sent the beam in a haphazard pattern, hoping for something to jump out at her. A place to start. She checked first behind a painting on a wall, looking for a concealed safe. It was surprising to her that people still kept safes in the most obvious places. But not here.

She turned her attention to the desk and took a few tentative steps toward it before the room flooded with light.

Her breath choked in her throat as she spun around. Fear clawed at her stomach. A man with tattoos covering his neck was leaning against the door frame, blocking any escape. He lazily dropped his hand away from the light switch and tilted his head sideways, accentuating the ghastly distortion of his face. "Well, hello there. Must be my lucky day."

There was a look in his eyes that chilled her blood. They were a mix of hatred and glee. He folded his arms and tapped his index finger on his bicep while he took in every inch of her. It wasn't the same look the guy at the bar gave her. This guy's look was feral and destructive.

She backed up, and he pushed off the door, following her until she bumped against a bookshelf. He reached a hand up and grabbed the shelf next to her head.

"Please," she pleaded.

"Oh, this one has manners." He ran a finger down her cheek, his fingernail like a knife. Then he grabbed her face, squeezing hard at her mouth. "I like manners. I also like begging," he said, shoving her head back hard enough into the bookshelf that she saw stars. "You think you could beg a little?"

Her head cleared after a few seconds, and she knew

if she didn't do something, she would die in a way she could only imagine in her nightmares.

She wrenched her leg up to knee him in the crotch. He was expecting it and easily pushed her leg aside, then he punched her in the stomach. She crumbled as the breath was knocked out of her, but he grabbed her by the throat and lifted her up. She grabbed hold of his hands, trying to scratch them away so she could get a breath.

"How rude of me. I haven't even introduced myself. My name's Stanley. What's yours?"

Chapter 12

NICK SCANNED the crowd for Murphy's hat when he entered the bar. He spotted it on the far side of the room. Nick tucked through the crowd and sidled up, dropping onto the stool next to him.

Murphy nodded stiffly, his arms resting on the counter with his shoulders hunched over the bar. He fingers flicked as though depositing ash in a tray. He wouldn't last long before needing to go outside and have a cigarette.

Nick ordered a bourbon and rubbed his tired eyes.

"Long day?" Murphy asked before he took a sip of what looked like a stale beer.

"Something like that." Nick pressed his fingers into his forehead and sniffed before resting his head on his hand.

Murphy looked at his watch. "Sorry to keep you out so late."

"Naw, I told you it was fine. I've got to head to Messina's on my way home anyway and grab a couple of things to deliver for Kennedy." He yawned, not bothering to cover it.

"Deliveries?"

"Artwork, I think."

"Maybe you should have a coffee instead."

Nick just shrugged and reached for his wallet when the drink was put in front of him.

"This one's on me," Murphy said, sliding some bills to the bartender.

"You're being awfully generous tonight."

"I'm in a rare good mood." He lifted his beer, throwing back the dregs of his drink. "How's Monkey?" He said the name like it was a hiccup, then punched himself in the chest a couple of times and burped.

"Recovering. Kennedy sent some guys after Brayson. They couldn't seem to locate him, of course. Although Kennedy didn't seem too concerned about it." Murphy just nodded. "Other than that, everything is pretty quiet."

"Disappointed?" Nick's eyes twitched toward Murphy, then he turned his attention back to his glass as he twisted it around between his fingers, wiping at the condensation. Murphy shifted in his seat. "Something you're not telling me?"

Nick turned his tongue around his mouth like he was tasting the words, trying to decide how to describe the flavor. "It's been a strange day is all."

"You've got something."

"Not something. Nothing really, I — " He thought about what Monkey had said and he thought of the pink-haired girl. He couldn't decide which was taking up more room in his mind. He'd have to give Murphy something. The guy wasn't stupid, but in the end, he kept what Monkey said about Kennedy to himself. He didn't want to get the kid mixed up in this business. "There was just this woman at the hospital."

"Ah, let me guess. You asked her out, and she turned you down?"

Nick laughed and scratched his head. His pride prickled, and he nearly gave into the temptation to explain, but he'd keep his tryst with Pinky to himself. "You got me in one."

"Guess a pretty boy like you's not used to that. But take some advice from a guy with my ugly mug, no woman is worth the trouble if she keeps you up at night." He sniggered. "Unless it's for the right reasons."

Nick laughed to keep Murphy happy, then tipped the rest of his drink back in one swallow. "I should get going."

"Don't go drinking and driving."

Nick gave Murphy a look that said "piss off" but responded with, "See ya 'round."

The foot traffic was thinning out as Nick walked to Messina's, whistling as he went. Thoughts of the pink-haired girl weren't far from his mind. The strange thing was, the way she had responded to him was almost like being turned down. Murphy was right. He wasn't used to that type of response from women. Probably the reason he was having trouble getting her out of his mind. But he reminded himself that he was glad to know he'd never see her again. There was something about her that made him want more, and he couldn't be sure he'd say no if it came to that.

"Punch him in the face!" a girl shrieked. Nick jumped back in reflex and reached for his gun, but the girl making all the noise wasn't looking at him.

Nick, lost in his thoughts, hadn't noticed the crowd.

He took another step backward as the girl staggered forward, sweeping her arms around in front of her as though she were swatting at a spider web. Her already skimpy yellow dress crept up with each giant step forward that she took and had about an inch left before it left nothing to the imagination.

Most in the crowd had their phones out, recording, as a tall skinny guy swung drunkenly at a shorter red-haired man who looked just as drunk. Nick was about to intervene when the girl in the yellow dress heaved to the side, vomiting toward the gawkers. The tall guy was distracted and gave Redhead the chance to punch him with a glancing blow to the head, which sent him stumbling into his sick girlfriend, both of them falling to the ground in the muck. The redhead stumbled away, and Nick decided this was a good one to skirt around.

He rounded the corner, passed two more bars that were less crowded on the street, then headed down the alley to the back of Messina's.

He pressed his fingers into his tired eyes before pulling out his keys and flicking through them. He handled a couple of them in the dim red light before deciding on the right one when he heard a bang come from inside. With the key poised at the lock, he stopped to listen. As far as he knew, the place should be empty. He pulled out his gun before unlocking the door.

Opening it a fraction, he scanned the short hall before slinking inside.

With his back to the wall, he crept down to the corner and snapped his head around the wall to confirm the hall was empty, then he stopped to listen. There was nothing. Maybe the noise he heard hadn't come from inside. But in a dangerous job like his, you never took these things for granted.

He snuck down the hall and passed the supply room, catching the strange sight in his peripheral vision that made him take a step back and give it his full attention.

"What the hell?" He had never seen the attic open before. He had no idea what was even up there. Casting his eyes up the ladder, he stood still, listening again for anything coming from up there.

His head jerked around when he heard another bang and a muffled yelp coming from down the hall.

He scanned the opening to the attic again before hurrying to where the new sound had come from. He'd have to go back and check upstairs once he dealt with whatever was down here.

When he peered around the next corner and saw the office door was open, he raced the rest of the way, his gun ready.

Dipping his face into the room, it heated when he recognized the back of Stanley. He had some poor soul up against the bookshelf. His body mostly blocked whoever it was, so Nick couldn't tell what state they were in, just that it was a girl, judging by the arm he could see.

He stuffed the gun into the back of his pants, noting the choking noises that meant he didn't have much time. He would have happily shot Stanley dead if he thought he could get away with it. Instead, he grabbed an ugly vase by the door that he'd always hated and lifted it as he heard Stanley whispering something fierce, close to the girl's face.

With an image of what Stanley had done to the cat fresh in his mind, his eyes focused on his target, and he smashed the vase home. It exploded and Nick jumped back as Stanley dropped to the floor unconscious and covered in bits of pottery. When Nick was confident Stanley was out cold, he lifted his eyes to the girl. She was still standing, surprisingly, with a look of horror on her face as she kept her frightened eyes on her foe. She rubbed at her neck and wrapped an arm around her stomach.

He didn't speak right away. He couldn't. He was too stunned.

Her eyes lifted and met his.

He shook his head slowly in disbelief. "What … the hell … are you doing here?"

She let out a shaky breath and looked back at Stanley. "Is he dead?"

"No," he said, not taking his eyes off her. He was having trouble calibrating himself. She was the last person he expected to see. Everything about the scene was wrong. She shouldn't be here.

"He was gonna … " Her voice trailed off, and she

fell back against the bookshelf, nearly toppling to the floor. Nick jumped over the body and grabbed her. He lifted her and carried her out of the room.

In the hall, he intended to let her recover on the floor, but she kept herself propped up against the wall like a frightened caged animal. He ventured a hand toward her, and when she didn't flinch, he pushed her pink hair out of her face. "Are you hurt?"

She shook her head and took a few steadying breaths. "No, not really. I don't think." She wrapped her arm around her stomach again, then looked at him as though seeing him for the first time. "I don't understand. Nick, right? Why are you here? Did you follow me?"

He tipped his head to the side. "Did *I* follow *you?* No. And really, don't you think I'm the one that should ask the questions? Were you after the artwork or something?"

"Artwork? No, I — I don't — You must have followed me. Why else would you be here?"

"Did you get a knock on the head?"

"But I didn't tell anyone. How else would you know I was here?"

"I didn't know you were here until just then."

"I don't … " She slipped to the floor, dizzy in confusion.

Nick crouched down next to her. "Hey, you're not okay. Let me take you somewhere. You think you need a doctor?"

"No, you're just not making any sense. Why are you here if you're not following me? How can I keep running into you?" A tingling panic sent jolts up her spine. "Something's not right." She scrambled up the wall.

"Whoa, whoa, whoa. Hey, it's okay. I'm not going to hurt you. Everything is going to be okay. It's just the shock. Can you remember breaking in here? I think you came in the attic."

"Yes. I know. I climbed up the wall and through the window. I got into the office and then that crazy guy turned up."

"Yes. He works for the guy that owns the place, unfortunately."

"But why are *you* here?"

"I have a key."

She took a deep steadying breath, but a thought pricked at her mind. "Why?"

Nick couldn't help but laugh. She must have bumped her head pretty hard. "Because Kennedy, the guy Stanley works for?" — He jerked his thumb toward the office door — "I work for him too."

She shrunk at his words, took a deep breath, and jerked her leg up, kneeing Nick in the crotch. He wasn't expecting it like Stanley had been. He doubled over and tried to grab for her when she slipped past him, but she easily ripped her arm out of his grasp and took off for the attic.

By the time Nick had recovered and worked out she'd gotten out the attic, he limped to the back door half-heartedly, already knowing she was gone.

"God dammit, woman. You gotta stop taking off on me," he yelled to the empty alleyway, then curled up against the door frame to recover.

At home, Erin spent the next several days hiding in bed. She had never been assaulted like that before, expecting to die. It was stupid and naive to think she could waltz in there and do what she wanted, but she had to do something. All she wanted was for them to be a family, for Peter to come home and for them all to just do what regular people did, like go to restaurants to have dinner, not to find evidence against crime bosses.

She finally pulled herself together enough to have a shower for the first time in days and brought a cup of coffee to her room, where she sat at her desk staring out the window while her drink went cold. Her fingertips drummed a random pattern on the cup as she twisted it around and around.

She should be dead. If Nick hadn't turned up when he did, she would be. But for all she knew, he was the one who had the diamonds that kept her brother in prison. She let her head fall onto her arm and moaned.

She was crazy to think she could face a crime boss. She wasn't a fighter. She couldn't do it on her own. Her only defensive move had gotten her away from Nick, but he wasn't the one she was afraid of. In her panic she had run from him, but there were other ways women got things. She could tell by the way he looked at her at the hospital that there was an attraction. She could have flirted with him and tried to get information. But that wasn't her mode of operation either. She wasn't much of a flirt, and she was concerned about her own attraction to him. Every time she pictured Nick, she became increasingly conflicted. He might work for this Kennedy guy, but he still saved her from Stanley. The way he responded at the hospital didn't make sense either. Nothing about Nick added up. The facts said she could trust him, but that couldn't be right when he worked for her enemy.

The doorbell rang, and her body tightened. She lifted herself from her chair to see the street from the window. Ryan's BMW was parked out front. He would help her if she asked. But she couldn't face him like this. She was too fragile and couldn't take it if he tried to make advances on her like he had been doing lately. She leaned back into her chair, away from the window in case he looked up when he left.

Puffing her cheeks out, she blew out some tension. She might not know what to do, but there was one thing she did know — she couldn't hide in her room forever. What she needed was to get her confidence back, and there was only one way she knew to do that.

Chapter 13

ERIN PULLED her hair into her usual messy bun and hopped down the stairs. It felt good to get moving, especially to a place she knew well.

It took her twenty minutes to reach the old stone building and the rising sun was finally bringing a small amount of warmth, but her breath still showed in the cold air. The place wasn't open to classes until the afternoon, so she'd have it to herself for a couple of hours.

She ran her thumb along the key she was given less than a decade ago when her trainer retired and wanted her to have the freedom to practice when she liked. It allowed Erin the quiet and space she enjoyed when practicing. No eyes judging and assessing. Just her.

The large room was chilly, so Erin jogged around the edge of the space to warm up, passing a couple small rooms on one side, including a locker room.

After a couple of passes, her body was warm enough, so she crossed to the middle of the room where there were two ropes about fifteen feet apart hanging to the floor from three stories up. Other stations for building balance and agility bordered the perimeter, but the rope was all she needed today.

She had first stepped into the building as a six-year-old. Her mom and dad were looking for an outlet for their energetic daughter. They called it a circus school back then, but from her first move on the rope, she was hooked.

She found it easy to climb the rope as a kid, and swinging around like a monkey became her new favorite pastime. But as she grew and learned about the control you could have in propelling yourself in whatever direction you wanted using something as malleable as rope, she knew it was for her. It was a challenge at first and then became something of an obsession as she made her way through tough teenage years. It was also a useful skill when she joined her brother, and it became a regular feature of her jobs.

She stood on her toes and reached up to grasp the rope as high as she could. Then, dropping her heels back to the floor, she held fast, taking most of her weight. She closed her eyes and breathed slow, even breaths, then lifted her legs and climbed until she was ten feet off the ground. She wasn't supposed to go too high on the rope without a spotter, but she had never bothered to heed that rule. It didn't make any sense to her when she was doing far more dangerous things outside of that building. Besides, she had no fear of falling because the rope always caught her. When she was on the rope, it became a part of her.

Pulling herself higher, she twisted her legs around

the rope and pushed out sideways, stretching her muscles. She ignored a twinge in her bicep as her body shook from the exertion. Often she would follow a routine that gave her a combination of strength training and skills practice, but today she needed to push her limits.

She took a deep breath, held it for a second, then let herself fall, the rope snaking through her legs until she twisted again and held herself steady, upside down.

Wrapping the rope around her leg and waist, she dropped her arms to let them rest a moment before ascending again as high as she could go, then she stared at the floor below. She would need to keep her focus so she didn't lose track of where the floor was. One injury she carried happened when she'd tried the drop and lost focus. She twisted too fast and lost direction. Before hitting the ground, she had wrapped her arm through the rope to stop her fall and yanked it out of its socket.

She pushed a long breath out slowly between her lips, let her head tip back, her mind on the ground below, then her body followed. She went from sideways to upside down, then back upright before starting it all again and picking up speed. She twisted and spun and finally, only a few feet off the ground, slowed herself to a stop.

She was out of breath when she stopped, but she held herself off the ground, allowing the giddy wave of the drop to dissipate. As the dizziness faded, so did the muddled thoughts, and her mind cleared for the first time in days as she lowered herself to the mat to rest.

She lost track of time as she lay on the floor, staring

up at the ceiling. She thought of her mom cheering her on at performances. Part of hiding out meant she hadn't been to visit her mom. She couldn't have done it without falling apart. Her mom had a way of looking at her that was unraveling. Then she'd have to explain, and there was no way she would. Not to mention that her mom had enough drama to deal with without her daughter adding to it.

But it had been long enough that her mom would be worried because Erin hadn't visited. Thankfully, after the workout she'd just had, the fear and worry had subsided enough that she should be able to hold a smile on her face. She was strong enough to visit without breaking. Hopefully.

The gift store at the hospital was full of useless items whose sole purpose was to make a sick or injured person, smile. Erin reminded herself that it was important, but she'd spent too much time within these walls and all the trinkets did now was remind her that her mother was sick.

In her desire to give the appearance that everything was fine, Erin had considered buying flowers. But she never bought her mom flowers. They'd be dead in a few days anyway. Another reminder she'd grown to hate. Not to mention her mom would know something was up if she did something out of character.

Heading for the elevators empty-handed, Erin practiced her smile in the reflection of the doors. It was an effort to push the smile into her eyes. She hadn't gotten it yet when the doors opened.

As she made her way through the familiar halls, she focused on the fact that her mom was getting better. Seeing her sitting up in bed and looking well would help.

Just before Erin reached the room, her foot stubbed on the ground as a jolt of fear attacked her again.

A nurse brushed passed her arm and turned to apologize. She had a sweet and easy smile on her face that turned out to be a lifeline for Erin, who grabbed hold of that joy and smiled back before the nurse continued on her rounds.

Erin held the smile in place and stepped into the room before her thoughts could get away from her again. But when she walked through the door, the smile that had come easily in response to the nurse melted off her face.

"Pinky, there you are," Nick beamed.

"Pinky, that's cute," Jodie said, smiling serenely at her daughter.

Erin looked at Nick. Her smile had somehow found its way back on her face, although it now carried a crazed quality. The worried look on her mom's face confirmed that her attempt at a mask had failed.

It took her a moment to find enough words to put together in a sentence. "Nick. How unexpected."

"Where have you been? Your mom and I have been worried."

"I — " She looked at her mom as her voice wavered. "I've been busy." She had to get Nick out of there.

"Sorry, Mom. I need to have a word with Nick, if that's okay?" She squeaked.

Jodie looked at her daughter quizzically. "You okay, sweetie?"

"Mm-hmm." She was afraid to say anything else.

Nick looked at Jodie. "Will you excuse me, please?"

"Of course. See if you can find out what's bugging her. You sure you're okay, Erin?"

"Fine," she blurted, then twisted out of the room.

"I'll see you later, Jodie."

"I hope so. Stop by anytime. I've got plenty more stories about Erin to share."

Erin could hear the two of them laughing. Nick still had a cocky grin on his face when he walked out past her. "What's gotten into you? I'm the one that keeps getting the raw end of the deal every time we meet," he said, flicking her hair as he went by.

A strange mixture of fear and anger warred within her.

She looked back at her mom's door one last time before turning to Nick. He was standing right behind her, and she bumped into him.

"You really need to stop doing that. It's getting a bit creepy." His grin remained, so her anger won out over her fear, and she pushed him down the hall to a quieter area.

"No need to shove, Pinky."

"My name is Erin."

"Erin." He crossed his arms like he was annoyed with her. That pissed her off more.

"What the hell do you think you're doing?" she whisper-yelled.

"Keeping your mom company while you disappeared off the face of the earth."

"You have no right." She was having trouble looking him in the eye.

Nick could see he intimidated her. He was surprised by her fear. After she kneed him the other night, he thought it was a repeat of their first encounter. An overconfident, beautiful girl using him however she could. With her arms crossed against her chest in a protective squeeze, he could see he had been wrong.

Her eyes darted around, keeping people in view in case he tried to hurt her.

Nick's face softened, and he dropped his arms to his side. "Erin. I didn't come here to hurt you. I came because I wanted to make sure you were all right." She still wouldn't look at him. "Okay, it was also because I was miffed you took off like you did, but Stanley is not someone to mess around with. He's dangerous. He would have killed you, and you didn't stay long enough to tell me if he had hurt you. I was worried about you, especially when you hadn't been to visit your mom in a couple of days."

She licked her lips, and her eyes lifted to him but then moved away again. "But you work there. For Kennedy."

Nick steadied his own eyes on her. "Yeah."

"So this Stanley guy is your co-worker, right?"

He leaned toward her. "You saw me smash that vase over his head. I didn't join him. I didn't ask him what he was doing. I knocked him out when I saw he was choking someone. I didn't even know it was you until he was on the ground."

Nick was right. He'd saved her. But it didn't make any sense, and there was still the possibility he had been a part of her brother's arrest. She shook her head. "How long have you worked for Kennedy?"

"Less than a year. Why?"

"Where were you before that?"

"New York."

Her shoulders tensed up again. "You swear?"

"Yes. I have no reason to lie to you."

She scoffed and waited while a doctor walked by. When there was no one in earshot she said, "But you're loyal to Kennedy."

Nick tipped his head up to the ceiling and cleared his throat. "No actually, I don't have any loyalties to him. I just do some work for him. That's all."

"Illegal stuff?"

"Sometimes. Well, mostly. But look, you were there for a reason. Maybe I can help. I'd like to help, and frankly, you could use it."

She gave him a blank look at the offer, then a sly smile spread across her face and she wagged a finger at him. "You know, I thought of doing something like this."

"Like what?"

"The nice guy routine. I thought if I flirted with you, you might give me the information I'm looking for."

He lifted an eyebrow. "But I'm not flirting."

"Same thing. You're being all nice so I'll spill." She

crossed her arms. "Not gonna happen. I'm not afraid of you." She was mostly telling the truth at this point. She seemed to waver in her feelings as they related to him. The thought occurred to her that he could have done a lot more damage to her and her family by now if he had wanted to. The terror that had filled her when she saw him with her mother had been more due to the surprise of seeing him there and not knowing why.

He could see she was loosening up. "So, there's nothing I can do to prove to you that I'm trustworthy?"

She looked at him for a moment, then pressed her fingers into the bridge of her nose. If he genuinely wanted to help, that would be a godsend. There was no way she'd ever go after Kennedy again on her own. If Peter had any chance of getting out of prison, it was with Nick. And for whatever reason, she found that, despite her anxiety toward him, there was trust as well.

She looked around the room. Out the window was a horrible view of the brick wall of the building next door, but it gave her an idea.

The corner of her mouth lifted. "Okay. I promise to tell you what it is I'm after, if you can beat me to the top of the hospital."

"That's an unusual proposition. You mean like, I race you up the stairs?"

"Outside."

He took a step back to take her full measure. "Outside? As in, climb to the top of the hospital from the outside?"

"Yup."

He looked out the window, his face in full smile. This

girl was unreal. "I take it you have some experience in this area?"

"Sure do. How about you?"

He shrugged. "I can manage." He'd chased and been chased enough to have plenty of practice scaling buildings.

"I'm going to tell my mom I'll be back later. I'll meet you out front."

He watched her go, a skip in her step, and rubbed the tip of his thumb across his bottom lip. He was in trouble.

Chapter 14

WAITING OUTSIDE, Nick was close to floating. He could tell by her build that she'd be quick. She had gotten into Messina's by climbing up the exterior of the building. Not the biggest feat, but still.

He stretched as he assessed the surrounding buildings. Growing up in a rough part of town meant he knew how to beat an opponent that had the advantage. Unfortunately, in this case, he wouldn't have the added motivation of knowing if he were caught he'd be beaten to a pulp. He'd have to find another incentive.

He looked across the front of the building but knew they couldn't climb there. There were too many people around. But there were a lot of other buildings to choose from.

It wasn't long before she joined him. He waved a hand around, pointing at their choices. "So, which one will it be?"

She scanned the buildings that she could see. To the left was one that would be hard to scale. Not for her, but she was curious to see his reaction. "How about that one?" she asked, heading over to it and around the back to take a closer look.

He followed, but his attention was on her instead of the building. He was going to enjoy this a little too much.

The building was four stories high, and the windows were flush. Nick ran a hand along the wall. "You can climb this?"

"Of course. Can't you?"

He laughed. "Damn. You really don't want me to win, do you."

"Does that mean you give up?" she challenged.

He turned to her and stepped closer, leaning in until his face was inches from hers. "I never give up."

"Good."

He caught a twinkle in her eye as she tugged off her shoes and stuffed them into her pocket. She walked several feet away from him then stopped. "Ready?"

He analyzed the wall in front of him and found his spot, dropped his head, and smiled. Then looked at her, ready. "Say when," he said with the jerk of his head.

She didn't say, just started climbing. He was several seconds behind her because he couldn't help but watch her start. He was screwed. He turned to his own place on the wall and started climbing. He'd have to focus, but he kept getting distracted when he'd glance over, watching her work. She was like a spider. Then she moved around the corner and was gone, which forced him to pick up speed. He wanted to win but was sure it was impossible. Her light weight was definitely an asset on this building with small holds.

He was sweaty and frustrated by the time he pulled himself up onto the roof. He'd slipped in a few places and for a moment images of Erin falling to the ground slowed him down, but that fear helped push him on. By the time he reached the top, his desperation was mounting. He didn't see her at first and almost panicked, until he spotted her sitting on the other side of the roof.

"You lose," she called out, breathing heavily. She must have sprinted across the roof so she could be sitting casually when he made it up.

He chuckled as he walked over to her, shaking out his arms. "You're good. That how you break into places?"

"You don't get to ask me questions. You lost." Her sly grin gave him hope that he still had a chance. If she knew something about Kennedy, he wanted to know what it was.

"Aren't you the least bit impressed that I actually made it up here? That was not easy."

"Maybe a little."

"Tough crowd."

"If it's any consolation, I only suggested this building 'cause I thought you'd say no."

"Well, that's something at least." He slid down to sit next to her. "But I really do want to help. Kennedy crosses lines I never would. And you gave me the opportunity to put Stanley out of commission, which I have been wanting to do since I met him. So I owe you." His lips tweaked. "But I wonder what you think a little thing like you can do to a big guy like Kennedy."

She huffed in exaggerated offense. "I've got very damning information on him." She rested her arms on her knees. "Sort of. I guess I can tell you I'm in over my head. That's something you already know."

"Yeah. I gathered that."

"You're actually the first guy I've properly defended myself against when I had to."

"Hang on a minute. There was no need to defend yourself against me. That was a totally unprovoked attack."

She covered her face with her hands. "I know. I'm sorry. I shouldn't have done that to you, but I panicked." She looked at him through a gap in her fingers. "Did it hurt?" She scrunched up her face, already assuming the answer.

"Getting kicked in the groin? Yes. It did. I know you're small, but you've got a mean knee jerk." She groaned. "In fact, I'm not even sure if I'll be able to have kids now. It's pretty terrible what you did. Still hurts." He shoved her shoulder with his. "Hey, I'm just giving you a hard time. You were in a scary situation. I don't blame you at all. I just didn't like it much. But it goes to show that you need help. Why don't you take a chance on me?"

"I like to minimize risk."

"My help doesn't minimize risk?"

"Does it?"

"Okay. Well, how about the fact that I saved your life. Twice."

"Twice?"

"The first time we met could have gone down very differently for you if I hadn't stepped in."

"You mean if you hadn't gotten in my way. But if you recall, I lied to you when I said that guy was after me, remember?"

"Wasn't he after you?"

"Yeah, but you know what I mean. No lives were saved that day. You just don't want to admit that a big guy like you got scammed by a little thing like me."

He held back the grin that was threatening. "If I hadn't been sidetracked by your looks, I might have been a bit sharper, and you wouldn't have gotten away."

"Oh, god. Now you *are* flirting with me to get information." Erin dipped her head.

Nick took the opening and adjusted his approach. "Erin. Come on. Let me help you."

She considered him for a moment. "Be honest. You don't want to help me simply out of the goodness of your heart."

"I never said I did."

"So there is something in it for you?"

"Yes. Does that change anything?"

"If you said there wasn't, I'd know you were lying." And someone on the inside would make all the difference. "Okay, I accept your help. But I don't want to get into it here."

"Why not?"

"Because my mom is waiting and I need some time to gather my thoughts."

"You're not going to bail on me, are you?"

"As I have discovered, I can't seem to get rid of you. Meet me down at the Navy Pier tonight at six, near the Ferris wheel. Now, I've gotta go say hi to my mom and tell her to ignore anything you've said and make her promise never to speak to you again." Erin grinned.

Nick pushed up off the ground. "Okay, but she really likes me." He held out a hand to help her up.

"Don't worry, I'll change that," Erin said, ignoring his hand and standing.

Nick put his hands on his hips and surveyed the roof. "So, how do we get down from here?"

"Jump," she said and ran to the other side of the roof, slipping over the side and disappearing.

Nick ran over. It looked like she had leapt off the building.

Leaning over the side, he saw the fire escape that she obviously already knew was there. He watched while she made her way down, not using it. There was something oddly fragile about her, and yet she did stuff like that. It boggled the mind.

Chapter 15

ERIN RUBBED her hands together then blew into them. Her knuckles were stiff in the cold. She should have worn a heavier jacket.

The cloudless sky faded to white at the horizon, where the sun was about to dip out of sight and take any remaining warmth with it. The night would be colder than she had expected.

A small number of people occupied the pier, but they were thinning out quickly. She scanned their faces again in the dimming light, searching for Nick. He was late, and her anxiety heightened as she questioned whether she should have agreed to tell him anything. If he turned out to be one of the bad guys, she was screwed.

She bit her lip hard and looked around again, wavering between staying or going.

A gust of wind whipped at her jacket, and she shivered. She was too agitated to stand still any longer so walked to the other side of the pier. The change in angle gave her a view up the side of a building and she spotted Nick, bounding into sight, with his hands stuffed in his pockets and looking as cold as she was.

She could tell he had seen her by the direct line he walked toward her, but he wasn't looking at her now. His head swiveled as he observed the other people and anything that might try to remain unseen. His attention to his surroundings gave her a certain amount of comfort that he was a guy who knew what he was doing, and it eased her enough that she noticed how good he looked in his leather jacket. Not that attraction meant anything. It was just a physical response to someone and had nothing to do with the type of person they were. At least that's what she told herself. But as he moved toward her with a confident stride, his hair a bit mussed in the breeze, and the memory of how he had helped her, she felt a buzz she tried hard to ignore. It was the last thing she needed, and it brought a frown to her face when he made eye contact.

He misunderstood. "Sorry I'm late. I got caught up."

"It's fine," she said, wrapping her arms around herself to try to block off the cold. And him.

"Here," he said and put a hand on her shoulder, directing her back the way he had come. "Over through there it's a bit more protected from the wind."

She nodded as she rubbed her hands up and down her arms to bring some warmth into them. "Looks like I'm not very well prepared for my own rendezvous."

"No, but you look good." He winked and Erin

clicked her tongue, annoyed at her inability to think of a comeback to negate the flip in her stomach.

Nick led her to the token machines. She leaned against one of them, out of the wind, and Nick took up position at a pillar across from her. "We can go inside somewhere if you're too cold."

"I'm fine," she said and rubbed at her red nose.

He looked around again then back at her. "I didn't expect you to be here."

"I told you, you know how to find me. So what's the use of avoiding you? I'd rather deal with my problems head on."

"Oh, so I'm a problem, am I?"

"You might come in handy for my current dilemma, but other than that, yes, I consider you to be a prob-lem." *Was she flirting?* She tipped her head to the side. "Maybe 'hassle' is the more appropriate word."

"I see. It's such a burden you bear putting up with me. Maybe I should go." He didn't move. His eyes were glued to her face, watching the struggle she was having to keep from smiling.

She shrugged. "I might be able to work it out on my own."

He bit his lip and smiled, dropping his gaze to the pavement before locking eyes on her again. "It could work. I'll have a look at my schedule and see if I'm free to turn up at just the right moment to help you again."

She smiled back at him until a shiver carved a path up her core. It wasn't from the cold. "Nick, I know I've been pretty standoffish with you, but I wanted to thank you for saving me the other night. That was one of the most terrifying things I have ever experienced. I know I'd be dead if not for you."

"I'm just glad I was there."

She shifted her feet. "Look. I'm not used to trusting anyone but myself and my family. Doing what I do, I don't really have friends, and I've never had to rely on anyone else besides Peter. Not for anything serious, anyway. But I need help now, and I've got no one else. So even though I don't know you well enough to know if your promises are worth anything, can you promise me I won't get hurt by getting involved with you? I don't want my family to suffer because I made a stupid choice in trusting you."

He moved close to her and spoke softly. "My promises *are* worth something. And I promise you, I'm not getting involved to hurt you. I do want to help you. And I will do everything in my power to make sure you're safe. I already told you I have my own reasons, but that doesn't mean I don't genuinely want to help you."

"Okay." Erin sighed. "Here goes. I'm trying to get my brother out of prison."

Nick nodded, but when she didn't continue straight away, he frowned. "What does that have to do with breaking into Kennedy's?"

"He might have something that will prove my brother's innocence."

Nick's jaw clenched. "He set your brother up." Nick had seen Kennedy do it before.

"Sort of. I mean." She suddenly felt stupid. She shouldn't have led with that. How could she explain to

Nick that her brother was breaking into the place, but he was innocent? "Like you said, he set my brother up."

"Murder?"

Erin winced. She wasn't really being fair to Nick. She was still trying to keep stuff from him, but if she expected him to help, he'd need the facts. "My brother was breaking into a jewelry store where there were a bunch of diamonds." Nick almost jumped out of his skin. He'd expected some connection to drugs. He didn't know Kennedy had his hands on diamonds. "He's in prison for a long time because of it."

"So your brother stole the diamonds and gave them to Kennedy?"

"No, he never took them."

"Wait. So he broke into the store, but didn't steal the diamonds?"

She threw her hands up in the air. "Forget it," she said, turning away.

"No." He put a hand on her arm and pulled her around. "I'm not picking on you or your brother. I'm just trying to figure out what's going on."

She took a deep breath and looked down. She had to stop being so defensive. "My brother broke in for the purpose of stealing from the store. Yes, he would have taken them if given the opportunity, but while he was still in the store, the police turned up and caught him while he was there. He didn't have the diamonds, but they never found them, so they suspected that my brother had somehow taken them. I recently found out Kennedy gave the police the tip-off as a distraction so he could steal the diamonds himself."

"But that doesn't make any sense. If they got your brother in the store, how could they prove he has the diamonds? What could he have done with them that they wouldn't have found the loot on him?"

Erin rubbed her hands together. "They didn't have to prove anything. He pleaded guilty."

"Why?"

"I don't know." She threw her hands in the air again. She was flustered and frustrated. "But the diamonds weren't there when the police went through. Now I know Kennedy took them somehow, but the court sentenced my brother to decades because he wouldn't tell them where he hid the diamonds that he never had in the first place."

He saw her eyes go glassy with tears and he moved in closer, ignoring the warning bells in his head. He took her hand. "Erin, are you sure he never took them?"

She pulled her hand away. "Positive."

"I'm not saying your brother would lie to you, but family can do strange things to protect those they love."

"He didn't take them."

"How can you be so sure?"

She would have to tell Nick what a coward she was. "Because I was there."

He let that information settle, but he didn't ask the question he wanted to. She seemed smaller than normal in that moment, and he would have given her the world if he could have. "Let me help you. I want to help you."

She wiped at her eyes. "Well … I guess … you haven't seen any diamonds lying around the place by any chance?" She laughed lightly.

"No." Nick searched his mind for anything that might be connected. "How'd you find out it was Kennedy who took them, anyway?"

"When I went to visit my brother the other day, a guy named James, who said he had worked for Kennedy, told me he heard a conversation about it."

Nick remembered a guy named James who worked for Kennedy. A driver if he recalled correctly. "When was this? I mean your brother's arrest."

"A couple of years ago. You know, if he *had* taken them, we would have been set for life. No more risk. We could have just lived off that. We were so close."

"That's what you think? You think your brother would have stopped stealing after that?"

"Why wouldn't he?"

"It's just … " Nick ran his hand through his hair. "You can't just turn that off. That rush you get. If you don't find it somewhere else, you tend to go back to it. It's like a drug."

"He only cared about providing for me and our mom. After my dad died, he had a lot of pressure on him. Then Mom got sick, and he ended up in prison." Emotion choked off her words, and she clasped her hands together and stared at the ground again.

"I'm sorry. I'm not trying to upset you." He thought about the diamonds. He hadn't come across any, but it was before his time. Whether Kennedy had them or sold them, Nick couldn't be sure, but there had to be a trail of some kind. Someone would know something. You don't pull off a heist like that without people knowing about it.

"They wouldn't be at the restaurant," he finally said. His eyes flicked back and forth as he tried to put pieces of information into place. "Unless he had a buyer for the lot, he'd most likely spread the sales out over time to avoid attracting attention. Couple of years, huh? Do you remember how much they were worth?"

"I don't know. Millions," she said in a small voice.

Nick whistled. "And you were there when all this was happening?"

Erin laughed, sadly. "Not much help though. I was supposed to be at college."

"College? Really?"

"Peter asked me to do this last job, but I had already moved on. I had been home for a break and was headed back. Had my flight booked and everything."

"What were you studying?"

Erin shook her head. "You'll laugh at me."

"What? No, I won't. Tell me." He laughed.

"No, you're laughing already."

He ran a hand down his mouth. "Okay, I'll stop. Look." He pointed at his deadpan face. "Serious. Now tell me."

She glared at him, then said, "Accounting."

"Accounting?"

"Yes, don't laugh. I'm good with numbers and finance and everything. I just wanted to know what it was like to have a normal life. Then my flight was delayed."

"You gave up on college because your flight was delayed?"

"I felt bad for not helping Peter out on this one last job. And I was also missing it."

"The rush."

"Yeah, I guess. When my flight was delayed, I took that as a sign. I decided I could take a later flight and surprise him." She shook her head. "I was hiding up in the ceiling of the jewelry store waiting to surprise him. That's when the police burst in. Peter didn't take the diamonds. I would have seen him." She closed her eyes and pressed her fingers into her forehead. "Then the police came in, and all I could do was sit there in the ceiling like a coward while they took him away. Because that's what happens when stuff goes wrong. I freeze."

"You didn't freeze. You kept yourself from getting arrested. There's a big difference. There was nothing you could do. Besides, you didn't freeze the other night when the security guard was after you."

"That was different." She moved her hands to press onto her cold cheeks. "First my dad, then my brother," she mumbled.

He heard what she said, but let it go. "Did you have a good view? Did you see what happened next?"

"After they took my brother away, there was a police officer, looked like a detective or something, who went through the place before the others came in to see what was missing."

"Maybe he took the diamonds."

"He could have, but I don't know. How am I supposed to figure that out? It's pointless. I spent so many nights going over that in my head, and I never got any closer to the truth. Then after Peter was arrested, my mom's health went downhill fast. I think Peter blamed himself, but it had nothing to do with him. Then I gave up finishing school to stay and look after her. With her hospital bills, I had to do something."

Nick's mind was racing. "The detective, did you get a look at him?"

"Not really, just mostly from on top and he had a hat on so I couldn't even tell you his hair color. My only chance to get at them is through your boss, Kennedy."

Nick nodded. "I can ask around. There are a few people I might be able to get some information out of."

Erin took a step closer to him and put a hand on his arm. He looked genuine in his concern for her situation. "Thank you, really. I — " Damn, she was blushing. She dropped her hand and pulled her jacket tighter around her body. "Thank you. That's very kind of you to help."

"Kind, huh?"

She looked up at him. He had his eyebrows lifted as he watched her. She tipped her head sideways. "Not kind?"

His laugh was light and lifted her spirits. He took a step closer. "What guy wants to be told he's *very kind*. And don't forget. I've got my own reasons."

"Well, like I said, as long as I don't get hurt." She stepped back and leaned against the ticket machine again.

"I already told you I would never hurt you on purpose."

"Then I guess we're good."

"You're not going to ask what motivates me?" he

said, taking another step toward her. What was he doing? Her face flushed as he took another step closer.

"I'm not sure I want to know," she said, trying to keep things light. His face was so close now she could smell mint on his breath. She swallowed. "So we're business partners then?" She squeaked out. She wasn't used to feeling so drawn to someone. This was not good. She was too vulnerable.

He pulled a hand out of his pocket, tucked a strand of hair behind her ear, then slipped his hand back in. "Your eyes are blue."

"So are yours. Are you going to back up, or am I going to have to knee you in the crotch again?"

His eyes flared, and he jerked back. "I'm back, I'm back. Okay, business partners. You're right." He looked off over the water. He would have kissed her if she hadn't put him off. What was it with her that made it so hard for him to keep his distance? "Now that I know what I'm looking for" — He turned back to her — "I'll see what I can dig up. How do I get in touch with you?" He had moved toward her again, but not as close. The air was still hot between them.

"We can exchange numbers. That's the way people usually do it." Erin pulled out her phone. "Actually, I am a little intrigued to know why it is you want to help me against Kennedy. You think you'll ever tell me the actual truth about your real motivation?"

Not likely. "We'll see." He'd dated a few girls over the years but never anything serious. He had made sure of that. And this was the kind of girl he could see himself being serious about. They were business partners, that was all. And when this was all over, they wouldn't see each other again. He would have to make sure of that. He'd promised her he wouldn't hurt her, and he meant it. The complications of making sure that happened went deeper than she realized, and he would make sure she never found out why.

Chapter 16

ERIN FELT hope for the first time in years. Despite her reservations about getting Nick involved, she was sure that he would find the answers she needed. Her risk had paid off after all.

She was in such a good mood that she was up early and began cleaning the house — something she struggled to do even in the best of times. Her intention was to do a full clean from top to bottom, but she got sidetracked when she dusted off the old picture albums. After finally putting the photos away, she hadn't made it out of the living room. Now, she stood at the fireplace wiping down the mantle while humming a chorus she couldn't get out of her head, while her feet danced from one side of the fireplace to the other. They'd be a family again. They'd have fires this year, maybe even roast marshmallows like they did when they were kids. She let that thought warm her even though she knew the possibility of Peter actually getting out of prison by

Christmas was impossible, but it didn't matter. The important thing was that he would be home *soon*.

She stepped back to admire her handiwork. The ledge hadn't been dust-free in a long time. She reached her hand out to run a finger along the edge of the mantle, where there were nail holes from Christmas stockings in years past, but her arm dropped back to her side when she remembered Christmas last year when she fell into a deep depression and became reckless for a short period. She was careless in her climbing. She shouldn't even still be alive. A ripple of regret surged through her at the memory of a close call that would have meant her death. But somehow she made it through and came out of the fog to recognize the importance and purpose of her getting a new lease on life. Her mom would be dead if she hadn't pulled herself out of it, and that was the one thing that had held her life together through the pain of it all. It was to help her mom get through her sickness. And the way things were looking, she might not have Peter home, but she had a chance of getting her mom home in time to celebrate the holiday.

She spotted a smudge and ran smooth circles over it when the thought came to her that she could invite Nick for some Christmas celebrations if her mom came home. Let him enjoy the beginning of the reuniting of her family that he had a part in bringing about. The thought squeezed at her heart. She didn't want to admit that their encounters had evoked feelings she'd tried to ignore and had apparently failed at. But she was too happy to worry about pushing them aside now.

She'd never dated much and had mostly given up on the idea. You couldn't get close to a guy when you couldn't tell him you stole for a living. And any guys she'd ever met who also broke the law were usually not the kind of guys she'd bring home to her mom. But Nick was different. Even though he worked for a crime boss, he seemed like a genuinely good guy. Who knew what could happen when this business with the diamonds was all over? Maybe they could both turn over a new leaf.

A knock at the door broke her daydream, and she walked to the door feeling lighthearted.

She swung the door wide. "Ryan." She was beaming.

"Hey there. What's got you in such a good mood?"

She pulled him inside and closed the door conspiratorially, leading him to the living room. "I might be able to get Peter out of prison." She put her bottom lip between her teeth, holding back the smile that was close to enveloping her face.

"What? Are you serious? How?"

Erin sat on the couch, tucking a foot under her. "I got some information on Peter's arrest. Information about who really took the diamonds." She licked her lips in anticipation of Ryan's surprise, but his face closed in and he sat slowly, not yet responding. She pulled her head back. "You don't look very excited."

"No, I am. I mean … " His sigh held a flickering disdain. "I'd like to know where you got this information from before I get my hopes up too high." He clicked his tongue. "It sounds too good to be true."

"I know. You're right. I can understand why you

wouldn't be as excited as I am, of course. I've had time to process. I was hesitant at first too. But Ryan, someone took those diamonds, and it wasn't Peter."

"And you think you know who?"

She nodded. "There's this guy, James, in at the prison."

"A guard?"

"No, an inmate."

"Erin — "

"Just hear me out. This guy, James, hasn't been there long, but he used to do some work for this other guy." She halted. "It just occurred to me that I don't know the guy's first name. All I know is his last name, Kennedy. Anyway, he's the leader of some sort of crime group or something."

"Kennedy?" Ryan's face was impossible to read, but it didn't matter because Erin wasn't paying attention.

"Yeah, turns out Peter was set up. Kennedy took the diamonds, and Peter went down for it. So if I can get my hands on the diamonds, or at least prove that Kennedy took them, then Peter's off the hook. They aren't going to keep him in prison long for breaking in and not stealing anything." Ryan's face twitched. Erin's shoulders dropped. "Come on, Ryan. It's at least worth looking into. In fact — "

"No, yeah, I mean. Look, Erin." He took her hand with both of his. It felt condescending. "I don't like to say it, but I think someone's taking you for a ride here. You are a beautiful girl and I wouldn't put it past any of those inmates to try and get close to you by offering you hope. But think about it for a minute. How would anyone know what Peter was doing when he went to get those diamonds? He made up his own mind about what jobs to do. Who knew what he was doing besides us? I didn't tell anyone, did you?"

"Of course not, but someone knew. They must have."

Ryan shook his head. "Just don't get your hopes up."

Erin wrenched her hand out of his, crossed it under her arm, then huffed back against the couch, deflated.

Ryan grabbed his chin, thinking. "If it means that much to you, I can ask a few questions. I know some people. But please." He leaned forward and put a hand on her knee. "Don't go doing something stupid."

"Like what, go after Kennedy?" She couldn't hold back the bitter sarcasm.

"Yes."

"Why would I do something like that?"

Ryan smiled. "I know you, Erin. It sounds exactly like something you would do."

He obviously didn't know her well enough to know the fear she had battled to go do something crazy like that. "I'm not going to do anything." She was glad she never got around to telling him about Nick. He'd celebrate plenty when Peter walked out of prison, but for now she'd keep the details to herself.

"I'm not trying to upset you, but … have you told Peter? Does he even know about all of this?"

Erin sighed. "Yeah, he knows."

Ryan leaned forward a bit further. "And what does he say about it?"

"He told me to let it go. That it doesn't matter."

"He's a good brother. Hey." He slapped her leg. "The reason I actually came over." He chirped up. "Was to see if you wanted to grab some lunch."

"Oh." Her mind raced for an excuse.

"Come on. You need to get out and be spoiled a bit."

"Well … I'm cleaning the house. If I stop now, I'll never get back to it."

A muscle clenched in his jaw. "I'll get you a cleaner. Now come on." He grabbed her hand and pulled her off the couch. "I'm taking you out so you can stop thinking about these horrible conspiracies with your brother."

"Ryan, I don't know."

"You do eat lunch, don't you?"

"Not always."

"Stop. I don't want to hear any excuses. Get your coat. Let's go."

Erin went reluctantly, but hated that with Ryan, she sometimes felt like she didn't have a choice.

Nick looked for the familiar gray hat and found it on the other side of the park. He approached casually and sat down on the far side of the bench from Murphy. "Diamonds," he said, looking out over the park.

Murphy twitched before licking the edge of the cigarette paper he had just rolled. He lit it before responding. "What about 'um?"

"Guy named Peter Hart was charged with stealing a pile of diamonds a couple of years ago."

"And?"

"I think Kennedy did it and framed Peter."

Murphy nodded. "Where's this come from all of the sudden?"

"I have my sources. Word is, he may have gotten a cop to take the diamonds after Peter's arrest."

Murphy's eyes narrowed as he watched a man throw a frisbee for a dog. "That's quite an accusation."

"I am aware what it is. My question is, is there any way for you to have a look into it for me. Find out who was involved in the case?"

Murphy ran a finger under his nose. "Not sure what you're looking into that for. Don't you have enough on your plate as it is?"

Nick considered his words before he spoke. "I'm there to find any angle that gets us Kennedy."

Murphy put the cigarette between his lips and held it there for a moment before sucking in. "That's old news." He slowly twisted his head toward Nick. "Shouldn't you be focusing on the present?"

Nick closed his eyes in resignation. "It's also kind of a favor for a friend."

Murphy coughed. "A favor? Must be some friend that's got you going after cops."

"You going to look into it or not?"

"I can look. Not promising anything."

"That's all I ask."

Murphy stood, studied a tree in the distance, then

squashed the cigarette under the toe of his boot. "It's a fine line you're walking."

"Always is in a job like this."

Ryan put a hand on Erin's back, ushering her into the swanky restaurant. She looked down at her ripped jeans and was suddenly very self-aware as she had to lead the two of them through the door. She watched the maître d' scan her outfit before her eyes caught sight of Ryan. The slight change from grimace to smile suggested she wasn't sure how to handle the pair.

"Good afternoon," the woman said, her focus totally on Ryan.

"Table for two. By the window."

"I'm sorry, sir, did you have a reservation?"

Erin stood firm, but in her mind, she had already slunk out the door.

Ryan took a step forward. "You're new here?"

"I don't see how that's relevant, sir. But if you must know, I was asked to join the establishment specifically because of my work — "

"I'll excuse your lack of knowledge once, and only once. You might want to go back into the kitchen." Ryan lifted his hand so his index and middle finger could scurry through the air in the direction he expected her to go. "And speak to Felix. Let him know that Ryan Thomson is here for lunch and then come back out and seat us at your best table."

"Sir." The woman barely got the word out between her teeth before doing exactly as Ryan said.

"That was a bit harsh." Erin murmured.

"These people expect you to be rude to them. It's how things get done around here. Now, don't worry about her. Let's have a nice lunch. Order whatever you like. I feel like spoiling you today after all you've been through."

"Yeah, you said."

When the woman returned, she smiled broadly at Ryan like nothing had happened and continued to ignore Erin.

Customer's always right, Erin thought as they were led to the table Ryan had requested, overlooking an indoor garden. It was a beautiful spot, and Erin thought she might have enjoyed it more if she weren't there with Ryan. She allowed herself a moment to imagine being there with Nick, but then ran her hands down her jeans, and decided she didn't belong here, no matter who she was with.

"So," Ryan said, opening his menu. "What else have you been up to? Do you need anything? Any more 'gadgets,' as you are so fond of calling them."

"No. I'm good." Erin looked down at the menu. Half of it she couldn't read. "I'm not very hungry. I might just have a salad."

Ryan dropped the heavy menu on the table, causing a thud that clinked the water and wine glasses. "This isn't still about that mess with Peter, is it?"

"I'm just not hungry." Erin raised her voice slightly above the din.

Ryan wasn't usually so pushy with her. He'd always stayed aloof. But there was one time she had seen him snap. Just the once. A security guard found them on a job. She, Peter, and Ryan. They had always had a plan for that type of thing. Usually they tried to avoid a confrontation of any kind, but Ryan always carried a stun gun. It was enough to slow the person down, but when he fired on the guard, after the man dropped, Ryan jumped on him. He kept kicking him until he was unconscious. Peter had to pull him off. The guard lived, but it was mentioned on the news that he was in critical care for a while and ended up on disability as far as Erin knew. Peter stuck up for Ryan, said he was going through some hard stuff, and she'd never seen him behave the same again, but it always made her wonder what was under the surface.

Ryan's eyes turned to the room for a moment. When he looked back at Erin, his face lightened. A small grin crept on to his lips. "I've seen you eat. A salad will not do for today. I don't want you wasting away to nothing." Ryan waved the waiter over to make his order. "I'll start with the marbré of duck, followed by the risotto. The same for the lady. Erin, do you have a wine preference?"

She let out a frustrated sigh. "I'll just have water."

He looked back at the waiter. "A bottle of the Vacqueyras, Domaine Palon."

The waiter reached for Erin's wine glass to remove it, but Ryan stopped him. "Leave it."

Erin waited for the waiter to leave before crossing her arms. "What are you doing?"

"Helping. You're too wound up. You need to have a glass and lighten up."

"You don't think I can make my own decisions?"

"After the conversation we had about Peter? No, I don't. I don't believe you are thinking straight. I, on the other hand," — Ryan flicked out his napkin and laid it across his lap — "have been thinking a lot lately." He reached across the table to take her hand, but she kept it tucked under her arm. He dragged his own back. His lips pursed, then softened. "I care a lot about both you and Peter, and I'd be no friend to Peter if I didn't look after his sister." Erin took a sip of water and averted her eyes. Ryan leaned forward. "You have so much going for you. So much potential. I've watched you grow over the years, and you've changed from a bratty little kid into a beautiful young woman. I think you just need someone to take you under their wing and guide you into every-thing you could be. But you'll have to trust me."

"So it's your wing we're talking about then?"

Ryan pushed his tongue against his cheek. "Do you know a better one?" He couldn't help the curve at the corner of his mouth.

Erin wanted to kick his shin under the table, but she restrained herself. "I think I do pretty well on my own."

"We both know that's not true." He lifted his eyebrows, and Erin was on the verge of walking out on him.

"Where is all this coming from? Why do you think you know what's best for me all the sudden? You come from a different world than I do, and I'm doing the best I can with what I have." She was going to add that she was doing a pretty good job of it, but she wasn't convinced herself.

"That's exactly my point, Erin. You ever read *Great Expectations?*"

"In high school, why?"

"Think of me as your rich benefactor."

"You know the benefactor turned out to be the convict."

Ryan laughed. "The work that I do isn't exactly legitimate, now is it? If I recall correctly as well, there's a boy named Pip." He touched his finger to his lips. "And I think Pip fell in love with a cold, unfeeling girl who broke his heart."

Erin sucked in her cheeks. "That's about right."

"He ended up with her in the end though, didn't he?"

"I'm not sure what you're trying to say. Are you Pip or the benefactor?"

Ryan laughed again. "Not sure yet." His eyes focused on hers and she had to look away. "I wish you'd admit that you need me."

"I don't need you. I don't need anyone." She sighed. "Ryan, I would really rather manage on my own. I appreciate the offer, and it means a lot to me that you care, but I don't want a rich benefactor or a Pip."

Ryan grabbed the edge of the table, making his fingers turn white. "So what happens when you keep going the way you're going, and you get caught and go to prison like your brother? You're going to let your mother rot away in that hospital? I bet you'll come running to me then."

The first course arrived, defusing the outburst that was about to come from Erin. But when the duck was put in front of her and the waiter walked away, Erin dropped her napkin on top of the food. "Now I'm really not hungry." She stood. "And don't you ever talk about my mom again."

She felt all the eyes on her as she weaved her way between tables, wondering if any of them were on her side or if her poor attire made her the scapegoat and Ryan the victim.

Her skin crawled as she expected him to grab her arm at any moment, but she got out the door without being stopped and gulped a deep breath of freedom when she made it outside. Not having access to Ryan's gadgets would make things more complicated, but it was worth it if that's how he was going to behave.

Chapter 17

NICK ARRIVED at Messina's with a plan.

It wasn't a good one.

In fact, it was probably the stupidest plan he'd ever had. And the fact that he was willing to go through with it concerned him slightly. He reminded himself that it was all part of the job and ignored what might be the real reason he was doing it.

He went over in his mind what he was about to do. A driver came by the restaurant once a week to pick up whatever Kennedy had that needed transport and dropped it off at the warehouse. Nick would sneak into the van and attempt to get a look inside the warehouse. He was sure there would be a few guys with guns stationed there with the arrival of merchandise, but if he got caught, he'd be finished in more ways than one.

At the back door of the restaurant, he found Kennedy talking to Paddy.

"It's a big shipment, so I need a few extra hands," Kennedy was saying as Nick ambled up.

He stood next to Paddy. "Anything I can help with?"

"Nicholas. Impeccable timing. Stanley had a mishap a few days ago. He's still recovering, and we're shorthanded."

"He all right?" Nick feigned surprised concern.

"He will be. We had a break-in. Some idiot girl with pink hair, he says. She must have had someone with her because he was ambushed."

"Geez, he's lucky he wasn't killed."

"Don't know what they were after. Nothing was taken, but my favorite vase was broken and that pisses me off more than Stanley's head." He forced his hands down into his pockets with a mumble, "Which appears to be unbreakable." He shook his head. "He'll recover, but that vase was priceless."

"That's rough."

"Yeah, well, I've installed cameras in my office now and I've added extra security down at the warehouse just in case they head that way. I was about to send Patrick off to help unload a shipment, but I need to make sure we've got plenty of men down there, just in case." He dropped a hand onto Nick's shoulder. "And I don't believe you've been introduced down there yet."

This would work far better than his plan. "No, I haven't. Sounds like a great idea."

"You'll accompany Patrick. He can show you around. You're a strong boy. You'll be a big help, no doubt."

Nick rubbed his hands together. "Great, when do we go?"

"Now." Kennedy nodded to Paddy and went inside.

Paddy looked Nick up and down. "I don't know what you're so excited about. Unloading shipments is about the worst job there is. I don't like being used as labor hire."

Nick shrugged. "It's new to me. And besides, what if we get ambushed? That could be interesting."

"Unlikely. And don't worry, it will get old soon enough. This is one of those shitty jobs I hate to get stuck with. And now I'm stuck with Guy Smiley over here." He slapped Nick on the shoulder as he walked past. "I'm driving."

<hr>

Down at Kennedy's warehouse, several shipping containers were waiting to be emptied. There were already three other guys there, all with guns, who Nick hadn't met before, but he'd seen around.

Monkey came out around the side of one of the containers.

"Hey, kid." Nick said, giving him a shove. "Good to see you up and about. How you feeling?"

"Good and strong," Monkey said with a bob of the head.

"That why Kennedy sent you down here?"

"He's not here on Kennedy's orders," a short guy with cropped hair and solid shoulders said. "You should scram you little weasel."

Monkey gave him a dirty look. "I can go wherever I want. Kennedy gives me free rein around here."

"You're a worthless little shit." The man scoffed and turned to unlock the first container.

"Don't listen to him, Monkey. Although I do agree that you shouldn't be unloading this stuff."

"Why not?" Monkey flexed his skinny arm. "I've been working out."

"No doubt. But I was thinking more along the lines of your gunshot wound. You don't want to make it worse. You need to let that thing recover. Trust me. I know from experience."

"You were shot? When?"

"While ago." Nick lifted his shirt and showed Monkey the oblong scar on his side, front and back. "Went straight through. Hurt like hell. I didn't rest long enough and paid for it though."

Monkey shrugged. "Doesn't bother me."

Nick put his arm around Monkey and pulled him aside. "You crazy kid." When they had moved away from the others, Nick lowered his voice. "Hey, what's really going on. Why are you down here? You trying to get yourself in trouble?"

Monkey squinted his eyes in confusion, then they went round. "I said something. Didn't I … I remember." He shrank back.

"No, it's okay. It's okay. I swear. What you do in your own time is none of my business. But I want to make sure you don't get yourself in trouble."

Monkey let out a shaky breath. "You swear you won't say anything? I'd be dead." He turned to see where the other guys were.

"I swear. But it doesn't matter down here. If these

guys have it in for you, they won't pull their punches while Kennedy's not around. I think you should leave it for today."

"I can't."

"Why not?"

"I heard Kennedy say this was an important shipment. I want to know what's in it."

"Look. I'm helping them unload it. How about I have a look and I can report back to you?"

Monkey scrunched up his mouth while he thought about it. "Really? You'd do that?"

"If it keeps you out of trouble, sure."

"You don't want to know why I want to know?"

Nick laughed. "Sounds like we all have our secrets. I'll let you keep yours if you let me keep mine, deal?"

"Deal." They bumped knuckles and Nick pushed Monkey in the direction of the gate.

The guys had already begun unloading when Nick walked over.

"You done babysitting?" Paddy asked.

"I thought it was worth taking the time to get rid of him. Should I go bring him back?"

Paddy shook his head as he lifted the manifest and ran a finger down to the bottom and flipped the page. "Jason will take the load in with the forklift. I'll need you to shift one portion of the stock to the shelving along the back wall.

"Got it. You know what's in the boxes?"

"It's not my job to comment."

"Right. Hey, have you ever heard of a guy named Peter Hart?"

Paddy's lips thinned. "Why?"

"I just heard his name come up in conversation somewhere. It sounded familiar."

"He was around before your time. Not long though, and I haven't seen him for a while."

Nick nodded, but by the look on Paddy's face, he thought he'd better drop it for now. Like Paddy said, it wasn't his job to comment.

Paddy got busy directing where to put everything while Nick and another guy named Rusty organized the boxes.

Another man Nick didn't recognize came in the warehouse and Paddy walked with him over to a crate. Nick monitored the two as he continued to work. The boxes were heavy enough that he was sweating and decided that Paddy was right about the job. If he had to do this on a regular basis, it would suck. No wonder Paddy made sure he was the one with the clipboard.

Paddy lifted the crate lid, and the new guy leaned over and put his hand in, moving things around. Nick had to get a look in that crate.

After the new guy left, Jason brought in a couple more similar crates and lined them up. Paddy looked up from the paperwork and caught Nick looking. Nick didn't bother looking away, that would be too obvious, so instead he called across the room. "We get a drink break soon?"

Paddy ignored him and turned back toward the crates, but Rusty pushed past him with another box, bumping him hard. "No breaks till the job's done, moron."

Nick rolled his eyes but said nothing. Just picked up another box and kept unloading.

By the time they finished, Nick's arms felt like lead. He slowed enough to be the one with the last box. Rusty put his own last box away and eyeballed Nick. "Now you can have a break." He didn't hesitate to walk away.

Nick took his time stacking the last box. No one was in the warehouse now, so he shoved the box into place and hurried over to the crates. They were all nailed shut except the one that Paddy had opened. Nick took another quick look around and opened the box enough to let a bit of light in.

Sneakers. That wasn't what he was expecting. He lifted the lid further and moved a couple of boxes out of the way, but there were just more sneakers. He lifted a lid off one box to check the contents, but it really was sneakers. Looked like expensive ones, too.

He dropped the lid back into place and turned. Paddy stood watching him with his arms crossed. "You do know how dangerous it is to be nosy in this business?"

"What?"

"Don't treat me like an idiot. I'm already giving you the benefit of the doubt not shooting out a kneecap right now. But you've been here long enough to know it's not a good idea to mess with Kennedy. If he wants you to know what he's got, he'll tell you. Otherwise, keep your nose out of it."

"Sorry, you're right. But sneakers? I mean, cigarettes I get, drugs sure, but sneakers?"

"Do you know how high the duty is on sneakers?"

"No, how high?"

"High enough that Kennedy thought it would be a good business move to get into the shoe business."

"Fair enough."

"You ask any more questions and I will shoot you."

Nick saluted Paddy who huffed and turned, walking out of the warehouse.

Nick followed. He'd like to hang on to his kneecaps a little longer if he could. He and Paddy might get along okay, but Nick knew that if it came down to it, Paddy was Kennedy's man, not his.

Nick glanced sideways at a set of stairs that led up to what looked like an office. He'd need to have a look in there, but with the added security that wasn't going to happen. Not yet, anyway.

He was hoping he'd have more to give to Erin. Sneakers were a long way from diamonds, but if they were getting out of paying duty on imported items, that could be enough for a search if it became necessary.

The best he could offer Erin right now was that he'd wait for another opportunity.

Chapter 18

AFTER HER VISIT WITH RYAN, Erin panicked and texted Nick, but when she didn't get a response straight away, she wavered between being afraid something had happened to him and wondering if he had bailed on her.

Two days later he responded, apologizing for the delay but saying he didn't have much. She felt an element of relief when he sent another text offering to meet and fill her in on what he did have. Anything was better than nothing.

When she drove into the empty car lot, he was already there waiting, wearing a white button-down with the sleeves rolled up, tucked into his jeans, and she had to admit, he looked good. He was also leaning on a classic Camaro. Guys who owned beautiful cars made her suspicious. She'd known too many who cared more about their cars than the people around them. But that didn't change the fact that the car caught her breath.

Peter had a love for cars that he got from their dad.

Erin was at an age where she was more interested in Barbies than cars, so everything she knew about cars she got from Peter after their dad had passed away. She adored everything her older brother was interested in. That included some of his favorite classics.

She pulled up nearby and got out but stayed behind the open door. She was unsure of herself or how she should respond, so kept it safe. "Nice car," she said, flatly.

"Aw, come on, say it like you mean it," he said, pushing off and walking toward her.

"I do mean it, actually. I wasn't expecting you to have such good taste."

"You know cars?"

"I know that one. Yenko, right? One of my brother's favorites. He'd be drooling if he were here right now."

Nick shook his head. "I can't take any credit. It's my brother's car, not mine."

"And he lets you drive it? If Peter had a car like that, he wouldn't even let me touch it." She put a hand up. "No, I take that back. He'd let me touch it to clean it."

Nick rested his forearm on top of her open door, leaving the door between them. "Well, *my* brother doesn't just let me drive it, he gave it to me."

She opened her mouth in an incredulous gape. "I'm assuming he's either stupid or dead." The look on Nick's face had her regretting her words. The casual way Nick had talked about the gift, it hadn't occurred to her that his brother might actually be dead. "Oh my god. I am so sorry. I didn't mean it. I mean, I did, but not like that. I'm so sorry."

He looked amused. "It's okay. It was a while ago. It was his pride and joy and I was honored when I found out he left it to me. Just the fact that he had a will was shocking, let alone being given this. I don't do it justice though."

Erin left the safety of her own car to get a closer look at his. Learning he had lost a loved one too shook the nerves out of her.

She lightly ran her finger along the hood as she moved to the window. Nick might not appreciate it as much as his brother, but he definitely looked after it. She dipped her head in to admire the leather interior.

"You want to go for a ride?" Nick asked, stepping up beside her.

It was tempting.

She looked at him.

Too tempting. "No, thanks. Maybe some other time." She rushed around the car to see the other side, but mostly because she needed the space from Nick. Her head scrambled when he got too close, and she needed to focus on what was important. At least for now.

Nick smirked as he watched her scurry around the car. Considering how they met and the way things went from there, it was nice to know she had warmed up enough that she had to be careful when he was close. He had better be careful too.

"I suppose you'd like to know what I've found out?"

Erin leaned into the hood toward him. "Yeah, have you got something?"

"Well, like I said, I don't have much yet. Kennedy does all his major business through a construction company, Barter Construction. He's got a warehouse down at the harbor where the more serious stuff goes down. The problem is, I haven't been with him long enough to gain his trust to the extent that I could get in there on my own and have a look around. I went down yesterday, but all I found were sneakers."

"Sneakers? Is that like … do they smuggle drugs or something inside the sneakers?"

"No. It's kind of like with cigarettes. Getting around the taxes on imports can be big business."

"But you didn't actually expect to find diamonds in a shipment though, right?"

"No, but it was the only opportunity I had. And right now, I'm looking for anything that might pan out in a way that will give me more access. I've got some connections outside of Kennedy's group, and I'm looking into a few different angles. I just wanted to let you know that even though things are going a bit slow, they're still going."

Erin crossed her arms and shrugged. "I guess my brother has plenty of time. I just don't want any diamonds that might still be hanging around to slip through our fingers. Is there anything I can do? I hate being useless. Could we break into the warehouse?"

"Slow down there, tiger."

Erin raised an eyebrow. "Did you really just say that?"

"I did. You got a problem with that, or may I continue?"

"By all means, please go on."

"Breaking in is an option, but it would be a last resort. Especially now."

"Why?"

"They've increased security because apparently someone broke into Messina's the other night and smashed Stanley on the head with a priceless vase."

"Wow, that sounds terrible. Priceless you say?"

"I know. Can you believe that such an ugly vase was worth so much?"

"I didn't actually notice the vase before it was shattered. I was too busy being assaulted. Wait. He doesn't know who did it, does he?" She moved around the car to get closer to Nick, feeling suddenly vulnerable.

Nick couldn't help stepping closer to her himself. "Some little mite with pink hair, apparently," he said, flicking a strand of her hair. "And an accomplice."

"That's bad." She touched a hand to the back of her head. Occasionally she considered changing her color to be less obvious, but she liked it and hadn't been willing to give it up.

"No, you're fine. There are plenty of girls in the city with pink hair. He wouldn't know to look anywhere near your direction, as long as you don't tell anyone."

Erin stared at the ground, reviewing everything she had said to Ryan. She had been so disappointed when he wasn't on her side. Now, she was glad she hadn't told him everything. It turned out to be a good thing that he showed her what a jerk he could be.

Nick touched her arm. "You okay?"

"Yeah, just a close call, that's all."

"I'll keep looking, but you have to know too that

you're not useless. You got the inside information in the first place."

"I still wish there was more I could do."

"There is one thing you could try."

"Yeah? I'll do anything."

"If you could get any more details about that day from your brother. Anything he might have seen would help."

"Oh, uh. How about anything but that?"

"You don't want to talk to him about it? Isn't this what he wants?"

"I'll ask, but he'll probably get mad at me for pursuing it."

"Why would he get mad? You're trying to get him out of prison."

"That guy James told him about all of this before I found out about it. Peter wants me to drop it. Said he's made peace with everything and doesn't want me to do anything."

"Wow. Your brother is going to hate me then. Hey, by the way, has Peter ever been mixed up with Kennedy that you know of?"

"Peter? Never. He might be a criminal, but he's not *that* type of criminal. He'd never get involved with a guy like Kennedy."

"What type of criminal does that make me?"

"No, I mean." She pinched her lips together at his smile. "Peter just didn't like being a part of a gang like that."

"I brought his name up to one of the guys."

"You did what?"

"Just casually. He said he knew a guy named Peter Hart was hanging around a while ago, but he hadn't seen him in a while. And this guy I spoke to was not interested in giving me any more information."

"Are you an idiot?" She shoved him. "What if they go after him?"

"They won't. I only asked Paddy because I knew he wouldn't pursue it."

"How can you know that?"

"Calm down. I wouldn't have brought it up if I thought there was a risk of him getting Peter into trouble."

Erin was pacing now with her hands on her head. "I've got to warn him."

"Erin." Nick grabbed her and pulled her around. "I told you, it's okay. Your brother is not in any danger, but I needed to find out if there was a connection there."

"Then you should have asked me. I could have told you there wasn't."

"And you think you know everything there is to know about your brother?"

Erin shoved him again, hard, and walked purposfully in the opposite direction. He didn't know how close to home that hit. She wanted to think she knew everything about her brother that needed knowing, but she was already sure he was keeping things from her. Would he go as far as getting involved with Kennedy and not say anything?

She heard the running crunch of stones under Nick's feet as he came up behind her. "Wait, Erin. Please. I'm sorry." She kept walking. "Erin, come on." She finally stopped but didn't turn. "Your right. I'm used to working on my own and doing what I think is best at the time. I haven't put enough thought into your part in all of this."

Erin turned, breathing hard. She looked up at the sky and bit her lip. Fear was just waiting at her doorstep for any little thing that might trigger it. She had to admit to herself that Nick was a professional. He knew what he was doing. "You really don't think he's in any danger?"

"No."

"He never said anything to me about Kennedy, but there was a time when he went off the rails a bit. I think he might have even started doing drugs." She then added quickly. "But I know he's definitely not doing them now. And I know he's not involved with Kennedy. And I know he didn't take the diamonds."

"Considering how much we don't know, it's nice to know there are some absolutes."

"He's going to kill me if he finds out I'm looking into this."

"Well, if you don't mind making him mad, I think it would be worthwhile."

"I guess."

"Look, I can't have you breaking into places. It's too dangerous for you. These aren't jewelry stores. You might be good at the getting in part, but you won't go to jail if you get caught. These guys will kill you without a second thought, and we can't have that happening. But I guess you already know that."

"Yeah, well, the knee in the crotch worked okay on you."

He made a face. "You like to remind me of that regularly, don't you? Did you try it on Stanley?"

"I did. He was expecting it."

"That is totally unfair. You disarmed me by making me think I was helping you, but the whole time you were lying in wait."

"It's true. That was my plan all along." She smiled, but it was weak. Just thinking of what Stanley had done to her still turned her stomach.

Nick observed the worried look on her face and sighed. "Maybe it would be worth teaching you some better strategies for getting the actual bad guys and not just us good guys. You know, just in case." He circled around her. "If you do get into trouble, there are other body parts that are vulnerable in case the knee to the crotch doesn't work."

Erin stood up a bit straighter. "Yeah. I figured. But when you're panicking, you sort of go for what you know."

"Have you ever learned any self-defense?"

"Nope."

Nick looked around the empty lot. "Well, here isn't the best place to learn."

"You mean, you want to teach me? Now?"

"It would make me feel better if I knew you had at least a small amount of training."

"I know a place. If you have time. You can follow me in your fancy car."

He looked at his car, then back at her and grinned. "Sure."

"Great." She turned to her car.

"Wait. Where are we going?" Nick asked, heading for his own.

"You'll see," she called out before jumping in and taking off.

Chapter 19

WHEN ERIN PULLED up in front of the old stone building, the first thing Nick noticed as he parked behind her
was the illustration of a figure hanging upside down from
a rope doing a split. He kept his eyes on it when he got
out of the car and studied it as Erin unlocked the door.

She turned to him after opening it. "You coming?"

Lines gathered on his forehead. "Where are we
exactly?"

"The gym where I train. They're closed in the
mornings during the week, so we have the place to
ourselves."

He dropped his eyes to her, his mouth slightly open,
then he lifted his face to the sign again. "What kind of
training do you do here?"

"Come in and see." She left him at the door and
went inside, leaving him to follow.

He walked in slowly, looking around at the minimal
equipment, and stopped in the middle of the room,

grabbing a rope hanging from the ceiling and tugging it lightly. "What's this for? Climbing?"

"Sort of. Let me show you." She slipped off her shoes, tucked her shirt in, and put her own hand on the rope, just below his. "Mind stepping back?"

He arched an eyebrow and took two big steps backward.

She felt like showing off, so she didn't. She'd made too many mistakes in the past when she tried to impress. Instead, she did a couple of quick basic moves a few feet off the ground so he'd get the idea. Then finished by wrapping the rope behind her leg and spinning upside down.

"Oh, I see. Like the sign out front."

She responded by rearranging the rope slightly and doing a split while she remained upside down.

His eyes widened. "Yeah, that's it." He nodded approvingly, then stopped because he realized he probably looked like he was gawking. Which he was.

He crossed his arms to adjust his pose. "Doesn't look too hard."

She crossed her own arms while she remained upside down. "You want to have a turn?"

"Nah, I wouldn't want to show you up."

She flipped back around and dropped to the ground. "You sure? I could use a good laugh."

"How can you say that? You don't know me that well. I could be a closet performer."

She walked over to stand next to him, facing the rope. "Show me."

He dropped his arms, then his head. "All right. But only 'cause I think you could do with a good laugh."

"Excellent." Her hands fluttered in a clap.

He walked forward and grabbed hold of the rope then looked at her. "You might want to step back a bit farther than that." She took a step back, and he waved his hand for her to go farther. "Keep going. I'm not sure what sort of collateral damage this will create."

She laughed and moved back against the wall. "How's this?"

He grimaced. "I guess it will have to do."

Erin put her hands behind her and leaned on them against the wall while she watched him jump up onto the rope. He free climbed about one story before stopping and looking back down at her. "What do I do now?"

"You're the closet expert. Figure it out."

He turned back and looked up to the ceiling. "Damn," he said to himself.

She gave him credit for the fact that he wrapped the rope around his leg and found enough purchase to lay himself sideways. But then he shook his head. "Enough of this. I'll just show you what I'm good at."

She watched him take off the rest of the way up the rope. He was a good climber. No wonder he was able to follow her up the wall. Climbing a rope wasn't the same as a building, but his skill still showed.

He reached a hand up to tap the rafter that held the rope, then he descended, quick enough that she was impressed. When he was still very high up, he fell off the rope. She jumped forward in a desperate attempt to do something, but then he hit the ground, rolled, and jumped up, throwing his hands out in triumph. "How was that?"

She opened her mouth in astonishment. "Okay. I'm impressed. I'll admit it."

"I'm just glad you're not laughing at me. But I do have one question."

"What's that?"

"What exactly is the point of what you do? The fancy stuff."

"For most people? Entertainment. For me? It comes in handy for the work I do."

"But why can't you just climb like I do?"

She got that twinkle in her eye again and it set his heart beating a little faster. "It's more fun my way."

He drummed his fingers on his arm as his eyes moved back up the three stories to the top of the rope, then he nodded. "I see your point. So. You ready for self-defense lessons?"

"Okay, fine, change the subject. So where do we begin?"

He moved around to face her. "Well, you know about the groin area. That seems to be your preferred shot. But look at my face." Erin almost smiled. "Where on this beautiful face," he said, drawing a circle in the air around his head as he stepped closer. "Could you hurt me the most?"

She took the opportunity to study his face freely but kept on the subject. "I guess a good eye gouge would work, or a punch to the nose."

"Yup. You can also punch the neck if it's exposed,

jaw, chin. But yeah, if you've got a clear shot to the nose, I'd recommend that. Not only does it hurt like hell, but it makes your eyes water instantly, which would temporarily blind your opponent."

"Do you know that from experience?"

"Heh, yeah, on both sides of the equation." He put a hand on her shoulder and pushed her around. "Then of course you've got kidneys," he said, touching her side. "Knees." He pushed a foot against the back of the knee of the leg she had her weight on.

"Hey." She threw her arms out as she dipped then straightened. She shifted her weight to the other leg but turned to face him so he couldn't do it again.

"If you can get a good kick into the knee, you're likely to inflict some damage, and it will slow your opponent. Gives you the opportunity to escape, too, if that's your aim. Which I would highly recommend."

"I suppose that's all pretty obvious. I just never had much occasion to think about it."

"That is a very good thing. I grew up needing to know how to look after myself."

"Tough neighborhood?"

"Not as bad as some, but I was a dirtbag as a kid. Wasn't good at staying out of trouble. What about you? How long have you been stealing stuff?"

"My brother brought me on my first job when I was fourteen."

Nick bit his tongue, then cleared his throat. "Fourteen, huh? What did he have you do?"

"He's amazing with safes and locks and stuff. Not as good at squeezing into small spaces, and the best way into the building he wanted to enter was through a small grate."

"So he used his little sister because she was small?"

"Not just because of my size, no. I was doing circus training they had when I was a kid. Here, actually. It was an after-school thing. I got really good at the corde lisse."

"Corde lisse? That's a circus thing?"

She grabbed the rope and lifted it.

"Oh, it has a name."

She gave him a shove. "Yeah, it has a name. It has always been my favorite. Not enough to make a career out of it or anything, but it comes in handy when I need to enter a building from the ceiling."

"Okay, I get that, but what does that have to do with fitting through a grate?"

"It doesn't. Not that part. I also had a bit of fun with the clowns. Stuffing into small spaces and things. Peter watched me perform, and that's where he got the idea into his head. I can squeeze into just about anywhere."

Nick looked her up and down. "Well, you are pretty small, but you're not *that* small."

"It's not just about size. You have to know where to put all your body parts so you can squeeze."

Nick laughed. "Sorry. I just got a picture in my head. You should be careful who you tell that to. Somebody might get the wrong idea."

"You're the first," she said, holding back a smile.

"Touché. The rope thing is pretty cool though."

Erin nodded, unsure what else to say. "I guess."

Nick slapped his hands together. "Well, if we're going to get anywhere today, we should get started."

They spent an hour practicing different maneuvers. Nick showed her how to disarm an opponent and how to get out of different types of confrontations. Erin was familiar with how her body worked and so was a quick learner. She was good at twisting out of his grip when she was given direction on how to do it.

"Not bad for a girl," Nick said, egging her on. He grabbed her wrist, and she twisted it like he showed her, but then he improvised and swung around to grab her waist to see how she'd respond. He had her arms pinned to her side.

"Hey, that's cheating."

"If you ever come into a situation where you need this stuff, I can assure you, the other guy won't play fair."

She squirmed around to get her arms into the position she needed them, then broke the lock he had around her. He put out his leg and tripped her as she pulled away and she fell to the ground.

She laid still, frustrated, while he stood over her, waiting for her next move. When she didn't make any, he reached a hand down to help her up. "You shouldn't give up so easily."

She used her own improvisation and yanked his arm, pushing the tipping point of his balance over and sending him tumbling forward. But he didn't let go of her and pulled her with him, and they both ended up tangled together on the mat.

Erin laughed. "Damn. I thought I had you on that one."

"That was better. You weren't doing what you thought you were supposed to do. You did what felt right."

They were too close. Nick pulled away first, even though he didn't want to. He noticed that Erin wasn't quick to untangle herself from him. But she made him promise not to hurt her, and he was coming very close to breaking that promise. Not only that, he wasn't about to make the same mistake his brother had.

He jumped up and started stretching to hide the fact that he needed some distance from her. "That's probably enough for today. You think you'll talk to your brother?"

Erin was still on the floor. Unsure. "Yeah. I can do that. He's my brother after all. He'll still love me, even if he's mad at me."

"I should get going, but I'll let you know if I get any further on my end."

"Okay. I'll get in touch once I talk to my brother."

Nick stood awkwardly for a moment then walked across to her and shook her hand. She looked at their hands, then up at Nick. He noticed the frown and understood it. He had to get out of there.

———————

Chapter 20

———————

PETER WALKED INTO THE VISITORS' area scanning for Erin. He didn't see her, but the person who was there had him stalking forward, close to rage. He sat down stiffly at the table. "How'd you get in here?"

"How long's it been, Peter? And that's the way you treat an old friend?"

"You're not my friend, *Ryan*. And I asked you a question."

"You really think you're in a position to ask me questions? Fine, I'll indulge you since I'm not completely unfeeling and you're stuck in here while I'm free to roam." He pulled at the sleeves of his suit jacket and rested his arms on the table, leaning forward. "It all comes down to who you know."

"I can't believe you even have the balls to come here after what you did."

Ryan smirked and stretched a long leg under the table, leaning back into a comfortable position. "Saw your sister today."

Peter flinched and felt a tremble through his body. If the guard weren't there, he wouldn't have hesitated to jump across the table and wrap his hands around Ryan's throat.

Ryan noticed and lifted a cocky shoulder. "She's doing well. Told me about a chat she had with a guy named James. You know him? Little fella."

Peter just grunted.

"Apparently, he got in Erin's ear. Convinced her that you were set up."

"You're not telling me anything I don't already know. I've told her to drop it."

"Right. And she agreed, did she?"

Peter knew better than anyone how strong-headed Erin could be, but she wasn't stupid. Now he just had to convince Ryan. Otherwise, she'd be in danger, possibly for her life. "I'm her brother. Of course she listened to me."

"You forget that I've known Erin for many years. I know when she gets something in her head, it's not easy to get it out. I also know for a fact that she hasn't given it up. Oh sure, she says she has. But I see that look on her face. She's hiding something." He rubbed his finger across a name that had been scratched into the surface of the table.

"She's not hiding anything. I would know."

Ryan looked up from the table. "You're not as good a judge as you think you are. So, unfortunately, she's become a liability. We can't have her sniffing around into Kennedy's affairs now can we?"

Peter dug his fingers into the palm of his hand. He

had to do something. "How can you even think of hurting her? She's like a sister to you."

Ryan sucked in air through pursed lips. "When she was a little girl, maybe. But Peter." He laid his hands flat on the table. "As her brother, you may not have noticed how hot she is these days. She's got it all goin' on. And I can't promise I won't have my fun before I'm done with her."

Peter slammed his hands on the table and jumped up. "Don't you dare touch her." The guard was there, threatening action.

"Or what?" Ryan said, standing slowly and leaning over the table.

Peter clenched his fist and focused on the guard to keep himself from doing something he might regret.

Ryan addressed the guard. "It's okay. He's not going to do anything rash." He turned to Peter. "Sit down. Prison has got you all wound up. I've got something to offer you in exchange." He nodded toward the guard, who slowly backed up.

Peter waited until Ryan sat back down before sitting himself. "This better be good or else I will make sure you are cut into a thousand tiny pieces."

Ryan laughed. "That's cute. The truth is, I don't want to hurt Erin. But if you want to keep her safe, you're going to have to do something for me."

"You mean for Kennedy."

"Same difference."

"And since when do you work for him?"

Ryan shook his head. "You've got it all wrong. He

still works for me, but I like to keep those loyal to me in business."

Peter sighed loudly. "I already took the fall for him. Just leave my family alone."

"Wish I could."

"No you don't." Peter muttered.

Ryan leaned forward. "You do this thing, and we can leave your family alone for good. Just hear me out. It's a small thing."

Peter shifted his jaw to the side. "Fine. What is it?"

"All we need is James out of the picture." Peter stopped breathing. "With James taken care of, things can go back to normal."

"I'm not a murderer."

"There's no time like the present."

The two men stared at each other, but Peter broke first. "How does James being dead keep Erin safe?"

"Erin is strong-headed, but she's not brave. Not when it comes to violence. I'm sure you'll be able to persuade her to give up her pursuit once she finds out James has been murdered. She's not equipped to deal with killers."

Peter had never hurt anyone in his life, but as he watched Ryan, he tried to decide the best way for him to die. He was one exception Peter would make if given the opportunity.

"You know, there was a time when you did what was necessary for those you cared about." Ryan stood preparing to leave. "It's your sister who will pay for your choice." He turned to go.

"Wait."

Ryan smiled, but dropped it when he turned to look at Peter. "Change of heart?"

"I'll do it." He pointed a finger at Ryan. "But don't come back again, and stay away from my sister."

Ryan shrugged. "I can leave your sister alone, but I can't promise she'll leave me alone. You should see the way she looks at me."

Peter jumped across the table onto Ryan. It got him twenty-four hours in solitary and bruised knuckles. But it was worth it.

"But I don't understand." Erin resisted the urge to stamp her foot.

"Ma'am, I'm sorry, but I can't discuss it with you."

"But I'm his family. How can there be a rule saying you can't tell a family member why you've put someone in solitary confinement? What if it's abuse?" Erin made her face as threatening as she could, but the guard behind the counter only looked bored.

"Call his lawyer."

There was no argument left, so Erin slammed her hand on the counter and turned to go. She had psyched herself up to bring up the diamonds with Peter, only to find out something awful enough to get him solitary had happened. At least he'd be safe in there. Whatever he did.

She was so jittery when she reached her car that she fumbled and dropped her keys. When she was settled in her car, she pulled up Google on her phone to see why someone could get thrown in solitary. Mostly what she found were articles about how bad and damaging it could be for a prisoner, which didn't help her mood.

Most likely he would have been in a fight, but the Peter she knew had infinite patience and preferred to settle things with his brains. But he did know how to handle himself, and if he was provoked — everyone has a breaking point.

Now she would have to wait until Friday to see him. She sat in her car and stared at her phone. She really wanted to see Nick again, but after the way he had acted the other day, it seemed as if he couldn't get away from her fast enough. She groaned and tapped the phone against her forehead. It would be easier if she could simply read people's minds, then she'd never have to guess.

She tapped her fingers on her lips and made the decision that she didn't care. He was helping her out, and it was her own fault she let herself feel emotionally attached to him. He wasn't helping her because he liked her; he was helping her because he had some other agenda. He had told her that.

She took a deep breath, trying to convince herself that she was lucky nothing had happened between them the other day. It was just attraction and nothing more. It must be if he was going to flirt with her one minute and then push her away the next. He wasn't someone she should be mixed up with anyway. And now, with nothing else but confusion and energy making her feel like a volcano about to erupt, she needed to find an outlet.

She ended up at her gym first to try getting it out on

the rope, but it wasn't helping. Sometimes there was only one way to relieve nervous energy. She thought back to Nick's comment that he didn't think Peter could ever give up the thrill he got from whatever illegal activity it was he was pursuing. But he was wrong about Peter. Peter was very level-headed. She was the one who was addicted to it. When it was only herself at risk, it gave her purpose, a feeling of accomplishment. But when the people she cared about were in trouble, she froze.

She slid off the rope onto the floor of the gym and lay there as she remembered her father, sprawled on the kitchen floor, dying of a heart attack. As a nine-year-old, all she could do was watch, horrified. Somewhere in the back of her mind, she knew there was something she should do, but she couldn't think. All she could do was watch as her dad's skin turn gray and he stopped moving. Her mom had walked in to find her huddled on top of him, sobbing. She didn't have any memory of that part. She only knew about it because her mom told her what had happened. After she saw the life leave her dad, everything went blank until the funeral.

Then came the day when the police stormed into the jewelers to arrest her brother. All she could do was look on from her hidden perch. But as she hid, she had the same feeling as when she was watching her dad on the kitchen floor. There had to have been something that she could have done to fix it.

Now, she wouldn't get distracted by Nick, and she wouldn't give up. She'd do what was necessary to help her brother. Finally, she had a way, and she wasn't going to miss her chance. But while she was waiting, she had to find a way to get free of the pent-up energy that was still coursing through her body. What she needed was a hit.

The El rumbled along its predestined route. The vibration shifted through Erin's body as she followed the path of the track. The street was heavy with both foot and car traffic as people went home from work or headed out for dinner, but she barely noticed. In her mind, she pictured the police that had clogged the street. She never saw them of course. She was stuck in the ceiling. But they would have been there, waiting for her brother to be brought out into the street to be transported to jail because they knew they'd find him there. Because Kennedy didn't care that Peter was a brother or a son. Kennedy only cared about himself.

She turned her head to get a glimpse inside. The gray of the streets outside contrasted with the lush furnishings of the building she was walking past, with its chandeliers and jewel-colored chaise lounges. She could remember seeing those chairs the first time they had checked out the building. She had spent the next day searching for a reasonably priced knock-off for the house. It seemed ridiculous now. Just the thought of the chair made her feel sick.

She picked up speed to get out of the street. She never intended going that way, but somehow her feet just brought her there. Now, after visiting the scene of the crime, she was more wound up than ever, so she hurried on to her intended target.

Changing her focus to the purpose of the outing, she neared her destination. As she dodged around the scaffolding plastered across the face of a building, she almost wished it were the one she was heading for. But tonight she needed the challenge of the climb and the control it would take to be discreet.

"Shit." She scowled as she approached the alley she had intended to slip into. It was gated by plywood to protect the construction materials that were being used on the building next door. It was locked by a padlock and chain. Usually going out on a job put her in a good mood, but tonight she was struggling to keep her head in the game. Every unexpected dilemma gave her the feeling of being ripped off. She leaned heavily against the wood, angry. She looked down and closed her eyes. If she didn't get her focus back, she'd have to call off the job. It was too risky to do while her head was in a spin. Then it occurred to her what was really eating away at her as her mind forced an image onto the back of her eyelids. It was Nick's face when they were tangled up. How he pulled away when things got too close.

"Bastard." She wanted to be mad at him, but she wasn't. She just felt unwanted. It wasn't a feeling she was accustomed to, since she never let anyone close before. Once this was all over and she didn't have to think about Nick or be in contact with him anymore, it would get easier. In the meantime, she had a job to do.

She pushed off the gate and squared her shoulders, then pulled out her phone and stepped close to the lock.

Moving her finger across the screen like she was texting, her eyes lifted to focus on the lock.

A couple passed by, arguing about who was responsible for the argument they were having. Erin glanced across to them and saw they were still holding hands. She couldn't help but smile. It must be nice to find someone you can argue with but still care enough about that you're not willing to give up intimacy. She grunted and determined to push Nick from her mind, turning her attention back to the lock. It was a cheap one, easy to remove. The trick was doing it unseen. Peter had challenged her in the past to try to pick locks blindfolded, more for the fun of it than the necessity.

Another small smile danced on her lips as she remembered one evening when the blindfold had shimmied up enough so she could see through a small slit at the bottom. It was the first time she had ever gotten the lock, and Peter laid on the praise so thickly that she was compelled to tell him the truth. He pushed her around playfully, but in the end, made her do it again. Right. And she did.

But she didn't always get it. Tonight she'd have to.

She put her phone away and stealthily pulled out her tools, hiding them behind her back. She leaned back into the lock, watching the cars and people go by while she worked.

To anyone passing, she was a people watcher, not a thief, although she realized at one point her face was compressed into a grimace. She took a moment to relax her countenance so she didn't scare anyone, then continued her work. Having to focus on her hands and her face slowed her down, but after nearly half an hour, the lock sprung.

She pressed her lips together to hold back the "whoop" that wanted to escape. After dropping the pick twice, she had been close to giving up.

With the lock out of the way, she waited for the El to pass. The reverberation hit her feet first, but when the rumble filled her ears, she dragged the wooden gate far enough to slip behind it.

The street sound was dampened, and she took the opportunity of solitude to stretch. Despite the frustration the gate had added to the last thirty minutes, it had the benefit of keeping her out of view for the beginning of her climb, the hardest part of the whole job. Not because it was a difficult climb, but because for part of it, if anyone looked directly where she was, even buried in the shadows, they'd see her.

She had to climb to the third floor and break into a boarded-up window. The train would be good for cover here too. People were more distracted during a loud noise, less likely to look around, but she'd still have to be quick.

This time, when she felt the vibration in her feet, she scurried up the wall to a spot where she was mostly concealed just as the air settled back into stillness.

She took a moment to assess the window. It wasn't well boarded. She leaned forward to get a good look at the street, then whipped back when a light drizzle began to fall. Drizzle made people look up. They also made holds slippery. Then the drizzle turned to rain. She couldn't wait it out, and the heavier rain meant people would run for cover or umbrellas. Either one would work for her, but she didn't want to be hanging off a wall in a downpour, so she moved to the window, making sure her grip was secure, then slipped in quickly.

The room was dark and musty. It was empty except for a dusty display case.

After shaking off the rain, she headed down a long hall that ended with an air vent. On the other side of the air vent, was a storage closet that belonged to a jewelry store. Because it was going to be a quick job, she didn't bother cutting the power. She'd be in and out before anyone turned up, and she didn't expect them to figure out that the robber came through a tiny vent.

That was something she loved about her job. When law enforcement couldn't work out how it was done. Like a cozy mystery novel, where the pieces don't add up if you don't have the secret ingredient buried in the text.

She slipped through the vent and jumped to the floor, landing on a broom and breaking the handle. She looked down at the destruction and had to laugh. A small hassle in the scheme of things. If that was the worst of the night, it would be a good night.

She shoved the broken broom back through the vent. It wouldn't do to leave evidence like that lying around. That type of slip-up got people caught.

Chapter 21

THE JOB WENT SMOOTHLY, and Erin was able to come away with several pieces that would cover the next medical bill and hopefully fill her car with gas.

Once she was clear of the busy street and had discarded the broom, she looked at her stash. One piece was a simple diamond tennis bracelet. If she were a bracelet person, she'd like it. The other was a ring with a large aquamarine surrounded by diamonds. It was pretty enough to admire, but too big for her small hands. When she was a teenager doing these jobs with her brother, she loved trying everything on, but he never let her keep anything. It wasn't a good idea to keep the goods on you for longer than you had to.

Her mood had changed dramatically now that she had finished the job successfully. If she were a little girl, she'd be skipping. Her confidence was high once again, and the win meant she was feeling better about the chances of succeeding in getting Peter out of prison. She was also pleased to find that she had been able to push her feelings for Nick aside, enjoying the adrenaline high instead. In her elated mood, she called Nick just to prove to herself that she could. She didn't notice the time.

"Erin, is everything okay? What's wrong?" Nick said as soon as he answered.

"Nothing's wrong. Why?"

"It's late."

"Oh." She pulled the phone back to check the time. "Sorry, I'm a bit of a night owl. I just wanted to call and say thanks for helping me out. I appreciate everything you're doing. I know you have your reasons and that they have nothing to do with me, but I'm feeling really good about it all," she rambled. "Really positive. I think this all might just work out. I might have to give you a thank-you card or something in the end."

"Do you realize you're talking really fast right now?"

"Am I? I guess I'm just on a bit of a high."

"I take it you're not talking about drugs."

"What makes you say that?"

"You're not the drugs type. Not street drugs anyway." He paused. "You just did a job. Just now. Didn't you?"

She had been strolling along at a quick pace, but she stopped when he called her out. "Not right this second, no."

"Mm-hm. It's the rush, right?"

She started walking again, but slower. "No, I just needed to get out some pent-up energy. I can offer you a piece if there is someone special in your life. To say thanks, I mean. They're pretty, these ones. They aren't always."

He waited until he was sure she was done talking. "No, I don't have anyone to give jewelry to." Erin winced at the jump her heart made. "And besides, it's for your mom, right?"

"Yeah, my mom. You're right."

"And don't think you owe me anything."

"Right. Of course."

"Have you spoken to your brother yet?"

"I'm going to see him Friday."

"I'm surprised you didn't go get it over with."

"I would have. I tried, but he's been put into solitary."

"Solitary? What'd he do?"

"Don't know. It's very unlike him, but I'm going to find out when I see him. I guess I should let you get back to sleep or whatever it was you were doing."

"You should probably get some rest yourself. Sounds like you had a big night."

"It'll take me a while to come down. I'll probably be awake for the next several hours."

Nick squeezed his eyes shut at the words that almost came out of his mouth. He wanted to see her. To spend some time with her. He could picture her bouncing around in her euphoria. "All right, well, I'll talk to you soon. Hope you get some rest."

"Yeah. Bye."

Erin hung up not knowing how she felt about that conversation. Not even sure why she really called Nick in the first place or what she had expected. All she knew was that she felt slightly disappointed. Her buzz dampened.

———

When Erin finally made it to visit Peter on Friday, he was waiting at the table when she walked in, which was unusual. His back was straight, his face was tight, and he had his hands clasped together on the table.

She scanned the room quickly to see if James or his brother was there. It would be nice to get the opportunity to thank one of them. She'd do her best to get Peter to agree to look out for him. James's information was definitely worth it.

She gave Peter a quick hug, but he didn't let her go right away. When he did, it was to hold her away from him so he could get a good look at her. There were lines on his face that she couldn't remember seeing before.

"How are you? Everything okay?" he asked.

Erin nodded, then sat stiffly in the chair and looked down at her hands. She wasn't looking forward to asking him about his arrest, but right now, she was more concerned with his behavior. It was unusual and upsetting.

Erin opened her mouth to speak, but Peter beat her to it. "What is it? What's happened?"

Her eyes lifted to his, but her body was frozen. The panic in his voice and on his face was unmistakable. "I'm … everything is fine. With me. I just … Why were you in solitary?"

She could tell by the look on his face that it wasn't

the question he was expecting, and his tone was oddly suspicious. "How do you know about that? Did someone tell you?"

"I came to visit on Tuesday. They told me where you were but not why."

"Oh." Peter picked at his fingernail. "I just had an argument with someone. He was rude, and I had to set him straight. But I'm fine."

"Really? 'Cause you don't seem okay."

"It's just been a rough week."

"You don't want to talk about it?"

"No."

Erin bit her lip and looked down at her hands, rubbing her thumb across the line on her palm. "Right, well, I want to talk to you about something, but I don't want you to get mad."

Peter shifted in his chair, and his eyes darted around her face unsure, where to settle. His breathing had quickened, but he didn't speak.

It was an effort for her to look him in the eyes, but she did it anyway. "You know how James said he — "

"James is dead."

Erin stiffened. "What? Dead? How?"

Peter took a deep breath and spoke as steadily as he could. He made an effort to sound casual, like it was no big deal, but Erin knew him too well. "There was a big brawl. He got stuck in the middle and was killed." He stopped when he saw the shock on her face.

"So he was right to be afraid, to look to you for protection."

Peter winced. "He was foolish. He was involved with

dangerous men, and there's always a price to pay when you get caught up with dangerous men. Now, Erin." He reached across the table and took her hand tightly. "You have to promise me you won't pursue it, or else you could end up the same way, and I couldn't live with that. If I'm going to survive in here, I need to know you are safe and Mom is being looked after. Promise me right now you're going to let it drop."

She squeezed his hands back, but this new information made her more determined than ever to get him out of there. It had never occurred to her that he could be killed here, but if it happened to James, it could happen to Peter. She looked him in the eye. "No."

Peter leaned forward so he didn't have to raise his voice. "If you don't stop this, who is going to look after Mom? You can't seriously be doing this to her."

Erin gritted her teeth. "I'm not doing this *to* her. I'm doing it *for* her. And for you. Why does everyone think they know what's best for me? You went and got yourself arrested, so you don't get to have a say. I'm out there trying to do it on my own, trying to make it work, and I don't need you to lecture me. I'm a grown woman and I can make my own decisions."

Erin watched as Peter got control of his anger. Exploding in here would only make things worse for him. He had to make her understand. "Did you ever wonder why I pleaded guilty in the first place?"

"All the time, but you would never tell me."

Peter looked around the room before settling back on Erin. "The police knew something was off with their charges against me, and their investigation was leaning toward Kennedy. Kennedy came to me and told me that if I didn't plead guilty, he'd kill you and Mom."

Erin leaned back in her chair and crossed her arms. "So you already knew Kennedy took the diamonds? The whole time? And you didn't tell me?"

"You're still worried about those goddamn diamonds? Erin, forget about the diamonds. I'm just trying to keep you and Mom alive as best as I can from in here, and all you're doing is making it harder."

"So you were mixed up with Kennedy then?" Erin shook her head. "I can't believe Nick was right."

"Who's Nick?"

"Nobody. It doesn't matter."

"These are dangerous men, Erin."

"But at least I know who they are."

Peter scoffed and ran his hand through his hair. "Really? God Erin, I really wish you weren't so naive."

"What's that supposed to mean?"

"Have you spoken to Ryan recently?"

"Ryan? Why?"

"Have you seen him? I mean, since he gave you the tech you've been using."

"Yeah, he stops by now and then. As it happens, he told me I should listen to you and drop it. Turns out you two have something in common. Telling me what to do. You guys should be best buds now. Why, you telling me he's dangerous? The guy who's been a part of our family for a decade?" She wouldn't normally be sarcastic to her brother in anger while he was stuck in here, but she couldn't hold it back.

Peter stared at her, his face hard as a rock.

Erin sneered. "Oh, please. Just because you guys had a little disagreement, doesn't mean he's the enemy."

"You need to promise me you won't see him again."

"I'm not *seeing* him. He stops by now and then. It's not like I'm inviting him over."

Peter closed his eyes and leaned forward. "Please, Erin." His voice was tense but soft.

It was obvious he was upset, so Erin decided to concede a little. "If it makes you feel any better, he was a jerk the other day and I'd rather not see him anyway."

"Good. And if he turns up at your door again, just pretend you aren't home or something."

"Pretend I'm not home? Peter, what's going on? There's something you're not telling me. You're afraid of him."

"I'm not afraid of him. I'm afraid *for you.*"

"Why? You have got to stop trying to protect me by not telling me anything. You're leaving me wide open by not being straight with me."

Peter rested his face in his hands. "I don't want you mixed up in this."

Erin lifted out of her seat. "Well, it's too goddamn late. Now tell me what the hell is going on."

Peter left his face in his hands for a moment then looked at her. "That job that got me arrested was Ryan's idea."

"Okay. But some of them were, weren't they?"

"What I mean is, he didn't get sick that day."

Everything around Erin slowed as the sound of her throbbing heart washed past her ears. She pressed her hands against each other, trying to retain control, but her voice shook. "Don't tell me that. Don't tell me he's been friends with you — with us — for so many years and he's the one who set you up."

"That's what I'm telling you."

Erin's guts twisted. "I'm going to kill him."

"No, Erin. You're going to leave him alone. You're going to avoid him."

"Why didn't you tell me before?"

"Because I didn't want you involved. I didn't expect you to hear from him again or make contact. I thought he was out of the picture. I thought the less you knew, the better."

"Why didn't you tell this to the police?"

"I told you, it wasn't them. It was Kennedy."

"It's not fair."

"You think these guys care about fair?" He reached for her hand again, and she was slow to let him have it. "Now that you know the truth, you need to drop it." He squeezed her fingers. "Hey, how's Mom doing, anyway?" he said hoping that would settle the matter, but Erin was ready for a fight.

"So that's it? You ask how Mom is after all of that, and I'm just supposed to go back to happy family? I can't do it."

Peter slammed his fist onto the table. "Enough."

"Peter Hart." The guard sped over, ready to grab him, but Erin jumped up.

"No, he's fine. We're messing around."

"Then you'd better bring it down a level."

"We will, sorry. I'm leaving soon anyway. It's fine." She couldn't let Peter get into more trouble. She wouldn't let it go. She still had Nick, but Peter didn't need to know about any of that. What she needed from Peter was for him to feel secure secure and not get into any more trouble. "You're right. You're right, I'm sorry," she said to him after the guard went back to his post. "I need to let it go. So yeah, Mom's good. She's getting better every day."

"Good. They still expecting she'll get to go home?"

"Yeah. They won't say before Christmas yet, but it's a possibility."

Peter's face lit up, and Erin realized it had been a long time since she'd seen him look genuinely happy. "That is the best news I've heard in a long time. Give her my love, would you?"

"Yeah, of course. Listen, I, uh … I should get going. Thank you for telling me the truth."

"I wish things hadn't gone this way, but I'll be okay in here if I know you're okay out there."

"Yeah. I'll have Mom home soon, and everything will be good." She forced a smile.

"So you promise to let it go and to steer clear of Ryan."

"Yeah, of course." She didn't like lying to him. When she turned her back to leave, she swallowed back the lump in her throat, but her sadness was soon swept up in fury as she walked into the parking lot. The idea that Ryan was responsible for her brother's arrest, especially after the way he treated her, made her head spin. He had lied to her every time she saw him, pretending he cared. No wonder he acted the way he had the other day. He was simply showing her who he really was. Her body convulsed at the thought of him trying to come on to her. She always knew his moral compass was a bit screwed, but she didn't expect him to be a traitor.

She slammed a fist on the roof of her car. She would have screamed if she were confident it wouldn't bring attention to her. She was going to explode if she didn't do something.

After driving for what felt like an eternity, she finally found what she was looking for. A nice, tall building in a quiet part of the city that she could climb as frantically as she needed to. She had no fear of falling. Falling would be a welcome blessing compared to the way her insides were ripping apart.

When she reached the top, she found a gash on her arm she couldn't remember getting but ignored it and curled up on the edge, looking out over the streets. A few tears fell over her cheek and onto the concrete ledge. She had let her hopes rise too far, not knowing the depth of what had really happened. If Nick couldn't find anything, it was going to be a long fall back to despair.

Chapter 22

IT WAS late in the day, and the sun had nearly set when Erin arrived home. The muscles in her arms and legs were shaky from the climb, but the emotional exhaustion she felt was more consuming.

It was scary enough to break into a building and be confronted by someone like Stanley, but to know that there was an enemy who was not only someone she trusted, but, after betraying her brother, had tried to worm his way into her life more intimately.

Peter was right. She had to stay away from him. He was sick in the head, and that created a new fear, as though she didn't have enough.

She pulled all the curtains closed in the house before washing and bandaging the cut on her arm. Then she sat on the edge of the couch with her head in her hands to gather her thoughts. She had decided one thing while she was on the roof of that building. Even though she'd stay away from Ryan, she wouldn't let him get away with it. Somehow, she was going to make sure he paid for what he had done to Peter.

She pulled a blanket off the back of the couch and wrapped it around her shoulders. She hated wasting money on heating when every penny spent on anything nonessential meant she had to find more for her mom. But it was getting cold.

She ran her finger around a pattern in the stitching and took a deep breath. If she could focus on the facts and remove emotion from the equation, she could make a decision.

If the job was Ryan's idea, and Kennedy was the one who took the diamonds, then there would be a connection there that Nick might know about.

Maybe when — She closed her eyes and rubbed her face. She needed to be realistic. *If* they found the diamonds, they could make sure Ryan took the fall for it. She grabbed her phone.

"Pinky, what's up?"

"You can stop calling me Pinky any time." She felt her throat closing. There was something about hearing Nick's voice that softened her up and made her feel like it was okay to lose it. But it wasn't.

"It's kind of grown on me. But I appreciate your calling me at a reasonable hour. Keeps me from panicking that something's happened."

"Something has happened."

"Oh, right. Your brother. What did he say?"

"I — " Her voice cracked.

"Was it bad? Are you okay?"

Erin swallowed the lump. "I found out some stuff. It's not good."

"Tell me."

She took a few breaths to steady her nerves. "That guy James, who told me about Kennedy? He's dead."

She heard Nick's sharp intake of breath. "That's not good."

"No. Poor guy."

"This is very bad."

"He knew by his size he would struggle in there, but I didn't expect it to be so bad."

"It wasn't me."

"I — " The oddness of Nick's response cut off her words. She had to clear her throat to continue. "I know it wasn't you."

"I'm just saying it because you haven't trusted me in the past, and I want to make sure you know since only me, you, and your brother knew about him."

Her head dropped. "There was someone else. I can't believe this is happening, but I think you're just about the only one I can trust right now."

"You told someone else?"

"There's this guy I know. I've known him for years. He's worked with me and my brother and has helped me out recently, but I just found out he set up my brother. He works for Kennedy — Oh god — " Bile rose into her throat.

"What?"

"It's my fault. Oh god. That's what you meant when you said it wasn't you. I told Ryan about James, and he had him killed because of me."

"Ryan?"

"I can't believe what I've done."

"Hey, don't worry about James. I knew him a little. He was a slime."

"That doesn't mean he deserved to die. Especially when it was my fault. I'm such an idiot. I should have known something was off about Ryan sooner. Why did I tell him anything?"

"The guy's name is Ryan?"

"Yeah. You know him?"

"Is he tall with wavy brown hair?"

"Yeah, you do know him. I was going to ask."

"You don't still have anything to do with Ryan, do you? He is bad news."

Erin paced through the living room. "He had been stopping by and helping out recently, but then he was a real asshole and I walked out on him, so maybe he'll leave me alone." She groaned. "I didn't know he was the one who set up my brother until today." She choked up again.

"So Ryan knows that you know the truth about the diamonds and about him?"

"No, he doesn't know I know about his part in it, but he knows that I found out about the diamonds, yeah."

"You're not safe." Nick grabbed his coat and his keys. "Where are you? I'm coming to get you."

"I'm at home."

"Okay, lock your doors and text me the address. Don't let anyone in who comes to the door. No one."

She hadn't felt panic when her overprotective brother worried about her, but hearing Nick's concern gave her the sense that she was in way over her head. A tingling sensation washed over her body. Her limbs felt like lead, and she lost all her nerve.

She collapsed onto the couch. "I'm so stupid. Peter was right. I never should have gotten involved. What was I thinking? Why did I think I could make a difference? All I'm going to do is get myself killed and then what will my mom do? I've been so selfish."

Nick was hurrying out the door but stopped when he heard the defeat in her voice. "Hey, you listen to me. You're doing a great job."

"No, I've just made a mess of everything, and we don't even know we can find any diamonds." Erin chewed on her nail. "I got so caught up in what I hoped would happen that I didn't stop to face reality. Not really."

"Hey, Erin. Erin. Listen to me. Now's not the time to fall apart. You'll have plenty of time to do that later. But not until I get to you. Right now, you have to keep your head. Do you hear me?"

"I don't know if I can do it."

"You can do it. I believe in you."

"No." Her voice shook. "No, I can't."

"Yes, you can. You're stronger than you realize. In fact — " He might be making a huge mistake right now, but she needed to know how he felt about her if it kept her going. "You're one of the most amazing women I've ever had the pleasure of knowing. And I've known a lot of women — wait — no, scratch that, that didn't come out how I meant it to." Erin couldn't help the laugh that slipped out. It took some of her anxiety with it. "I mean it, Erin. Even from the first time you crashed into me that night. I haven't been able to get you out of my head."

"Really?"

"Yeah. So, you can hang in there because what I'm trying to say is that you're great. You're doing great. I'll be there soon, and you can laugh at me for making a fool of myself."

"Good. Sounds good. I could use a good laugh." Her eyes drifted out the window through a crack in the curtains, and the blood drained from her face.

"Hey, just don't go overboard — "

"Nick." The word was barely a whisper.

"Yeah?" He leaned on his doorpost, enjoying the sound of her voice.

"It's Ryan."

He pushed off the door. "What? Where?"

"He's here."

Nick sprinted for his car with the phone pressed furiously against his ear. "Is the door locked?"

"Yes." Erin flattened herself against the wall, out of site, and breathed hard against the terror. "Hurry."

"Okay. I'm on my way. Don't answer the door. Don't let him know you're there. And don't forget to send me the address."

Erin's fingers shook as she typed, and she misspelled her street name when there was a knock at the door. She had to take a breath before she could steady her hands enough to delete it and type again.

"Erin, you in there?" Ryan called, knocking again.

Erin closed her eyes and held her breath.

"Come on. I know you're in there. I just want to talk to you. I know you've been through a lot."

Erin let a slim stream of breath through her lips to steady herself. Her body was tingling all over with tension.

"I'm only here because I got a call from Peter. He's worried about you. He said something about a guy being killed inside and was worried it had upset you. I need to be able to tell him you're okay."

Erin turned her head toward the archway into the kitchen. She could get out the backdoor, but she'd risk being seen through the front.

At the sound of a rustle at the door and a click, Erin's blood turned to ice. Ryan had a key. How'd he get a key? She ran sweaty hands down her pant legs. Ryan might be dangerous, but at this point there was no way that he could know how much she knew. He couldn't. She'd just have to bluff long enough for Nick to arrive. She could do that much.

With one last breath she let the fatigue and fear she genuinely felt draw her face down, and she came around the wall to the now open door. She squeezed her hands into fists to try to stop the shaking. "Ryan. Sorry. I fell asleep on the couch, and it took me a minute to come out of it." She noticed a cut through his eyebrow and a bruise on his cheek. She tipped her head to the side. "You been in a fight?"

He touched his fingers to the wound. "Oh, that's nothing."

"I, uh, I didn't know you had a key."

"Peter gave me one a few years ago. Just in case," he

said, tucking it back into his pocket and closing the door. "I wouldn't normally intrude, you know that. But Peter was so concerned, I thought I had better use it. Make sure you were okay. Especially when you didn't answer. And, well, after the way we left things the other day, I also wanted to apologize."

Erin was struggling to make eye contact but forced herself. "I appreciate your concern, but I'm not feeling well. I don't think I'm up for a visit."

"So you aren't okay." He took a couple of steps toward her. "Let me look after you. Can I get you anything?"

She waved him off but didn't move. "That's okay. I don't need anything but rest."

He put a hand on her shoulder and led her over to the couch. "Listen." He sat her down then joined her. "I really am sorry about how lunch went. I just got a little carried away. I know you are an independent woman who doesn't need a guy like me making decisions for you. But I wanted the opportunity to look after you. I guess it was a little overindulgent on my part and I'm sorry."

"Don't worry about it. It's not a big deal."

"You sure I can't get you anything?"

"No. Nothing."

"Mind if I make myself a cup of tea?"

"Uh." If she turned him away, he'd know something was up. "Okay, go ahead."

Erin flexed her fingers as she watched him head for the kitchen. Her instinct to bolt was making her leg jittery, but Nick had told her not to lose her head. If she ran out the door, Ryan would come after her and she couldn't be sure he wouldn't catch her. That would be worse than putting up with his presence for now.

She eyed the poker at the fireplace and considered bringing it close, but she had to keep calm and not alarm him. When Nick got here, he could sort Ryan out. She just had to stall, so she picked up a magazine instead, flipping through it but not looking at it.

Ryan came back into the room, but Erin kept her eyes on the magazine. He sat in a chair across from her, which lifted a weight. Having space between them helped.

He set his tea down and cleared his throat. Erin looked up. He tipped his head to the side. "I have to be honest with you, Erin. I'm not here just to see if you're okay. I also want to make sure you're not pursuing this thing about Peter being set up. He told me about James being murdered. These are dangerous men. I'll admit, I thought you were clutching at straws, but this? This is worse."

Erin closed her magazine. "Oh that, yeah? No, you and Peter were right. I just wanted him to be free, and he's always telling me to accept it. But yeah, you're right. It's way too dangerous. I'd rather be able to look after my mom and know that Peter's okay, even if he is in prison."

Ryan watched her, so Erin looked back at the magazine. It was so quiet she could hear not only the ticking of the clock but her own pulse that was racing. It sped up when Ryan stood and moved over to the couch, sitting too close. Erin scooted back, a feeling of nausea rising into her throat. "Look, Ryan. I appreciate the visit, but I've got a headache, and I'd planned on going to bed early."

Ryan put his elbow on the top of the couch and rested his head on his fist. "You never were a good liar."

Her breath caught in her throat. "I'm not lying. I truly do not feel well. Why would you think I'd lie about that?"

Ryan nodded, then reached up and touched the back of his fingers to her temple. Erin held back the flinch but couldn't quite keep the grimace off her face.

Ryan brushed his fingers to her cheek as he took his hand back. "I can't say I'm disappointed. I told Peter I'd leave you alone if you backed off, but that's not really what I want."

Erin's eyes flitted to the front door. "I'm not sure what you mean."

"You have no intention of backing off, and that's fine. It gives me an opportunity to come clean with you." Erin thought of the poker at the fireplace but was too terrified to move. "There are two ways this can go and one way it can't. I can't let you keep pursuing this issue, but I also do truly like you. I've had a thing for you for a while, and even though I've attempted the gentle-manly way of courting you, you don't seem to be getting the picture."

"I don't — "

Ryan put his fingers to her lips. "Now, I might sound full of myself, but come on. I know I'm a good-looking guy and I've got money and power. Not to mention that

I truly care about you, Erin. I don't see what your problem is."

"My problem? I don't have a problem with you. I just don't see you that way. And you're right. I should let this thing go and I promise you I will. So we're good."

Ryan let out a breath, then leaned back, biting his lip. "There's this girl I met at a club a while back. Beautiful girl. Nice, funny, body to die for."

Erin frowned. "Okay."

"I saw her a couple of times. She was good in bed, but it just didn't click for me. There wasn't that much going on with her upstairs." He pointed at his head, then pointed at Erin. "Not like with you. You're a smart girl, too smart maybe. Anyway, my point is. I see her around at clubs and stuff when I'm out, and she's always coming up to me and asking me what went wrong. She asks me what she can do to fix it." He scoffed. "She just can't get it through her head that I'm not interested." He lifted his eyebrows when he stopped talking.

Erin's eyes shifted away from him and then back. "I … still don't understand. Are you trying to make me jealous?" She smiled uneasily.

Ryan shook his head. "She would have done anything for me. Anything I asked, just to be with me."

"Maybe you should give her another chance."

He ran a finger up her arm, pausing at the bandage. "Things would have been so much easier if you were more like her."

Erin's face reddened. "You want me to have a body to die for and nothing upstairs?" She forced a tight laugh.

"You already have the body, Erin. There's no doubt about that. You're a beautiful woman. I watched you grow from a string bean little fourteen-year-old into the gorgeous woman you are today. If only you could have been happy with me. Wanted me so bad, you'd do whatever it took to be with me." He leaned forward. "The offer is still open for you to let me take you under my wing and protect you."

She looked at the door again. She had to find more time. "Let me think about it."

Ryan shook his head. "If you could have been more like that girl, then I wouldn't have to hurt you now." He grabbed her arm on the bandage. Erin winced and tried to pull away, but his grip tightened.

Her mind screamed at her to run. She twisted her arm around like Nick had shown her, ignoring the pain. She got free and tried to jump up, but Ryan grabbed her wrist, twisting her around so she fell on top of him.

"It will hurt less if you don't struggle," he said into her hair, then he shoved her backward onto the couch, but he still had only the one wrist. Erin glanced up and saw his throat was exposed. She took a deep breath and rammed her fist up into it.

His grasp loosened as he choked. She wriggled out from underneath him and sprinted for the front door until pain ripped through her body and her muscles locked. She tripped over her legs that had stopped responding and fell. Before she could figure out what had happened, Ryan was on top of her.

Chapter 23

RYAN HELD the stun gun over Erin's face, waving it back and forth. "I lo — " His voice cracked, and he coughed. "I love this thing." He tossed it aside and sat back on her hips, keeping her pinned with his weight while he rubbed his neck. "A throat punch." He coughed again. "Impressive. I don't mind a girl who likes to fight back. It's kind of hot." Erin struggled, but she was still recovering from the electric shock. "You should rest. I'm told those things hurt pretty bad. I don't know personally, of course, but it's what I've been told. Would you agree?"

"You son of a bitch. Get the hell off me." Her words were thick with fear.

He put his hands on his hips and puffed out his cheeks as he blew out a breath. "Uncle?"

"What?"

"You know, 'uncle.' Do you surrender?"

"No, I don't goddamn surrender, you sick bastard."

She tried to reach up and hit him, but he grabbed her wrists and shoved them over her head, leaning close.

His eyes dipped to her lips. "What am I going to do with you?"

She wrenched her arms around frantically, trying to loosen his grip, but he was too strong. She stopped moving as a tear escaped, and her panic subsided into something much colder and more permanent. Ryan reached down and wiped the tear away. Erin tried to pull her face away from his reach, but it was useless.

"I really like you. I'm mean, really." His eyes were looking a little wild. "It could still work. You and I. If you're willing to submit to me, properly. We might be able to work something out."

She was trying hard to hold tight to the last shred of courage she had, but it was slipping away.

He cocked his head to the side. "What do you think? You want to give it a try?"

Her despair was strong, but his arrogance infuriated her. "Go. To. Hell."

Ryan laughed, sighed dramatically, then shook his head. "Oh well. You can't say I didn't give you a chance. Peter's going to miss you. But don't worry, I'll look in on your mom now and then."

Erin thrashed around, but her size compared to Ryan's meant he was barely affected. "Don't you dare go near my mom, you psycho."

His smile turned hungry. "You sure you want to be moving around like that while I'm sitting on top of you? I mean, I'm all for it," he chuckled, "but it seems a bit drastic for you. Are you trying to seduce me?" He winked.

Erin let out a squeak when he pushed his hand underneath her shirt, rubbing across her belly. "Please don't," she whimpered.

"Don't worry. I'll be gentle. I've got some spare time this afternoon. I made sure my schedule was open, so we would have some time to play before the inevitable." He grabbed her wrists again and pushed them over her head, moving his face close to hers. "I've dreamed about this moment for a long time. I had hoped it would go differently, but I don't know. I think I might enjoy this more." He leaned down to smash his lips into hers, but she was yanked to her side as he flew off her and fell to the ground, unconscious.

She grunted and pulled away, confused until she saw Nick standing over her, a look of horror on his face. He dropped to her side. "You okay?"

Erin breathed out something close to a sob, then sat up and took in Ryan's unconscious body as she scooted away. "Is he dead?" She grabbed hold of Nick's shirt, pulling him close.

"Doubt it. I kicked him in the head, but I'd say he's only unconscious." Ryan groaned and twisted on the floor, lifting his arms up to cover his head where it was bleeding. "Not dead. You want me to kill him?" Nick asked, looking serious. "I'm happy to kill him. I mean. I probably shouldn't, but I will."

"N — No. No." She attempted to stand but fell into Nick.

"Did he hurt you?" Nick asked as he helped her up and pulled her to the safety of the open door.

"Hit me with a stun gun. So yes, that hurt a lot."

"Disgusting prick."

Erin pressed her head into Nick's shoulder. "I can't believe you saved me. Again."

He was focused on Ryan but turned to Erin and ran a hand down the side of her head. "Sorry it took me so long to get here."

Ryan groaned. Erin breathed in deeply, walked over, and kicked him in the ribs. He grunted but was still not fully conscious. "Think he has brain damage?" She kicked him again. "I hope you do. You sick pig," she yelled at him.

Ryan moved again, and Erin jumped back to the safety of Nick. "I don't want him to die. I want him to pay for what he did to my brother. What I'd like is for him to rot in jail. He can testify at my brother's retrial."

"I don't imagine he'll agree to that."

"I don't care." She shivered, and Nick wrapped an arm around her. "He pretended to be our friend." She couldn't hold back the tears.

"I know. I'm sorry." He wrapped his other arm around her. "Right now, though, we need to get you out of here." He lifted a hand to her clammy cheek. "You're not safe."

She pushed away from Nick and shook her head, trying to clear the fog. She had a million thoughts pounding through her mind about Ryan and her family and Kennedy, but she couldn't think clearly. She pressed a hand onto her forehead. "I'm not sure. I'm not sure what to do now."

"You trust me, right?"

"Yeah, you're the only one right now."

"Then come with me." He pulled her around to leave.

"Wait." Erin approached Ryan cautiously. She spotted the stun gun against the wall and grabbed it, reloading it like Ryan had shown her in the past, then pressed it against him, using it to move him enough that she could get into his pocket and take the house key back. "Can you pull him out of here? I don't want him in my house."

"For someone who's confused, you sure know what you want to do with him."

"That's the one thing I am clear on."

Nick looked out the door. "Your neighbors won't mind my dragging a half-conscious man from your house?"

Erin walked out the door and looked around. "It's dark out here. Let me turn all the house lights off. No one will see. Just leave him in the yard. If he wants to press charges for the way he's been treated, he's more than welcome."

Erin kept the gun trained on Ryan while Nick dropped him in the yard. Then she made sure the dead-bolt was in place before going with Nick to his car.

"You finally get to take a spin in the Yenko," Nick said when they drove away.

"Yeah. I wish it were under different circumstances."

"Gotta take what you can get."

"So, what about you? Have I messed up everything for you? What are you going to do now that Kennedy knows?"

"Me? Did you tell Ryan about me?"

"No. Thank god."

"Then I can keep doing things as normal. Ryan never saw me here. Kennedy knows you're onto him, but I haven't said anything to anyone."

Erin dropped her head into her hands. "This is so far beyond what I ever imagined. I can't believe there are people like that out there. People I know, who I considered to be my friends. I am not equipped for this. I'm just a regular girl."

"Mm. I don't know about that."

"Well, maybe not regular, but I'm just a burglar. I can't do the fighting thing."

"I have to disagree."

"No, you were right. Self-defense isn't enough with these guys." She looked at Nick. "I punched Ryan in the throat."

Nick snickered. "You did?"

"Yeah, but I wasn't strong enough to save myself."

"You know, fighting isn't always physical. The way you're going after Kennedy, that takes guts. You've got a lot of fight in you. You just have to know your strengths and weaknesses and how to use them to the best of your ability."

"I guess." She leaned her head back in the seat. "Why are you so nice to me?"

"I told you, I've got my own motives."

"For helping me, yeah. But … " She couldn't bring herself to bring up what he had said on the phone.

He wouldn't look at her. "I have to keep you going, don't I? You're part of the deal."

"Right. The deal." She turned to look out the window.

"Don't worry, I'm still going to do everything I can to help you get your brother out of prison."

"And what about the next time I get in trouble?"

"You're planning on continuing the trend?"

"Not planning on it, but trouble seems to be finding me wherever I go. So now I've come to count on you to knock out any guy who gives me trouble." She smiled. "But, I don't know … " She looked down at the fingernail she was picking at. "I guess I've gotten used to having you around."

"That's a real change of heart from the first time we met." He laughed.

"No, the first time we met, I appreciated you. It was the second time that I didn't like you so much. And can you blame me? The way you acted?"

"Oh man, I still remember seeing you sitting there at the hospital. I thought it was my lucky day. I had to get back at you for what you did."

"What I did? I didn't make you do anything you didn't want to do."

"I guess that's true. But had I known what I was in for … "

"You would have left me alone?"

He stared out at the broken line on the road ahead, glowing in the headlights.

Nick's sigh was quiet. If it hadn't been silent in the car, Erin would have missed it. "But?" she said.

"What?" Nick looked at her.

"Your sigh. It hinted at a 'but' of some kind. What you said on the phone, when I was panicking. That was just to keep me from flipping out."

"No."

"But?"

"But. Erin, you're really great, but I just don't have the ability to give you more."

"Of course. That's fine. You're not interested. I can take it. I'm a grown woman. I just wanted to make sure we were both on the same page."

"Don't misunderstand me. It's got nothing to do with interest."

"What does it have to do with then?"

Nick's hands tightened on the steering wheel. "It has to do with the reason I have this car. My brother got mixed up with a girl who had ties to a gang. It cost him his life."

"I don't have ties to a gang."

Nick shook his head. "I promised myself I wouldn't risk anything for a girl."

"Isn't that what you're doing right now?"

"I told you, I've got my own mot — "

"Motives. Yes, you've said. So that's it? Your brother got mixed up with one wrong girl with horrible consequences, and you let it decide the rest of your life?"

"Yes."

Erin tsked and crossed her arms. "Fine. I'll respect that."

"Thank you." He hoped she never discovered that wasn't the only reason he couldn't be with her.

"So, where are we going?"

"My place for now. You're not safe at home, and you need to get some rest. We can come up with a game plan tomorrow."

Chapter 24

NICK PARKED in front of a townhouse with a shiny black wrought-iron gate. It was a nice part of town that Erin had never been to.

"We're home," he said, pulling the key out of the ignition.

He ushered her through the front door of a tidy but sparse open living space with stairs that probably led to a bedroom.

"Make yourself at home." He dropped his keys onto a table near the door.

"Thanks." She pulled a stool out from the kitchen counter and sat down, stiff-backed.

She looked at the pictures of still lifes that hung at random around the room. It reminded her of a hotel.

Nick was still standing by the door. "We can organize a hotel room tomorrow. We'll book you under another name, and you should be safe."

"Should be?" She smiled wearily. "You sound like you've done this sort of thing before." She frowned.

"You okay?" He took a step closer, but only a step.

"What about my mom? You think they'd go after her to get to me?"

"It's possible, but I've got an idea. I'll make sure she's safe. Let me worry about that."

"You sure?"

"Trust me. I'll make sure she's safe."

Erin nodded. "It's a lot to take in. I feel like I'm in witness protection or something." She laughed but didn't see the look that crossed Nick's face. "I never expected it to get like this. I don't know why I thought it would be easier." She rested an elbow on the counter. "I was afraid to do it in the first place, but once I did, I guess I thought it would go like my other jobs. I've never gotten caught."

"Going after the bad guys is different."

"Yeah. I guess I've always only had law enforcement as my enemy, not other criminals. The law isn't so bad when you compare it to the chaos and danger I'm in now."

Nick decided it was time to change the subject. "Can I get you a drink?" he asked, moving into the kitchen.

"Water would be great." She looked around the room again. "This isn't what I expected your place to look like."

"No? You put a lot of thought into what my place must look like?"

She pursed her lips when she looked at him. "You know what I mean. I didn't picture you as a still life kind of guy."

Nick laughed. "What did you picture?"

"I don't know, warmer, but more intriguing. You don't seem like the type to spend much time at home, but I thought your place would feel like home. I thought when you were at home, you'd want to feel at home. This place is kind of cold and impersonal." Erin went stiff. "I don't mean that in a bad way," she added quickly. "There's nothing wrong with cold. It's its own style."

Nick placed the water in front of her on the counter and leaned down onto his folded arms. "You're quite perceptive, actually. As a matter of fact, this isn't my place. I'm just staying here for a bit."

"Why's that?"

"Long story." Nick pulled out his own stool. "My place is a loft with worn out wooden floors and a few giant abstract paintings. Nothing too out there. Like you said, warm. I've got views of the water, too. I miss that while I'm here."

"Views of the water, huh? Is that cause you have money or you got lucky?"

"More luck than anything. I knew the right person at the right time."

Erin nodded, then wrapped her arms around herself, shifting uncomfortably on the stool.

Nick picked up her glass of water and brought it over to a couch in front of a giant TV. "I said make yourself comfortable. Those stools are anything but."

She slid off the stool without saying anything and walked over to the couch, tucking her foot under her as she sat.

Nick plopped down on the other end and took a sip

of his own water. "You want to watch something? Or are you ready for bed? You can take the couch or my bed. Whichever will make you most comfortable."

She bounced a little on the couch "This is good. I'm not picky."

"You sure?"

"What, that I'm happy with the couch or that I'm not picky?" Nick rolled his eyes and stood. "Wait." He sat back down when she put a hand on his arm to stop him. "I wanted to say thank you. For everything."

"You have said that a couple of times now."

She shook her head. "I know. It's just … I've never …"

Nick smiled and scooted a little closer, slapping her on the knee. "Come on. Spit it out."

"You're helping not just me but my mom and my brother. I've never trusted anyone besides them before. Because my profession is illegal, I can't risk getting close to anyone."

"Not even Ryan?"

"Exactly. I did trust Ryan, sort of, and looked what happened. But I also never felt fully comfortable with him, if that makes sense. With you it's different." Nick tensed. "I don't mean anything by that, I just appreciate that I can trust you. You might have your own reasons for helping me, but I do consider you a friend. And you've saved me several times now. You always turn up right when I need you, and I've never had that before." She tucked her hair behind her ear and smiled. "I appreciate you so much. I couldn't do this without you."

She reached out and took his hand. He looked down

at her delicate fingers wrapped around his and he rubbed a thumb along them. His mind was screaming at him to get up, but he found himself stuck. He looked up at her and when she bit her bottom lip, he came unstuck in all the wrong ways. He knew he was being foolish. It was wrong what he was about to do, but for the moment, he didn't care. He leaned forward and slid his hand around the back of her neck, pulling her to him, and kissed her lightly on her lips. They were as soft as they looked, and he stayed there in that moment, allowing his desire for her to grow until reality slapped him in the back of the head and he drew away, dropping his hand into his lap. "I shouldn't have done that. I'm sorry." He stood and walked around the back of the couch. He needed space from her.

She was dazed and shook her head lightly. "It was nice. Really nice."

"No, it was amazing. But it was stupid." He let out all his breath. "If I could, I'd take you in my arms right now, but — You need sleep and I need to make a phone call."

His body was buzzing, but he ignored it and dropped a sheet, blanket, and pillow on the couch for her. Leaving her in her confusion, he went out into the cold dark with his phone.

Before making his call, he ran his hand through his hair. He had just made everything more complicated than it needed to be. For a split second, it was worth it, but he shook that thought off. Now that he had the taste of her, he was having trouble thinking straight. Squeezing at his temples, he took one last deep breath and made his call.

"Murphy. I need something from you."

"It had better be proper police business."

"It's the girl I told you about."

"What girl?"

"The one from the hospital."

"You mean the one who turned you down?"

"Uh, yeah. Erin's her name. She's mixed up with this diamond heist. I don't have time to explain, but Kennedy knows, and she's in danger. She's safe for now, but her mom, Jodie Hart, is in the hospital, and I'm worried they might send someone that way. I need you to post a couple of officers at her mom's door."

"I'll get straight on it. Did you know she was involved when you hit on her?"

Nick rubbed a hand across his forehead. "No. She's the one who told me about the diamonds."

Murphy sniffed. "You didn't share that piece of information with me earlier."

"Didn't think it was relevant."

"You expect me to do your dirty work, looking into bent police officers, when you're not giving me all the facts?"

"I told you, it wasn't relevant. And I'm under no obligation to share every bit of information with you."

"Your compatriots at the FBI know about this?"

"They know what they need to know, and unfortunately, Murphy, I'm not at liberty to discuss anything further than what I deem necessary for this investigation. Speaking of which. Have you even looked into the case?"

"Of course I'm looking into it. I said I would, didn't I? But obviously I have to be delicate about it. It's not something I can rush."

"Whatever you say."

"Where's the girl now?"

"With me." Nick could hear Murphy's throaty laugh.

"Guess it worked out for you in the end, didn't it? Don't let her keep you up too late."

"Let me know if you hear anything."

"Sure thing, Nick. Have a good night."

Erin spent most of the night staring at the ceiling. Nick was determined to keep his distance from her, and she would not make him suffer for that. He said the kiss was a mistake. It was her own fault, anyway. He said he didn't want anything to happen, and she didn't keep her distance.

It was still dark when she heard Nick come down the stairs and into the kitchen. She smelled the coffee and called out for him to make her one too.

"You sleep well?" Nick asked as he delivered the drink.

"Not really. You?"

"Same."

She wrapped her hands around the hot drink and lifted it to her face, letting it warm her before taking a sip. "I know I've got to hide out for a while, but what happens if we don't find anything? I can't hide forever."

That was something that had been preying on Nick's mind as well. So far he hadn't been able to find anything that would close the deal on Kennedy, not in a way that would help Erin. He had some evidence of other crimes that Kennedy could go down for, but not enough to convince law enforcement to make a move yet. The diamonds would make his case, but he had nothing.

"You won't be safe with Kennedy on the streets."

"So, are you trying to organize a takeover or something? I've been trying to work it out. Why you're helping me. Or is it personal?"

He looked into his coffee. "Bit of both these days."

"Wait. He wasn't involved with your brother's death, was he?"

"No. I'd have killed him by now if he were."

"Fair enough." Erin was stiff, not knowing how to respond after the night before. "Well." She stood up and stretched. "If you keep bashing his guys over the head like you've been doing, there won't be much to take over."

Nick's mood lightened at the joke. "Then you need to stop getting in trouble." He laughed but wouldn't look at her.

"Listen," she said, sitting back down. "About last night."

"Erin, I — "

"No, it's okay. I wanted you to know. It's okay. It must be hard for you, and I don't want to make it harder. I meant what I said about you being a friend, and I don't want to lose that. In fact, if you do manage to take over from Kennedy, I mean, if that's what you're after, I want to offer you my services if you ever need them."

Nick looked at her then. He wanted to tell her he'd love to have her on his team. She'd be a great asset if she would be willing to work on the other side of the law, but at that moment, every fiber of his being felt false in her presence. It had never bothered him before. He had never had trouble creating his fake persona, pretending to be someone he wasn't, until now.

His phone buzzed, and he glanced over to where it sat on the coffee table. "Sorry." He picked it up and read the text from Murphy: *911 in the alley. Bring the girl.*

Nick glanced at Erin. "Sorry. I need to respond."

"Yeah, that's fine."

Nick's fingers slid across the screen: *I'm not bringing her. She doesn't know who I am. I need to keep my cover.*

Your orders are to bring the girl was Murphy's response.

Nick swallowed hard and dropped the phone back on the table. "Thank you for what you said. I consider you a friend too. And if I ever have need of your expertise, I will definitely look for your help."

"Good. Now that that's settled, we need to sort out a place for me to stay."

"Yeah, we'll do that, but first I've got to meet with someone."

"Okay. You want me to wait here?"

"No, I don't want to leave you alone." He stood and began folding the blanket to avoid looking at her.

"I assume it's not Kennedy or one of his guys?"

"No, someone else. But he's safe, it's okay. I just don't want to leave you alone right now."

"Okay." Erin stood and helped Nick tidy up.

He didn't speak again, so she folded in silence but kept watching him, unsure of why he was giving her the silent treatment. She had thought the conversation they just had would have cleared all that up.

When they were done, he grabbed his jacket and keys and went out the door without a word, expecting her to follow.

She wanted to ask him what was wrong, but the hard set to his face kept her mouth shut until the silence was driving her mad and she couldn't handle the discomfort anymore. "Promise me everything is okay." The words burst out of her mouth, and he looked at her for the first time since the text.

He smiled and patted her on the knee. "I promise." The words were bitter in his mouth.

Chapter 25

ERIN SCANNED street names as they drove through the city. Some areas she knew, some she didn't. They pulled into a parking garage. Nick pulled into a spot and stopped, but he kept his hands on the steering wheel, focusing out the window. "It's a few blocks away."

She put her hand on the door. "Okay." He didn't move. "Is everything okay?"

He finally turned to her and opened his mouth but then closed it again. Then said, "I want you to know that I only ever wanted what was best for you. I know things haven't worked out between us the way we probably both hoped, but I do care about you."

"You sound like you're about to die. Or I am."

Nick smiled sadly. "No. You'll be all right."

"What about you?"

"I'm always all right." He got out of the car, ending the conversation.

They walked the few blocks in silence and when they reached an alley, Nick put a hand on her shoulder. "Wait here."

He walked to the other end of the alley where there was a chain-link gate. He checked possible hiding places as he went to make sure it was clear, then he motioned for her to join him near the gate. "You can wait here while I talk to my guy," he said, then walked back toward the street.

She didn't mind small spaces, but the way Nick was acting made her feel as though the walls were closing in. Whomever he was meeting, it had changed his mood.

She took a deep breath in through her nose and out through her mouth and focused on the surrounding buildings to find an escape route to set her mind at ease. It was a simple one. The gate itself was easy to climb, although it led to another back alley, which looked like it could be a dead end. The building to the right was only three stories high with a fire escape and higher buildings surrounding it. Most of the climb that way would be a concealed exit, which was an added benefit.

She turned her attention back to Nick when a man came around the corner, smoking a cigarette. He had a gray hat pulled low over his eyes.

They were twenty feet away, and she could see the new guy watch her before talking to Nick. Nick tried to change position so the man had his back to her, but the guy wouldn't budge. He was determined to keep her in view.

She couldn't hear anything of what they were saying, but Nick gestured her way and then the man looked at her, blowing smoke in her direction. He dropped his cigarette, shaking his head while Nick continued speaking.

She crossed her arms as she waited and watched as Nick grew more agitated while the man in the gray hat didn't change. He looked her way again before stepping on his cigarette and walking toward her. Nick grabbed him on the shoulder to stop him. They whispered for another minute, and then the two of them approached her. Her muscles tightened, ready. She felt trapped but couldn't imagine any scenario where Nick would let that happen. Her gaze moved to the escape route briefly as the two men closed in. Nick was stiff, but the other guy strolled casually closer.

When they reached her, Nick ran his hand down his face. "This is Murphy," he said.

"So you're Erin." Murphy's eyes dropped to her feet then moved slowly back up. "Not much to ya."

"Murphy," Nick threatened.

Murphy looked back the other way, toward the street. "Sorry, Nick," he said, turning back. "If there were any other way."

Erin flinched then shifted her body toward her escape. Without looking at the route, she pictured her first five moves to get up the wall. "Any other way to what?" she asked Nick.

Murphy shrugged. "Thing is, Erin, Nick's been made."

"Kennedy knows you're helping me?" Erin made a tentative step toward Nick as if to protect him.

Murphy snickered. "Oh, that's right. She doesn't

know," he said, watching her. Nick tipped his face to the sky.

"What don't I know?"

Nick licked his lips and finally looked at her. "Murphy's a cop, Erin. I've been working undercover."

Her anger dipped into disbelief. She took a step back and lifted her hands in defense. "You're a cop?" The words barely came out.

"Sort of. I'm a field agent. I work for the FBI." Nick could see she was about to bolt. Part of him would have gladly let her go, but he was too concerned for her safety to let her take off. He took a step forward. "Just give me a second to explain." She shook her head but didn't move. Nick figured he'd better talk fast. "I've been trying to get evidence on Kennedy for about a year now. When you brought me the information about the diamonds, I mean, that was huge. I really have been trying to find out about that. All I had so far were small things. If I found the diamonds, I was going to do what I could to get your brother out of prison. Helps you and me."

Erin was breathless. "How does you being a cop help me? I — I thought — "

Murphy tipped his hat up and spoke. "Miss, you are in danger. I'm going to need to take you and Nick in."

She glanced at Murphy, but her gaze shifted back to Nick. "You're no better than Ryan."

She sprang back and lunged for the first foothold behind a dumpster.

Nick and Murphy both tried to grab for her, but she was in her element on the wall. It was only a few seconds before she was up to the second story with a fire escape to block her from the men below.

"Erin wait," Nick called out. "You're not safe."

He had told her to fight with her strengths, and that's what she was doing. He would never catch her on her turf. Beside him, Murphy pulled his gun. Nick pushed his arm just as he fired.

"What the hell are you doing?" both men yelled at each other.

"She's getting away, Nick. What's got into you?"

"What's got into me?" It was the first time he'd seen Murphy wound up. He didn't think the man had it in him. He checked to see that Erin hadn't been hit. She had made it onto the roof. "She just found out I betrayed her. What do you expect her to do? Not to mention we're supposed to be protecting her. She doesn't deserve to die because she's terrified."

"She's a criminal — "

"She's not the criminal we're after. And what the hell, Murphy? Deadly force on a burglar?"

"I'm doing my job. I'm sorry that you can't see that, but Kennedy isn't the only one breaking the law here. And you let her get away."

Nick stepped away from Murphy and shook his head. "I guess you'll just have to write me up in your report." He threw his arms down at his side and stomped around the alley. "Their first move is going to be to kill her, and now I've got no way to protect her. You should have let me deal with it."

"It's because I let you deal with it that I had to pull

my gun. If you would have let *me* deal with it, I could have gotten her to come quietly."

"Quietly, huh? You mean in handcuffs."

"Hey, that's the job, Nick. You know that. So don't give me your bullshit because you've fallen in love with the enemy."

"She's not the enemy."

"The way she's got you acting, I'd say she is."

Nick yelled at the wall in frustration.

"Hey." Murphy grabbed his arm. "I was told to bring you both in. I did what was necessary, but I won't take the fall for messing this one up. That's on you."

Nick cocked his head at Murphy in disgust. "Don't worry. I'm more than willing to take responsibility."

Murphy pulled out another cigarette but had trouble lighting it. His hands were shaking. His cigarette kept bobbing between his lips as he mumbled curses every time he couldn't get his lighter to work.

He finally gave up on the smoke and gave Nick a shove. "Come on, let's go."

Nick ripped his arm out of Murphy's grasp but kept moving forward with him. "How'd they find out?"

"I don't have those details. I was just told to bring you and the girl in."

Erin watched the two men arguing on the street below. She slammed her hand onto the concrete roof. The sting was a welcome distraction to the raging storm inside her.

She watched Nick wrench his arm away from Murphy, then Murphy led the way out of the alley. She stalked them from the roof until they were out on the street, then sunk to the ground in a heap of exhaustion greater than any she had ever known. The helplessness that washed over her was complete. Not only had everyone lied to her, including her brother, but she couldn't even trust herself to make the right decisions. If Peter had been straight with her from the start, she would have stayed out of it, and she would have stayed away from Ryan and never run into Nick. But she had to face the fact that her decisions meant she had put everyone she cared about at risk.

A ripple of fear penetrated through her bones. Kennedy knew about her, and that meant he'd know about her brother and her mother. It could easily have been her brother instead of James who was murdered in a staged brawl at the prison. And her mom was completely vulnerable. Anyone could walk into the hospital and find her. Nick had said he'd take care of it, but now she knew Nick's word meant nothing. All he cared about was handing her over to the police. But she couldn't blame him. He was doing his job. If she was going to blame anyone, she would have to blame herself. It was her own fault. She had killed them all. She may as well just go home and wait for them to come find her.

"I'll drive myself to the station," Nick grumbled, turning back in the direction they had come.

"Can't let you do that. This is high priority. They

may have already gotten to your car. I'll have a team pick it up and get it back safely to you." Nick squeezed the bridge of his nose and leaned on the wall. "Come on, Nick. We've got to move."

"She's not safe."

"No, she's not."

"Not from anyone." Nick dropped his hand and glared at Murphy.

"Hey, give me a break. It's about time you start acting like the Fed you are."

"We have to find her." He pushed off the wall and headed toward his car. He'd take the risk.

"Whoa, Nick, come on." Murphy trotted after him and grabbed his arm. "I told you, I can't let you do that." Nick pulled away and picked up his pace. Murphy had to jog to get around in front of him. He put his hand on Nick's chest to stop him but had to take a few deep breaths before speaking. "Damn cigarettes." He blew out a breath. "How about you tell me where she might be, and I'll send a team out looking for her. Our best guys, Nick. The ones who know what they're doing."

"Who, SWAT?" Nick scooted around Murphy.

"Hey, hey. No. No guns. We'll take her in peacefully." Nick considered for a moment. "Come on. You cannot get to her on your own. Not with Kennedy out looking for you. Not to mention she doesn't trust you anymore."

Nick wanted to take a swing at Murphy, but the man was right. He was just doing his job. "You tell them they can't hurt her."

"Of course."

Nick didn't want to admit that Murphy was right, but he didn't want the police to treat Erin like a criminal. "You promise me they'll treat her like a witness. 'Cause that's what she is. You send your best guys."

"I promise. Just tell me where she is."

"That's part of the problem. I don't know. She wouldn't go home. She knows that's not safe." Nick shook his head. "She might try seeing her mom, but with the police there for her safety, she'd never go in."

"Okay. We'll send some plain clothes to keep close to her mom. Is there anywhere else you can think of?"

"There's a gym on the other side of town. Maybe she'd hide out there, but I don't know."

"Does she have any other family anywhere?"

"I don't think so. But listen, once we get back to the station, I want to lead a team."

"You can ask when we get there, you never know. But what we need most from you right now is to get as much evidence on paper as we can. If Kennedy knows that we're onto him, he's going to be making changes, and we have to get to him before he can. The best way you can make Erin safe is to get Kennedy off the street." He slapped Nick on the arm. "Come on."

Nick looked in the direction of his car, but then followed Murphy around to a side street, where they stopped beside a white delivery van.

Nick hooked his thumb toward it. "This is our ride? Since when do the police drive around in delivery trucks?"

Murphy sucked on a tooth then slid the side door

open to reveal Paddy pointing a gun at Nick's face. "Paddy?" It took Nick a second to register.

Paddy hopped out of the van, keeping his gun trained on Nick. "I can't believe you're an undercover cop, you goddamn son of a bitch." He lifted the gun and smashed it across Nick's head, knocking him out.

Murphy lit a cigarette while Paddy and another man dragged Nick into the van. "See Nick? I know how to take a man in."

Erin was numb when she walked into her house. Ryan's blood had dried on the floor. She stared at it, trying to feel something, but all she could think about was how completely Nick had betrayed her and made her feel like a fool. What did he think he was doing kissing her, a criminal, when he was an FBI agent?

She threw her keys at the wall and went into the living room, dropping onto the couch then sliding to the floor. She wondered who would find her first, Kennedy or the police. The rational side of her brain knew the police would be best, but she couldn't stand the thought of seeing Nick again, turning up in a blue uniform, even though she knew he was FBI, so he must wear a suit, if the movies were right.

"Dammit." She kicked her foot against the coffee table, buckling the leg, then leaned over to lie on the floor and wait for the end.

Chapter 26

BY THE TIME the van arrived at the warehouse, Nick had regained consciousness but felt sick from the concussion, and his head was throbbing.

Murphy slid out of the van first and looked back at Nick with disappointment written across his face. "Let's go," he said, flicking his fingers and heading for the wide door.

Paddy handcuffed Nick and dragged him out. He didn't speak, but Nick could tell he was taking it personally. For a man who was good at keeping his personal feelings separated from work, he wasn't doing it well right now.

Nick felt the urge to apologize. But how do you apologize for upholding the law? When he first began doing undercover work, he never expected that a job trying to do the right thing and bring the bad guys to justice would hurt people he considered friends.

He turned his focus to Murphy instead of wallowing in self-pity. Thinking back to the conversations he'd had with his police contact over the year, there were little things Nick would have picked up on if he had been paying attention. "Hey Murph, you gonna tell me when you sold out?"

"It's not selling out, Nick. It's called getting what's mine." Murphy called back to him.

Nick closed his eyes and stumbled along as he pictured Erin, hoping she had found somewhere safe. She was clever enough to stay hidden, but as far as he knew, she didn't have anyone else besides a brother in prison and a mom in the hospital, and now she didn't even have him, the one person outside her family who she thought she could trust. He had promised her he would never hurt her, and now he'd told Murphy every place he knew of that she could be. The best outcome for her was if she hated him enough to leave the city. The thought of how she must feel about put a knot in the pit of his stomach.

Nick scanned the warehouse as they led him in. It looked the same as the last time he was there. No new shipments had come in, and nothing had gone out yet. Not even the sneakers.

They passed three armed men at the door before entering the maze of crates that ended in a large open space on the far side of the warehouse.

Sunlight was pouring through the skylights. Paddy jerked him to a stop in a square of light, then left him on his own to stand several feet a way next to Kennedy, who was already accompanied by Stanley.

Nick squinted at the three men. He locked eyes on Stanley first, who wore a menacing grin, one that Nick was uncomfortably familiar with. It was the look he had on his face when he was torturing the cat. Nick refused to be intimidated by the man, but he still shifted his gaze to Paddy, who shook his head and looked down at the floor.

A shifting shadow brought Nick's attention sideways, where he spotted Monkey, crouched by a crate with a scowl on his face. Nick winked at him to try to judge where his loyalties lay. Monkey's frown deepened, but he also nodded subtly.

"Welcome, Nicholas." Kennedy said. His hands were clasped in front of him. He appeared mildly amused, but the look didn't reach his eyes. "How good to see you today."

"I'm sorry I can't say the same. But I can't say I'm surprised."

"Not even a little? Don't tell me you saw all of this coming."

Nick grunted. "Come on, Kennedy. We might not be friends, but I've learned a lot about you over the year, and one of those is not to underestimate you." Nick was making it up as he went along. If he could puff up Kennedy's ego enough, he might buy himself, and maybe Erin, some time.

"You didn't see it coming fast enough to save your-self though, did you? I was told you were one of the FBI's best men. I thought you would show a little more tenacity." Kennedy laughed.

"Maybe I have. I'm surprised you haven't cleared out of here already since you seem to know so much.

You don't think the FBI will swoop in here any minute and take you down, along with your stock?"

Kennedy looked across the room at Monkey and snapped toward him. Monkey unfolded himself from his squat and walked over with his shoulders slumped. "I'm not an idiot, Nicholas. With Murphy feeding me information and only passing on enough to keep you from becoming suspicious, it's been a smooth ride from my perspective. Besides, if the FBI were coming for me, they'd be here already."

Paddy stepped sideways to make room for Monkey, who had sidled up next to Kennedy.

"Don't look so glum, son," Kennedy said, wrapping an arm around the boy's shoulders. "I know you liked Nicholas, but this is an important lesson to learn. You can't trust anyone. Isn't that right, Patrick?" Paddy blinked before looking at Kennedy. "Poor Patrick here must have had some faith in you. You should have seen his face when I told him the truth about you. He was pissed."

Paddy ground his teeth but said nothing.

Kennedy ruffled Monkey's hair. "So, Monkey, your first big lesson is to surround yourself with the right people. People who keep tabs on each other for you, so you don't have to. And make sure you don't put too much trust in any one person. For example, Murphy here has been a great asset. Not only did he let me know the FBI was sending in a man, he made sure he was the contact person. But no matter how good he does his job — no offense, Murphy — I never fully trust him." He slapped

Monkey on the back. "So cheer up. You're learning a lot today. Far better than the education you'd be getting in school. And today you get to have a little fun."

Stanley jerked at Kennedy's side, and he began shifting from one foot to the other. Kennedy looked at him and balked. "Jesus, Stanley, you're like a goddamn excitable puppy. I give you plenty to play with, but today I'd like to give Monkey here an opportunity to mature. He's at an age where he needs to be exposed to the raw inner workings of this business." He shoved Monkey toward Nick. "Go ahead. Let's see what you've got. Give him a touch-up. He betrayed your trust."

Monkey dragged his feet toward Nick until he stood at the edge of the light.

"Go ahead," Nick said. Monkey took another tentative step forward. "It will go easier for you if you throw a few punches. I'll be okay."

"Don't be shy," Kennedy called out. "If he fights dirty, we can always rip his arms off."

Monkey swiveled around to Kennedy and nodded, then walked up close to Nick. "You're really with the FBI?"

"Yeah. Sorry."

Monkey punched him in the chest half-heartedly. "That's why you helped me."

"Yeah, but you're going to have to hit me harder than that if you want to convince Kennedy you're pissed."

Monkey tried again, but he wasn't used to punching, and when Nick flexed his stomach to take the impact, Monkey felt like he was punching a wall.

"Come on, Monkey. You can do better than that," Kennedy jeered.

"Can you do something for me?" Nick said, just before Monkey tried again. This time Nick focused on not protecting himself and let the blow push out his breath. He folded a little to help the illusion that Monkey was getting somewhere.

Monkey's head dipped almost imperceptibly in response to Nick's request. "Find a guy named Peter Hart, at the prison. You think you can find a way to get a message in there?" Monkey punched again. The mention of Peter's name sent Monkey's fist to its target more forcefully. "Nice shot." Nick said with a grimace. "Tell him his sister, Erin, is in danger."

Monkey's eyes widened to saucers. "Erin's in danger?"

"Hey," Kennedy called out. "What's with the chitchat? Nicholas, are you trying to mess with his head? You afraid of a scrawny little kid? Just wait till I send Stanley over. Stop your chattering, and stand up and take it like a man."

Monkey punched again, but now he was distracted by his fear for Erin.

"No, no, no," Kennedy said, walking forward. "You've got to get your shoulders and hips into it." Kennedy rested a hand on Nick's shoulder, then thrust his fist into Nick's guts without warning, buckling him to the ground. "Try it again."

Monkey waited until Nick was up. Nick dropped his head in a nod, and Monkey punched into his stomach.

"You're doing okay, kid, but you should expand your repertoire."

Kennedy threw a right hook and punched Nick in the jaw, dropping him to the floor. His head spun, and he had to lay still for a minute.

Kennedy shook out his hand and hooted. "That's how it's done, my boy." He shoved Nick with the toe of his boot. "Sorry, I took all the fun out of it for you, didn't I." Monkey chewed on his lip and shrugged. "Well, you can have another try when he's recovered. In the meantime," Kennedy pulled a hundred-dollar bill from his wallet. "Why don't you go get yourself something to eat and think about how you can improve."

Monkey snatched the bill and sprinted for the door. Nick, moderately recovered, watched him go as he shifted his jaw around to make sure it wasn't broken.

"Good kid, that Monkey," Kennedy said, stuffing his wallet back into his pocket. "I just need to teach him to be a bit more savage. Might have to send him out with you, Stanley."

Murphy cleared his throat and stepped forward. "Mr. Kennedy. I'd like to stay, but honestly? Too much blood makes me squeamish. Odd for a cop, I know. I blame it on my old age." He laughed. "But you also said yourself, you don't really trust me, so if you'll just give me my bonus, I'll be on my way."

"Your bonus?"

"Yes, as we agreed."

Kennedy crumpled his lips and looked down at Nick. "He wants his bonus, Nicholas. Should I give it to him?" He exhaled and lifted his head to meet Murphy's stare. "Don't get me wrong. What I said to Monkey about your service was true. I've had officers in my pocket before, but you? You take the cake. So I have happily paid your wage."

"And I've appreciated it."

"But now we're talking about bonuses."

"Need I remind you, Mr. Kennedy, that you offered the bonus?"

"Indeed I did. A generous one at that. But correct me if I'm wrong. Didn't we agree that you'd bring me both Nicholas and the girl?" Kennedy spread his arms and looked around mockingly. "I don't see any ladies present, unfortunately."

Murphy's jaw tightened. "Nick told me where we can find her. Just send some guys to pick her up."

"That's not what the bonus was for."

"Then half."

"I'm sorry, I don't do things by halves."

Murphy took an aggressive step forward. "I've done enough for you. We agreed I would keep an eye on Nick while he was in your employ and to keep you informed. I've already done more than you asked. Now you owe me half my money, at least."

Kennedy pulled his gun and shot Murphy in the middle of his forehead. Nick cringed as he watched Murphy drop.

Idiot.

Kennedy put his gun away and stretched his shoulders. "Didn't I say you could trust no one? God, some people are too greedy for their own good." He snapped his fingers toward Paddy. "Patrick, give Nicholas a hand up. Then get a couple of the guys to clean up this mess."

Paddy walked over and hauled Nick up by his armpits then shoved him sideways, nearly toppling him back over.

Kennedy smiled fondly. "He's upset at you, Nicholas. I was the only one who knew what you were. I mean, Stanley never liked you, but I didn't even tell him. I couldn't trust he wouldn't tear you to pieces. But Patrick? He doesn't take too kindly to turncoats." Nick didn't respond, just rubbed his throbbing face on his shoulder, his hands still cuffed behind him. "I need the girl, Nicholas, and I'm willing to make a deal with you to get her." Kennedy pushed his fingers into his temple like he was getting a headache.

Nick watched as Paddy and another guy dragged Murphy's body away, leaving a trail of blood. Then he turned back to Kennedy. "You're going to make a deal with me? You hear that, Paddy?" He called over his shoulder. "He wants to deal."

Kennedy spread his hands. "What'll it be, Nick?"

"I know you're not going to let me go. So I don't think there is anything you have to offer that would interest me."

"Oh no?" Kennedy nodded his head back toward Stanley. "You do realize there are worse things than death?" Stanley grinned and stepped forward. "You don't give me the girl, and I'll make you suffer. And then, because we will eventually find her anyway, I'll make you watch while she suffers. Or, you tell me where I can find her, and we kill you both quickly."

"Don't tell him where she is, Nick," Stanley said. "You should keep that information to yourself. Please. I've been so longing for this day."

Kennedy lifted an eyebrow at Stanley. "See, that's why I'm the boss. I think of the bigger picture, rather than my own desires. Nick, it's still early in the day and I've got a few things to do, so I'll give you a few hours to think about it."

Chapter 27

MONKEY CROUCHED BEHIND A HEDGE, ignoring the branch that was poking the side of his face. When he was in his element, he was completely focused. He liked that about himself, liked the pride that Peter had always shown for his skills.

He scouted the street and the surrounding houses. A car passed, and he followed it with his eyes, squinting into the windscreen. Then he focused on two cars parked nearest to Erin's house. The sun's reflection on one made it hard to see inside, and the other had dark tinted windows. He was sure he had seen movement from inside.

He'd been with Kennedy long enough to know how he worked. Kennedy would have guys on the house by now.

Monkey backed out of his hiding place and snuck around the corner to a neighboring street with a house that backed onto Erin's. He might not be any good at punching, but he was an expert at sneaking.

He crept over a fence into the yard of a drab blue house. A rocking horse was tipped on its side near a dilapidated swing set. He could hear a baby crying inside.

Crouched low, he confidently flew through that yard and over the fence into Erin's backyard, where he perched himself on the garbage can and peered into the kitchen window. No lights were on that he could see from that angle, but if it had appeared that anyone was home, Kennedy's guys would have already gone in. No one really expected her to be stupid enough to be there, but Monkey knew she had nowhere else to go. It was also the easiest place for him to check. Nick wanted him to get a message to Peter, but that could take days.

He looked back the way he came. If Peter was his only option, she'd probably be dead before he could get help.

He picked up a rock from what used to be a flower garden next to the house and knocked it lightly on the windowsill and waited. "Please be here. Please be here," he whispered, his breath fogging the window.

Nothing.

He knocked again, harder, but there was no sign of life.

The rock dropped to the ground as he leaned his forehead on the window in defeat.

"Tommy?" Came a loud whisper from above. Monkey lifted his head and saw Erin hanging out the upstairs bathroom window. "What are you doing?"

"Erin. Let me in."

"What's wrong? Are you in trouble?"

"No, you are."

She dipped her head toward him. "How do you know that?"

"Nick told me."

Her face puckered. She was unsure how that name made her feel. "How do you know Nick?"

"Just let me in and I'll explain."

"I'll be right down."

"Wait." Monkey reached up in her direction, and Erin's head popped back out the window. "There's someone watching the house out the front. Make sure they don't see you."

Erin nodded and disappeared again.

Monkey was agitated, waiting at the door. His long arms ranged up and down his legs.

Erin opened the door to let him in, and he slipped underneath her arm, sitting quickly at the kitchen table. His leg immediately began bobbing up and down. "It's bad."

"Tommy, hang on. The first thing I want to know is how you know Nick."

"Why does that even matter? Your life is in danger."

"It just does."

"He was — is my friend."

"You've been working with the police?"

"No. He's not with the police, he's with Kennedy."

Erin frowned. "And how do you know Kennedy?"

"I've been working for him."

Erin jumped up from the table. "What? Since when?"

"For a while. I've been working undercover."

Tommy's lips curled into a stupid grin. "Kinda like Nick."

"So you know Nick's an FBI agent?"

"I didn't. Just found out today. Kennedy said he had a big surprise for us. Said we had a traitor in our midst." Tommy's laugh was guttural. "For a second I thought I was gonna shit myself."

"Tommy, language."

"Sorry, but I was scared shit — I mean, stiff. You know, 'cause I thought he was onto me. But then he started talking about Nick working for the FBI." Tommy scowled. "Punched Nick in the stomach for it, too." He jerked his chin up. "But we're good now."

"Oh, Tommy."

"He sent me to tell you you're in danger. Actually, he sent me to tell Peter you're in trouble, but Peter told me to look after you, and by the time I would be able to get to him you'd be in even bigger trouble, so I thought I'd better come myself."

"Okay, I get the picture. How'd you know I was here?"

"Didn't. I was just checking."

Erin shook her head. "Well, I already know I'm in danger. I screwed up. Big time. And Nick found out that Kennedy knows about him, and he's gone back to the police, so he's probably using you to try to find me so he can send me to prison." Erin's voice was flat. She dropped back into the chair.

"You're wrong."

"I was there, Tommy. A policeman named, uh,

Murphy, I think, came and got him. Said he'd been made."

"Yeah, Murphy. He works for Kennedy."

"No, he was Nick's contact with the police or something. Listen, you should just go home. You're already in deep enough trouble. You need to get out while you still can. And stay away from Kennedy."

"Murphy" — Tommy cocked his head and looked up at her as though scolding a child. — "is a crooked cop. He brought Nick to Kennedy, and Kennedy told me to punch Nick, and Nick told me to find Peter and tell him you're in danger. So here I am."

"Hang on. So you've just come from Kennedy?"

"Yeah, Murphy brought Nick in, and I recognized him."

"Nick?"

"No, Murphy. Are you even paying attention? He was the cop involved with the diamond heist."

"Murphy was?"

"Yeah."

Erin put her hand to her mouth as the pieces started coming together. "And there he was, right in front of me. Wait, how do you even know that?"

"I told you, I work for Kennedy. But that's not important right now. What's important, is that you're in danger, and we have to figure out how to keep you safe." Tommy was bouncing.

Erin let out a slow breath, then licked her lips. "So now Kennedy has Nick."

"Yeah, but he wants you, too. Murphy was supposed to bring you both in, but I guess you're too good. Not that I'm surprised." Tommy's face reddened, and he looked down into his lap. "So now they're looking for you."

"They were already looking for me." Erin was lost in thought for a moment and a question came to mind she was afraid to ask but did anyway. Now wasn't the time to be emotional or squeamish. "You think Nick's still alive?"

Tommy shrugged. "Probably. For now. Kennedy will want Nick to tell him where you are."

"You think he will?

"No way. Not Nick. He's one of the good guys."

"How can you be so sure? Won't they … torture him or something?"

"Doesn't matter. I know Nick. He's tough, and he's not the kind of guy to squeal on his friends."

Erin wiped a sheen of sweat off her top lip. "But they won't let him live forever, whether he talks or not. Where is he?"

"A warehouse down at the docks."

"You think there's any way he could be rescued?"

"Really? You want to rescue him? Can you do that?"

Erin laughed nervously. "I don't know."

"Okay, yeah, I'm in."

"No, you're not 'in.' You just show me where to go. I want you safe."

Tommy made a raspberry with his lips. "Whatever."

"I'm serious, Tommy. You're just a kid."

"You know, you're the only one who's ever made me feel like a kid." Tommy pouted.

Erin put a hand on his arm. "Is that such a bad thing?"

He grunted an "I don't know."

"Come on. I still need your help. Show me how to get out of here without being seen."

Tommy's face lit up, and he rubbed his hands together fiendishly. "At your service, milady."

When they arrived at the warehouse, Tommy pointed out two guys with guns at the front door and whispered, "They've got guns." Erin looked at him with the corner of her mouth twisted in until he drew back and said, "What? They do."

"I actually picked up on that when I saw them."

"You got a plan for getting past guys with guns?" Erin's gaze drifted up to the roof, and Tommy's eyes followed. "There're windows up there, but I don't know if they open."

"No? You've never ventured up there?" She gave him a companionable shove.

"You're the crazy one, not me. I'm scared of heights."

"Really?"

"Yeah, but don't tell anyone. Come on." He crouched low as he led Erin around to where she could get to the back of the building.

When they were out of sight of the two men, Erin stood up straight and stretched her limbs. "The roof is my best shot. You've been inside, right?"

"Yeah."

"Up at the ceiling, you ever notice if there were any cables or anything?"

"Yeah, they've got a crane type of thing that runs across the top so they can move heavy stuff. There are cables attached to that, hanging off and stuff."

"Great. If I don't make it out of there … " She wasn't sure what to say. Was she really going to risk her life for the guy who betrayed her? But it wasn't just about him. She couldn't leave things as they were if she had any opportunity of pulling her family out of the hole she had dug for them. This was her last chance. She was dead anyway.

She put a hand gently on Tommy's shoulder and squeezed. "Maybe tell the FBI. I don't know if they'll believe you, but if I don't make it out, it might be the only way to keep my family safe."

Tommy stood up straight, pushing his shoulders back. He looked like he was about to salute, but he didn't. "I won't let you down."

"I know you won't." She took a deep breath. "See you soon." Then she sprinted for the building before she could hear Tommy's response.

Tommy watched her spring up to the top of a shipping container and felt his heart swell. He was proud of this girl who was kind of like a sister but also kind of not. He wouldn't let her or Peter down if he could help it.

Erin pulled herself to the top of a container before grabbing hold of a pipe and boosting herself up to where she could get a grip on a vertical ledge that would bring her almost all the way to the roof. Her fingers gripped the ridge of metal and she shimmied her way up using a large duct for support when she needed it.

It was an easy climb all the way up to the last six feet, where things got tricky. Metal sheeting was used to cover the wall and there wasn't much else. Electrical wires hung nearby, deceptively alluring, but she'd seen too many bats strung along power lines to risk grabbing one.

She dropped her feet off the wall and moved hand over hand across the face of the building. Letting her legs dangle meant she could give them a rest before pushing them to their limit with her next move. She found a spot that had a better handhold and, when she grabbed that, paused for a moment to catch her breath before stretching her foot up to where her hand was. She'd done it on numerous occasions with the circus group in order to shove herself into a small space, but it wasn't often a position she used as a spring.

With her foot secure, she was nearly upside down and she let her eyes drift to the ground below. The side of her mouth crooked up in a smile as her body catapulted its natural drugs into her body. The spike was just what she needed.

She took a deep breath, contracted her muscles, and using her other leg for leverage, shot straight up, making the long reach for the roof. Her fingertips grasped onto a lip of the metal sheeting, sending a cutting pain into her fingers. She winced, but quickly lifted her leg again to anchor it onto the roof and pulled herself up.

She closed her fingers in a fist and pressed her hand against her mouth before risking a look at the damage. A red welt ran across the crease of her knuckles, but miraculously, there was no blood.

She rubbed at the pain then turned her focus to the skylight. Tommy was right about the windows.

She jogged across the roof, stopping short of the glass, then crouched.

The window was covered in grime. Probably a good thing, as it would obscure her presence from anyone below.

She used the heel of her hand to clear a place so she could get a better view. She wasn't surprised by what she saw, but she couldn't help the fear and anger that shook her lips.

Chapter 28

TWO MEN HELD another man up. It was Nick. There was a third who she guessed to be Stanley, although it was hard to tell at this angle. Stanley punched Nick in the face. She could tell by his posture and response that his hands were cuffed in front of him, but he didn't bother blocking any blows. What would be the point? Erin knew from her brief encounter with that monster that if Nick defended himself, it would only stir Stanley up more.

Nick's head hung, and he watched a string of blood fall from his mouth. He ran his tongue along the inside of his lip where it was split.

"This is your last chance, Nick." Kennedy said, stepping forward. "You know he has a blood lust for you. You say the word, and I'll set him free. Or, tell me where the girl is, and I'll make him stop."

Nick smiled as he considered the irony that he now faced.

Kennedy twitched. "This is fun for you, is it? You think this is a game?"

Stanley punched Nick in the kidney, and he grunted. His legs dropped out from underneath him, but the two men continued to hold him up until he got his feet under himself again.

Nick shook his head. He had sworn he wouldn't lose his life for a girl like his brother did, and yet here he was, facing not just death, but most likely a pretty hideous torture. It didn't matter that he truly didn't know where she was. But the fact remained that he wouldn't tell them even if he did.

Stanley reached out and slapped Nick on the cheek. "Looks like I wiped that smile off your face, eh?"

Nick squirmed at the ache in his side, then he tipped his head back to look up to the skylight and take in the last warmth of the waning sun. Possibly the last rays he'd ever see. His legs gave way again when he saw someone in the window. For that split second, the shape reminded him of Erin, but that was impossible. She wouldn't be here. She couldn't be here.

"I'm running out of patience." Kennedy was saying, but Nick's focus was averted when he saw a large glass pane had been opened and the figure, who he was now convinced was in fact Erin, was leaning through it. He muttered under his breath. What the hell was she thinking? He let his eyes rove around the warehouse to make sure no one else gave the roof any attention. But at the sound of a loud screech, all heads shot in her direction. Nick watched in horror as Erin tumbled down into the room. It was a wild minute of confusion where guns were lifted and pointed, but no shots were fired as everyone was trying to figure out what was going on.

She looked like she was in a free fall, but then he noticed the cable. Nick had seen her do it on a smaller scale. His eyes sped ahead to see where she would land, behind boxes. In the confusion Erin caused, the guys hanging on to him had loosened their grip and with all attention on the plummeting woman, even with his hands still cuffed, Nick elbowed one man behind him and was able to shove him into the other while taking his gun, before sprinting for cover. If he could make it to Erin before they could, there was a chance. She had given them a chance.

Kennedy's voice echoed through the room, shouting orders as Nick used crates for cover.

He dodged around the large container of sneakers and swung around, running straight into Erin, who bounced off him and fell back, hard.

She jumped up and pulled a clip from her hair. "We should really stop meeting like this," she said as she grabbed for his hands, then stopped. "Look at your face."

He couldn't help the laugh that slipped out. Her confident antagonism, considering the situation they faced, was oddly amusing. "Does this mean I'm forgiven?"

She flattened her lips and stuck the end of the pin into the tiny hole in the cuffs. "Hold still."

"Wait." He yanked his arms up and fired over her head.

She clamped her hands over her ears.

"Come on." He grabbed her and pushed her in front of him as he checked around the next box. A shot was fired, chipping the wooden box they were next to. Nick pushed Erin down and spun around, shooting at another man as he ducked for cover.

Erin and Nick maneuvered around behind some shelving and crept their way along it. Nick's head was in a constant swivel, checking for gunmen. When they reached the end of the shelf, he pulled Erin up close to him and checked for anyone before leading her around. He knew the door was up ahead and would be heavily guarded. He checked to see how many bullets he had left and winced. "Two bullets. You don't have a way back up to the skylight by any chance?"

"One-way trip. Unless the idea of climbing up as a clear target for gunmen is appealing to you?" Erin hadn't allowed fear any place to take hold and was surprised to find, even with the look on Nick's face, she was more determined than ever to get out of this. "What if you killed two guys with those bullets and we could take their guns? Just kill everybody off one by one."

"I'm delighted by your confidence in my abilities, but unfortunately, this isn't the movies."

They were both peering around the corner when a voice spoke from behind them.

"An impressive effort, but I'm not sure what you thought you'd accomplish, Nicholas."

With his hands still cuffed, he lifted them both, dangling the gun from his finger. He turned, keeping Erin behind him. "What can I say? You wanted the girl, and I found her."

"A valiant effort, I'm sure." Kennedy motioned for Nick to drop the gun and push it over.

Nick did what was required, then straightened, continuing to keep Erin behind him, even if it only delayed the inevitable. "I don't understand what all the fuss is about. She's just a silly girl with silly notions. She's got nothing on you."

Kennedy spread his hands. "Oh, of course. I should just let her go because she'll let all of this go and we can all move on."

"Exactly. And come on, it's not like she could get anything from you, anyway. Besides that, you've got me. The FBI agent. That's a big deal. Well done."

Stanley stepped forward. "Kennedy has offered Erin to me as a special favor, considering how things have gone down."

Erin fisted the back of Nick's shirt and tucked herself in behind him. Nick could feel the press of her forehead between his shoulder blades.

Kennedy put a hand on Stanley's shoulder. "You're always getting ahead of yourself. I admire your enthusiasm, but we're not done here yet." He nodded at Paddy, who approached Nick, reaching around him to pull Erin out. Nick blocked him, pushing him aside.

Paddy took a step back. "You really want to play it

this way, you lying son of a bitch? Fine." He went in hard, but even cuffed, Nick didn't make it easy. By the time Paddy had Nick pinned to the floor with his palm pushing Nick's face into the cold cement, he was breathing hard and there was blood on his mouth.

Nick's eyes found Erin again, and he thrashed around when he saw that Stanley was dragging her back to Kennedy by her hair.

Another guy joined Paddy, and they pulled Nick to his feet and hauled the captives back into the open.

Kennedy's focus was now on Erin, who was still being restrained by Stanley. "So you're the infamous Erin. Peter's sister?" Erin didn't respond. "That" — Kennedy pointed toward the roof — "was amazing. I've never seen anything like it. I was going to just kill you and dump you somewhere, but now I'm not so sure." He crossed his arms. "I've got a business proposition for you." He took a step closer to Erin, who didn't move. She held her chin in the air, and Nick nodded at her in recognition of her courage, even though she couldn't see him.

"You've got something, a skill set, that I have to admire. I'd like to have you on my team, and I'm prepared to make sure your brother gets out of prison to acquire your services." Stanley croaked his dissent. "And I'll keep you safe from that animal." He nodded at Stanley.

"Erin, don't listen to — " Paddy punched Nick in the stomach.

Erin turned and tried to go to him, but Stanley twisted her arm up behind her, making her gasp.

Kennedy nodded toward Paddy, who dragged Nick back, out of the way. Then Kennedy approached Erin and lifted her chin. She yanked it away and the pain shooting into her shoulder increased. She yelped and tried to twist out of it. Kennedy raised his voice. "I can give you your brother and make sure your mother has the best care. Don't be stupid."

"You're the reason my brother is there in the first place." She choked out through the pain.

Kennedy tsked then motioned to Stanley to let up. "I'm a businessman. A businessman does what is necessary to see his business grow. Your brother knew that when he got involved with me, and he sacrificed what was necessary so that I could carry on with my business."

Erin glared at him. "My brother would never have worked for you."

Kennedy considered her carefully as he pressed his index finger into his chin. "Seems you don't know your brother as well as you think you do. But," — He flicked his fingers out but rested them back on his chin — "it doesn't matter. Business is business. I'll give you some time to think it over. I expect you'll change your mind when you consider your other option."

"What, you kill me?"

The corners of Kennedy's mouth turned up into a wicked grin. "Close. Have you forgotten so quickly? You, my little darling, go to Stanley. But I will kill your brother. And your mother." Erin tried to kick out at Kennedy as Stanley's iron grip tightened again, and she folded over to try to move away from the pain in her shoulder. "I told you, my way is better."

"So if I sell my soul to you, we all live. And if I don't, we all die."

"More or less. Nick will die either way. It's nothing personal, but he does work for the FBI. One less of them in the world would do us all good. Given your line of work, I imagine you agree. Now, I'll give you twelve hours to think it over."

Stanley shoved Erin forward. "What about Nick? Can I have him?"

Kennedy looked between Erin and Nick. "Not yet. I think Nicholas has some residual value. He obviously wants to protect her. I'll leave the two together for now. He might help her see the light. See you in the morning."

Chapter 29

A CLANG ECHOED through the small space as a bar was slid into place on the outside of the shipping container, locking Erin and Nick in. The improvised cell was dimly lit by the diminishing light that filtered through a small vent high on one wall.

Erin pulled the pin out of her hair and went to Nick to undo his cuffs. She wouldn't look him in the eye, and Nick didn't say anything.

When the cuffs clicked open, she tucked the pin away and walked to the vent. She stretched toward it but couldn't quite reach. Then she walked to the other side of the container and pressed her hands into the wall and rested her forehead on the cool metal.

Nick leaned back against the opposite wall. "Erin, I'm sorry you're stuck in this mess."

"Why? It's not your fault. I chose to come here," she said quietly.

He wanted to ask her why but didn't think it was the right time. "Then I'm sorry I lied to you."

"Really?" She turned to him and took an aggressive step forward. "So if you could go back, you wouldn't do it again?" She already knew the answer to that.

Nick crossed his arms. "I didn't really have a choice."

"Oh, right, of course you didn't. Because a gun was held up to your head."

"I told you I had motives I wouldn't share with you. You were okay with that at the time." Nick didn't want to be mad at her but couldn't help defending himself. He needed her to understand.

"Yeah, because you gave me the impression you were a criminal. I thought you had criminal motives."

Nick laughed but tried to hide it with a cough. "And that's better than the alternative?"

"It is when you're a criminal." She threw her hands up. "And what was that kiss about, huh?"

Nick dropped his eyes to her feet. "That was a mistake."

"Right. This whole thing is just one big mistake. I thought you were a bigger person than trying that kind of angle to get close to the enemy."

"You know that's not what I was doing."

"Do I? Was that whole thing about your brother even true?"

"Yes. Absolutely. Everything I said about that was true. It's just that it was also true that I couldn't get involved with you because of my job. Turns out it didn't matter in the end anyway."

"Why, 'cause now you know your life is over?" She was being a brat but didn't care.

"No, because in the end, it turns out I'm willing to give up my life to save yours anyway." Nick rubbed his face with his hand until he reached the injured parts and dropped it back to his side. "Kennedy was wrong about me trying to persuade you one way or the other, but I wouldn't blame you if you took his offer. There's no reason for you to choose your death and the deaths of your entire family over working for Kennedy." He stuffed his hands in his pockets." I mean, he'd probably just have you doing the same stuff you're doing now."

She sucked in her cheeks and leaned forward. "Will you shut up already? I'd slap your face if it weren't already bruised and bloody. I do have a little bit of dignity, ya know." Nick smiled as Erin carried on her rant. "You really think I would work for a man like Kennedy? Do his dirty work? Peter would rather die in prison than be free and see that his sister isn't. It would kill him. And my mom?" Erin shook her head as tears tripped her up.

Nick reached out and took her hand. No point avoiding her now that death was only a few hours away. "Come here." He pulled her into a hug and was surprised when she didn't resist.

"Did you really mean that?" she said into his chest.

"Mean what?"

"That you'd give up your life if it would save mine?"

"Yes. The only reason I wanted to take you to the police was to protect you. But then here you are trying to save me. You're one of the strongest people I know. You're prepared to die with your chin up." He pushed her back and brushed the tears off her cheek, then ran a finger along her jaw. "I know plenty of people, seemingly powerful people, who would take Kennedy's offer in a second. Would rather any kind of life when faced with death, or worse."

Erin rolled her eyes and pulled away. "No need to get all gooey. My courage on the issue doesn't come from where you think it does."

"Doesn't matter where it comes from. You're still choosing death."

She grinned and took a step back. "Not yet."

"Right. Okay. Great time to get pedantic. Yes, you still have till morning to decide, but sounds to me like you've made up your mind."

"You say that like there isn't a third option."

Nick lifted an eyebrow. " … Third … option?"

"You give up too easily. I thought FBI agents were made of tougher stuff," she said, striding the couple of steps to the front of the container.

"Maybe you've been watching too much James Bond," he said, joining her.

"Isn't that MI6?" She pressed her ear to the door. "You think they've cleared out? Or would they leave someone here?" She knocked and waited.

"No point leaving anyone when we're locked in." Nick's eyes narrowed. "Why? Do you have superpowers I don't know about?"

"Kinda. Think you can pull that vent off?" she asked, pointing with a jerk of her head.

Nick looked from Erin to the vent and then back again. "You're serious? You can fit through there?" Nick walked over and assessed it. "That's a really small space."

"You going to remove it or not?"

He eyeballed her and clicked his tongue then reached up and wrapped his fingers around the grate, pulling gently to get a feel for it. Then dropped his arms. "Close your eyes."

"Why?"

"I don't want you to get distracted."

"By what?"

He pulled his shirt off, and Erin pulled her chin in quizzically. "I'm not sure what you're trying to say."

He didn't let her apathetic response to his naked torso slow him down. "You really are a strange woman." He used his shirt to get a better grip on the vent and to keep the metal from cutting into his hands.

Erin slapped her hand on her leg. "I could have used that shirt when I was climbing to the roof. Nearly sliced the tips of my fingers off on a sheet of metal."

"You can borrow it next time." He grinned and put a foot on the wall.

"I don't expect I'll have the opportunity to climb on the roof again."

"You never know." He yanked back. The vent cracked, and the metal shrilled. He stopped and waited. They both held their breath, listening. No one came, so he put two feet on the wall and pulled a couple more times, feeling it give. Erin watched approvingly at his physique, which she knew he was hoping for, but she wouldn't give him the satisfaction of knowing about it.

With one last tug, he pulled the grate out and fell

into the other wall, making a loud bang. They waited and listened again. There was still only silence.

"What now?" he asked as he put his shirt back on.

"Now you give me a boost."

Nick lifted her, although the agility with which she pulled herself up made him wonder if she was just allowing him to participate so he felt included.

He held her feet steady as she wriggled her shoulders through and then helped push her the rest of the way.

She tumbled to the ground and took the time to look around before moving to the front and removing the bar. It was heavier than she expected, and she had to get her shoulder into it before it moved.

The door clanged as she pulled it open and revealed Nick standing in the doorway clapping.

Erin lifted her arms, swirling her hands in the air before making a dramatic bow.

"Impressive," he said, joining her in freedom.

"My mom would be proud. I never liked performing, but she loved to watch me."

"Next time I see her, I'll tell her what she missed out on."

She punched him hard in the arm. "Don't you dare. She would have a heart attack. She doesn't know I still use my skills. Or what I use them for. So how do we get out of here?"

"We still have a few hours to spare, and I've been wanting to get into the office in here."

"You mean the diamonds might be here?"

"I have no idea, but I think it's worth a look, don't you?"

"Yeah. We've got what, about eleven hours?"

"Oh good, time enough for a nap," Nick said, stretching.

Erin turned and gave him a look.

"What?" he asked. "A snack then?"

Erin shook her head and headed toward the stairs to what looked like an office.

Nick slipped ahead of her to climb first. He put a hand on the door and frowned. "The diamonds won't be here."

"You can tell that just by looking at a door?"

"Maybe I'm just that clever."

"No, there has to be another explanation."

"You're terrible. You won't give me an inch. I don't know if I can go on, I'm so heartbroken."

Erin shrugged. "You look good with your shirt off. There, does that make you feel better?"

"Yeah, actually, it does. Just for that, I'll show you how I know the diamonds aren't here." He stepped back and broke the door with one kick.

"Oh. Not very secure."

Nope. But maybe we can find something else. You said you're good with accounting?" He walked in and clicked on a desk lamp. "Now, where to start," he said as he riffled through drawers, pulling out files, scanning them, then putting them back. "Come on, Miss Accounting, start looking." He shoved a file toward her. "This is around the time your brother was arrested?"

She snatched the file out of his hand and checked the range of dates. "How'd you know when he was arrested?"

"I got Murphy to check it out for me."

"Murphy, the jackass. Did you know he's the one that took the diamonds for Kennedy? If I ever get my hands on him — "

"He's dead."

"Oh. Well … good. I think." She laid the folder on the desk and flipped through a couple of pages.

"So he was the first one on the scene I take it?"

"Sounds like it. How'd he die? Kennedy?"

"Yup."

Erin let that information settle before running a finger down a page that looked promising. "There are some big numbers here. Maybe he sold the diamonds over time."

"Dammit." Nick rubbed his forehead and sighed. "I don't know what I was thinking. The chance of him having any of the diamonds is pretty low, and any that he's already sold would be impossible to find."

"Why not just get the FBI to get a search warrant to find them?"

"Not without cause."

"I thought we had cause. What about the information James gave me?"

"A dead man's comments to you so he could get protection in jail doesn't count."

"What about attempted murder?"

"Whose?"

"Ours. Well. Yours. I'd like to stay out of it where the FBI is concerned. But Kennedy had planned to kill an FBI agent. That should get them inside, right?"

"Maybe, but it's not that straightforward. A warrant

has to say what we're searching for and why. It doesn't give free rein on a search. I could get a search warrant for a lot of stuff, but it's not clear cut as far as finding diamonds goes." Nick checked a few more drawers. "I don't know. Without knowing what I'm looking for, this is pointless. Do you think you can figure out anything with your accounting knowledge?"

"Honestly? I didn't even finish my degree, remember? And it was just a basic degree anyway."

"Then maybe we should get out of here."

"And then what?"

"Then we can get you and your mom in witness protection and — "

"No way. I'm not going with you back to the FBI."

"Erin, do you know how many times I broke the law working for Kennedy?"

"So?"

"So, I'm not going to tell anyone about what you've done in the past."

"What about the future?"

"What about it? Just stop stealing stuff."

"What if I don't?"

"Why are you being so obstinate?" His voice was rising. "Then just tell me you will, okay? I'll believe you and we won't talk about it again."

She glared at him. Her voice was low and brutal. "Maybe it's better if we never see each other again then if you're happy for me to lie to you."

Nick let out a frustrated grunt and dropped his head. "Erin … " He ran a hand through his hair. "I can't afford to think about that right now and neither can you."

She didn't respond and Nick didn't know what to do with the silence, so he kept pawing through paperwork, not paying much attention to what he was looking at. "We still have a few hours. I guess we can keep looking. Maybe we'll get lucky."

Erin dragged herself over to a cabinet. She'd lost her fight. Finding the diamonds would be everything, but she didn't care about that at the moment.

She pulled the cabinet door open and spotted a small box with a gold latch. Her heart sped as she flicked open the latch with her fingernail and lifted the lid, disappointed. The box was covered in velvet and held a revolver. She picked it up and twisted it around in her hand.

"I found a gun," she said, feeling the weight of it in her hand.

"You ever fire one before?" Nick asked as he walked over to see it.

"No."

He held his hand out. "Then you're better off giving it to me." She looked at him but didn't hand it over straight away. "Please."

She slapped it into his palm and walked over to the door, putting a hand on either side of the doorjamb and staring out into the dark, wondering what she had come here for in the first place.

Nick checked to see that the chamber was full and tucked the gun into the back of his pants. "Don't stand in the door like that, move to the side where you've got some cover. If you hear or see anything, let me know."

Erin kept looking between Nick and the door. They had hours, but it felt like seconds. She was used to pressure, getting in and out, but this was different. She hadn't expected anything from Nick when she decided to try and save him. Ultimately, it was her family that she'd come to save. But even with that knowledge, she couldn't work out why it mattered so much that Nick didn't seem to care if they never saw each other again. Why did he matter to her so much?

Nick pulled another folder out and read through the contents before he growled and shoved it back in the drawer. "There's nothing here." He walked around the desk and over to Erin. "When we get out of here, I'll make sure I do everything in my power to go after Kennedy. I might even be able to pull some strings and get your brother's sentence reduced."

"Why?"

"What?"

"Why does it matter to you?"

Nick moved closer. "Because you matter to me."

"Then why are you trying so hard to push me away?"

"I'm not pushing you away. I'm trying to focus."

"So that idea about witness protection, that wasn't pushing me away?"

"You need to be safe and that's the only way I know how to keep you safe while Kennedy is free."

"But that's ignoring the facts."

"What facts?"

"That I'm a criminal and you're an agent of the law."

He pursed his lips. "An agent of the law?"

She tried to hold back a smile. "When *you* say it, it sounds stupid."

"You're right, I'm sorry. Coming from you, it's very sophisticated."

"We should go."

Erin turned, but Nick put a hand on her arm and pulled her back around. "You're right. It is complicated. That doesn't change how I feel about you."

"If we were just two ordinary people, right?"

He put his hand in her hair and rubbed it between his fingers. "Maybe we can be for a few minutes."

"How?"

"Right now, we're both captives. Not ordinary, but at least we're on the same side." He leaned down and kissed her. She wrapped her arms around him, pulling him closer, knowing that this was the only moment they had. When they left the warehouse, they were back on two different sides of the line, and it would all be over.

A loud clang filled the darkness and ripped Erin and Nick apart. Both of them dropped to the ground and Nick pulled out his gun.

Chapter 30

NICK DOVE for the light and clicked it off.

"Follow me," he said, grabbing her hand. They needed to get down the stairs, fast.

Once they were at ground level, Nick pulled her along behind some boxes to allow time for their eyes to adjust to the dark.

When Nick could see better, he led Erin along as they made their way through the maze of containers toward the front of the warehouse. He was grateful he had the chance to unload the cargo the other day. He had some idea of the best way to move through the warehouse without being spotted.

When they were only twenty feet from the door, Nick put and hand on Erin's shoulder and pushed her down while they waited, listening for any sign of movement.

Erin put her mouth close to Nick's ear. "Could it have been the building settling?"

"Probably, but it's best to be overcautious. All right,

let's get out of here," Nick said as he tucked the gun back into his pants. "Come on."

He led her to the front door and twisted the nob. It was unlocked. He opened it as quietly as he could but shot up straight and reached a hand around to push back at Erin. Paddy stood on the other side of the door, his gun pointed in Nick's face.

"Back up," Paddy said.

Nick and Erin raised their hands and moved back. Several men entered with Paddy, followed by Kennedy, who was shaking his head. "I had a feeling. I don't know why, but I was thinking about Erin dropping from the ceiling like she did. Impossible. And I thought to myself, 'what other impossible things might she be able to do?'"

"Screw you." Erin snarled.

Kennedy laughed at her. "Tough words, girl." He reached an arm sideways to one of his men. "Give me your gun."

Erin was standing half a step behind Nick and could see the revolver tucked into the back of his pants.

"Where are the diamonds?" Erin demanded of Kennedy as he took possession of a gun.

"Diamonds?"

"Yeah, the ones you set my brother up for. The ones that Murphy stole."

"That's what this is all about? I thought you were just mad at me for putting your brother in prison and had a ridiculous idea of getting revenge. You really believe there were diamonds?"

"Why else would my brother be in prison."

"Well, okay, you've got me there. There were

supposed to be diamonds, but they vanished into thin air. Poof. Someone had to take the fall."

Erin gritted her teeth. "So Murphy kept them? Is that why you killed him?"

"Hah! No. Murphy's dead because he wore out his welcome. He doesn't have the balls to steal from me. So where does that leave us? Your brother didn't have them, and Murphy didn't have them. I certainly never had them in my possession, unfortunately. Maybe another cop took them? Who knows? There is only one thing I do know for sure about those diamonds, and that is that your brother will be in prison for a long time, paying the price. Unless I kill him first."

Erin pulled the gun from Nick's waist, fumbling with the trigger. Nick reached over before she could raise it and chopped down on her arm, so she dropped it before Kennedy or his men returned fire. "Oh my god, Erin. What are you doing?"

"What the hell, Nick? What are *you* doing?"

"Keeping you alive. You want to get shot?"

Kennedy was laughing hard. One of the other guys grabbed the gun away from Erin.

"I don't care. I'm going to die anyway. I'd rather go quickly and with the satisfaction of knowing he was dead."

Kennedy took a deep breath as his laughter died away, and he lifted his gun, pointing it from Erin to Nick then back to Erin. "I know I made promises to Stanley, but he's not here, and I find it troubling that you can break out of a shipping container. You are a bit of a Houdini, and I'm not going to risk it. It's easier to just get the whole thing over with so I can get on with my life." Kennedy moved the gun back across to settle on Nick. "But I think I'll kill you first."

Several gun shots rang out, and everyone dropped to the floor. Nick dove on top of Erin, covering her as best he could, which wasn't difficult, given their size difference.

When quiet returned to the room, he looked around to assess what had happened. Kennedy lay several feet away. His eyes open and staring. Nick twisted and saw men in black fatigues moving out of the shadows.

Erin squirmed under Nick. "What's going on?"

"Nick Lucas? This is the FBI. Stay where you are until we've assessed the safety of the situation."

Erin pushed at Nick, trying to get up and run. "I've gotta get out of here."

Nick grabbed hold of her. "You need to stay. They'll have the place surrounded. Just follow my lead." He helped her stand but held fast to her so she wouldn't bolt. "Trust me," he whispered in her ear.

"Little Nicky," called a deep voice.

"That's not Mikey, is it?"

"You know I never liked being called that."

"Then we're even."

A tall man with broad shoulders came out of the shadows. "I've got guys around the perimeter. Is there anyone else we should be looking for?"

"I don't know how many guys Kennedy brought with him, but if a guy named Stanley is around, you'll want your men to be careful."

Michael nodded to one of his men, who pulled out a

walkie-talkie and moved away to update the team. Then he focused on Erin. "Who's this?"

Nick put a hand on her shoulder. "Erin Smith. She's one of my informants. It's my fault she's here. She's not even involved with Kennedy. Erin, this is Michael Carter with the FBI. I used to work with him in New York." He turned back to Michael. "I forgot you were transferred here to Chicago."

Erin was unsure what to do, so she put her hand out to shake Michael's. His face was serious, but when he took hold of her hand, a small smile crept on his lip as he looked from Nick to Erin.

Nick stepped forward. "Erin has to get going, otherwise she'll be found out. She's expected somewhere, and I need to keep her in the good books."

"The good books with whom?"

"Different job."

"You know we'll need a statement from her."

"I know how it works, but she needs to go, otherwise her life will be at risk." He turned to Erin. "I'll be in touch."

Erin swallowed and took a small step backward. "Uh, yeah. Okay. Nice to meet you, Michael."

Nick watched until she was out of sight as Michael informed his guys to let her through, then he put his hands on his hips while he studied Nick. "Informant, huh?"

"Yeah. Different job."

"You said. You know we aren't allowed to get involved with our informants."

Nick laughed and shook his head. "I'm not involved."

Michael pushed his tongue into his cheek. "I recently met up with an old friend of mine, Cole Sullivan. He was helping out this woman. He looked at her the same way you look at Erin. The only difference was he was willing to admit how he felt."

"Cole Sullivan, huh? Never heard of him."

"No, you wouldn't have. He's not FBI, and he lives in LA."

"Sir." A short stocky man came jogging through the door. "We got two more men on the perimeter, but we're clear now."

"Either of them Stanley " — Michael looked at Nick. — "I didn't get his last name."

"As far as I know, he doesn't have one."

"Right, anyone named Stanley?"

"No Stanleys, sir."

"Okay, let's get this cleaned up. I'll be with you shortly. Nick, can you give me a quick recap so I know where things stand here?"

"Well, looks like you just took out my primary suspect. I have reason to believe he stole diamonds and set up another man by the name of Peter Hart. We need to find those diamonds if we can. There's a pile of other stuff, but the main reason I'm here now is because Kennedy found out I was an informant, and he was going to kill me, so thanks."

"How'd he find out?"

"My contact with the police was one of his guys. Kennedy killed him today."

"What about Erin? Why was she here?"

"I told you, it was a mistake."

"You haven't answered my question."

"She heard I was in trouble and came to see if she could help."

"Your informant — "

"Yes."

"Heard you were in trouble and came to help?"

"Yes."

"Okay, we'll take it from here. I'll need Ms. Smith's contact details."

"No. I'll get her statement. I told you, I can't have her compromised."

Michael let it drop for the moment. "Director Martin wants you back in the office by the weekend so you can complete your interview and give a full report."

"Martin? I'd be better off helping you here."

"Not my orders."

Nick rubbed his forehead. The only place that wasn't injured. "Okay, I'll be on the first plane to New York." He looked back at Kennedy's dead body. "Hey, how'd you know where to find me, anyway?"

"A young man by the name of Tommy Kincade."

"Don't know him."

"He knows you. I walked into the building as security was escorting him out. Good thing I took time to listen."

Nick made a mental note to find out who this Tommy Kincade was. Probably a fake name, but he couldn't worry about that now. He had to focus on the job, which was to go back to his office in New York and give an account of his past year undercover. They wouldn't send him back to Chicago for another job. The reason he caught this assignment in the first place was because he had no connections here. At least, he didn't used to.

"Well, it was good to see you, Michael."

"You too. I'll be in touch about Erin."

"Yeah, sure."

Nick turned to head out the door as Michael called out to him. "Hey, Nick. I don't suppose you've heard of a guy named Silas Lincoln?"

Nick stopped and processed the name. "Don't think so, why?"

"Apparently he's giving Cole's friend Bristol a hard time."

"Bristol? That's an unusual name."

"Yeah, you should see her file."

There wasn't much for Nick to pack at his place. He'd never settled in, but the fact that Erin had been there made it harder to leave than he would have guessed.

There was a knock at the door that Nick wasn't expecting. He checked through the blinds and saw an FBI agent by the name of Griffin standing at the door with Monkey. Nick jumped for the door. Monkey would have gotten caught up in the roundup they did of Kennedy's guys. He hadn't even thought of the kid.

He whipped the door open. "Monkey, you okay?"

Monkey got a stupid grin on his face and bobbed

his head up and down in a goofy nod. Griffin put his hand out to shake Nick's. "The kid's fine. Actually, a bit nosy, if you ask me. He insisted I bring him to see you."

"He's not in trouble, is he?"

"Who, Tommy? No way. Why would he be?"

"Tommy?"

"Hang on, Tommy," Griffin said, taking Tommy by the collar. "You said you and Nick were friends."

Nick slapped Tommy on the arm. "Some friend I am, eh Tommy? Not even knowing your real name. Tommy Kincade, right? My hero?"

"The one and only." Tommy said, pulling away from Griffin and rocking back and forth on his heels.

"When I told him you were headed back to New York, he insisted on seeing you before you left."

"Come on in. My flight leaves soon, but I have some time."

"Can I leave you two for a bit? I've got some things I need to take care of."

"Yeah, sure. You can come get him in about an hour."

Griffin tipped his hat and headed back to his car.

"Tommy, eh?"

Tommy's grin was toothy. He strode around and flopped down on the couch. "Nice place you got here."

"So you're the one who went and told the FBI? I thought I told you to go find Peter Hart?"

"Nah, that would have taken too long. I went and saw Erin instead."

"Erin? So that's how she knew how to find me. I

wondered, but wait, how'd you know where to find her?"

"I didn't know where she was, so just went to her house to see if she was there."

Nick knocked his fist on his knee. "And how'd you know where she lives?"

Tommy's face went crooked. "What d'ya mean?"

"Where'd you get her address from?"

"I didn't need it. I've been there lots of times."

"What?"

"I've known Erin for years."

"You're kidding. You two know each other?"

"I used to be a pickpocket for her brother."

Nick slapped his hands to his ears. "Never mind. Don't tell me."

Tommy looked around the room again. "Can I have this place when you go?"

"No. Listen, Tommy, can you do me a favor?"

"Oh cool, yeah, 'cause I've got a favor to ask you, too."

"I don't know why that makes me nervous, but what I need for you to do is stay out of trouble from now on."

"Yeah, no problem. I'm in tight with the FBI now. I've given them a ton of helpful information on Kennedy."

"Okay, great. That's great. So what's your favor?"

"Get me a job with the FBI."

"I thought you said you were in tight."

"Yeah, but they haven't offered me a job. I want to be an agent like you."

"I don't think they hire minors."

"Really? Maybe I can settle for being an informant."

"You don't want to be an informant. You want to go to school. Get a good education, and then you can apply to the FBI."

"Exactly. I already got a good education, now I just need the job."

"You don't go to school."

"I got a street education. That's better for the FBI, isn't it?"

"No. The FBI likes college graduates."

"You're no help. I'll just have to stick with Peter and Erin."

Nick shook his head. "I'm going to miss you, Monkey."

"I'm gonna miss you too. But don't expect me to get all soppy. I'm not into that kind of stuff."

"Good. Neither am I. But look me up if you ever end up in New York."

"You think you'll ever come back to Chicago?"

"I don't know. I hope so. There are a few very important people here."

Tommy waggled his eyebrows. "Like Erin?"

"Stop. But yes, and you."

"That's cool. Erin's cool."

"She's pretty too."

Tommy blushed and picked up the remote control. "You have Netflix here?"

"Nope."

"What is wrong with you?"

"I don't know. Lots."

.   .   .

Tommy was still bugging Nick about the job when Griffin came back to get him. Griffin gave him a shove toward the car. "He's been trying to convince me of the same thing the whole car ride over here."

"He's a good kid." Nick said, pulling Griffin away from Monkey, who was leaning on the car like a gangster. "If you've got anything he can do. He's a good kid. Been brought up in an adult world. He'd be a great asset."

"If I can think of anything, I'll make sure to look him up."

"Great."

Back inside, Nick sat on the couch with his head in his hands. This had been his first long-term undercover job. He was trained not to get attached. Of all the things he could have screwed up, he didn't expect it to be that.

Chapter 31

IT HAD BEEN ALMOST a month since the incident. Nick had sent a text to Erin saying he had the FBI looking for the diamonds, but that was all she heard from him. It would have helped if she could steal something. That was always a great release for her, but the idea of breaking the law now carried with it the knowledge that it pushed her further away from Nick. It shouldn't matter. Nick was out of her life for everything except finding the diamonds. Tommy told her about him leaving for New York. The chance that he would come back was small, and she tried to convince herself of that fact. But she couldn't let go. Not yet.

She had plans to visit Peter but was hoping to bring him good news about the diamonds. Kennedy had to be lying. Diamonds don't just disappear, so she kept putting it off. He'd know as soon as he saw her that something was up, and she wanted to avoid telling him anything until she had something positive to add. Although Kennedy being dead would probably make his day.

Erin had vacuumed the entire house and had moved on to dusting. She stopped and looked at her dirty rag, wondering if she had cleaned enough, when her phone dinged from the other room.

She ran to the kitchen table and checked her message, beaming, then tossed her rag. Best excuse to stop cleaning she had ever had. She swung her arm through the strap of her bag and ran for the car. At least there was one thing she could be grateful for today.

Erin had trouble finding parking at the hospital and was jittery when she finally entered her mom's hospital room, suddenly afraid the doctors had changed their minds. She found her mom sitting on the bed with her legs hanging off the side.

Erin stopped in the door. "You've already packed. I told you I'd take care of it when I got here."

"Are you kidding, sweetie? I can't wait to get out of here and back in my own bed." She closed her eyes, and her lips twisted into a luxurious smile. "It's been too long."

Erin ran over to her mom and hugged her hard. "I can't believe I get to bring you home. This is the best day of my life."

A nurse entered the room, and Jodie stood unsteadily. "Hold on, Mrs. Hart. You can't leave yet. The doctor still needs to see you one more time."

Jodie groaned. "It's always one more time. Poking, prodding, measuring, testing. All just one more time."

The nurse smiled and wrote something on the chart. "It's for real this time. At least until your next appointment. But we're going to miss you."

"Would it be rude if I said I wouldn't miss you?"

"Not at all. I hope you don't. I hope you go live an active fun-filled rest of your life." She frowned and dropped her voice into a grumpy funk. "I never want to see you here again."

"Yes ma'am."

"Except for checkups." The nurse winked.

"There's always a catch."

"It wouldn't be real life without a catch, now would it?"

Erin enjoyed watching the two women jousting. Her mom had rarely had the energy for it over the last couple of years.

After the doctor gave Jodie the all clear, the nurse helped her into a wheelchair, and Erin wheeled her out.

Jodie twisted her head around to look up at Erin. "I haven't seen that Nick guy in a while. He still around?"

"No, Mom. I told you, there was nothing going on there. I won't even see him again. Let's just get you home. Besides, he lives in New York."

"That's not far."

"It's far enough, and it's not the only thing, but I really don't want to talk about it."

"That's too bad. I liked him. Not like that guy Ryan that used to hang around your brother. He had a thing for you, ya know. Stopped by here once a month or two ago. I pretended I was drugged up and couldn't talk." She snickered.

"I didn't know you had such treachery in you. Well done. I agree, he is a bit of a sleaze."

"Took you long enough to realize it." She reached up and squeezed Erin's hand. "I'm just so glad I'm going home with you today."

"Me too."

When Erin pulled onto their street, she saw the Yenko and her heart raced.

"Oh! Isn't that Nick?" Jodie said, tapping Erin on the arm. "I thought you said he was in New York."

Erin looked up at the house as she pulled against the curb and saw Nick leaning on the railing at the front door. When he noticed them arrive, he headed down to the street.

Erin wasn't sure what the feelings were that were coursing through her. She'd have to just play it cool. "I don't know what he's doing here." Jodie looked at her daughter and pressed her lips together. "Stop it, Mom."

"What? I said nothing."

"Your looks speak louder than your words sometimes."

Jodie shrugged as Nick pulled the passenger door open.

"Good afternoon, Jodie," he said, holding a hand out to help her from the car. "It's good to see you."

Jodie smiled. "We were just talking about you."

Nick's eye flicked up to Erin. "Is that so?"

"It's lovely to see you. Erin said I'd never have the pleasure of your company again."

Nick's eyes swept back to Jodie. "I could never stay away from you long."

"Oh, listen to you. But I can see through your wily ways."

"Oh, can you? That's disconcerting."

"But what I see is that deep down you are a good man. You're heavy on the charm, and there's no point denying the fact that you are a very attractive young man, but I know the truth."

"Can't hide anything from you, can I?"

"And don't you forget it."

"You don't have to worry about that."

Nick carried the bags inside and helped Erin settle Jodie onto the couch. He pulled a blanket off a nearby chair and draped it over her legs. "You want me to start a fire?"

"No." Erin said, heading for the kitchen to get a cup of tea for her mom. "It hasn't been used in so long. It needs to be cleaned and checked," she called out through the door.

"I know a guy. You want me to call him?" Nick asked, following her into the kitchen.

"I can take care of it." She reached up to get a mug from the cupboard.

Nick leaned on the counter next to her and watched as she filled the kettle and turned on the stove.

Erin looked out the window at the snow that had just started to fall. "I thought you were in New York?"

"I was. But I had to come back and get my car." Erin nodded and watched the kettle, hoping it would boil quickly. She didn't know how to be alone here with him. It made her heart ache.

"Erin, I wanted to tell you in person. The FBI has found a lot on Kennedy in their search, but they haven't been able to work out anything related to the diamonds. Kennedy's guys all say the same thing, that he never got any diamonds. I'm sorry. I don't think they're going to find what you need."

Erin gripped the side of the counter and squeezed until her knuckles turned white. "That's okay." She let go and turned to him. "You did your best. I've got Mom home, and that's a big improvement."

"I've also asked for a couple of guys to watch your house."

"Why?"

"They haven't found Stanley or Ryan."

She stepped toward him, wanting the safety of his proximity, not realizing she had come to rely on it. "You think one of them will come here?"

"No, I think they've cleared out to avoid being caught. But I wanted to make sure you and your mom were safe."

She nodded. "You have another undercover job coming up?"

"Don't know. For now, I'm back in the New York office."

"Right."

Nick shoved his hands into his pockets. "I've gotta get going, but call me if you need anything." He leaned forward and kissed her lightly on the cheek. "I'll see you later."

Erin wanted to call him back as he walked out of the room. This was it for real. Now that the diamonds were an impossibility they had no more reason to communicate. But she didn't speak.

She listened as he said goodbye to her mom, then turned back to the window when she heard the door shut. She stared at the snow until the kettle whistled and startled her. When she saw him at the house, a small part of her thought it meant something more than him giving her an update and leaving.

But at least now she had closure. She could let him go, just like she now had let go of her brother getting out of prison early. If she didn't have her mom, it would have been much harder, but for now, she would enjoy the things she did have. And she'd get that fireplace fixed.

She took a breath and put a smile on her face, then sat with her mom in the living room for the first time in too long. She had enough joy right now to fill her heart and keep her from lamenting her loss.

Chapter 32

ERIN DRUMMED her fingers on the steering wheel, getting up the nerve to go inside. Now that she knew there was no chance of getting Peter out early, she had to face him. She didn't know why it made her nervous. He had told her many times to let it go. He'd be happy now that she had. She turned the car off and got out to face her brother.

It was a bitterly cold day as she marched through the parking lot. She wore her big puffy jacket, but the cold wind seemed to find its way through to her bones.

Inside the prison was warmer, but with the chill she now felt, she was loath to give up her coat.

Sitting in the all too familiar room, she ran her hands up and down her arms to warm up. Cold from the metal chair seeped through her pants. She was about to stand when the buzzer sounded. Peter came in looking worn out. He hugged her tightly. "I'm so glad to see you. It's been a while. You doing well?"

"Yeah. Having Mom home is great. I love being able to get up in the morning and have coffee with her. She's still weak, but in good spirits and improving every day."

"That's good. I'm glad to hear it." But sadness clipped at his eyes.

"You're not doing so good?"

"I'm fine."

Seeing him like this was going to make it harder to tell him she couldn't get him out. "There's something I need to tell you."

Peter breathed deeply, as though steadying himself. "I guess I should expect bad news by now."

"Good news and bad, actually."

"Let's start with the bad then."

"Uh. I think I better start with the good. Otherwise you might throttle me."

Peter's eyes sparked, lessening the weariness for a moment before the fight drained out and it returned. "Okay, the good news then." He rubbed a hand across his chest.

"Kennedy's dead."

Peter shot forward. "Kennedy's dead?"

"Yeah. Good news, right?"

"You're sure?"

"I was there."

Peter's face turned a couple different shades before finally settling on red. "You were there?" he asked through clenched teeth.

"You are focusing on the wrong things here. I am

safe, everything is okay, and Kennedy is really dead. But … the bad news."

"I don't know if I can take it."

"It's not that kind of bad news. It doesn't change anything."

Peter's shoulders stooped further. "Okay, the bad news then."

"I can't get you out of prison."

"That's your bad news?" He laughed.

"That is bad news."

"No, that's *no* news. Geez, Erin." He wiped a hand across his mouth. "I thought you were going to say something like you had — I don't know — gotten caught shoplifting or something."

"Well, that wouldn't really be that bad considering."

He laughed and shook his head, then went still. "So Kennedy's really dead?"

"Yeah. I was trying to get the diamonds, but the douchebag said he didn't have them, which we both know is bullshit, but the FBI looked — "

"FBI?" Peter almost yelled. "Why is the FBI looking for them — You know what? Never mind."

"I was hoping the FB — I was hoping that they would be found so we could prove your innocence, but they haven't found anything."

Peter sat back and pressed his fingertips together, staring down at the table.

"You okay?" Erin asked, reaching across the table.

"You and Mom are safe?"

"Yes."

"The FBI isn't ... you know ... causing you any problems?"

"None."

"And Kennedy's dead?"

"Right, yes, definitely. So everything is great, except that we can't find the diamonds."

"Kennedy wasn't lying."

"What? About what?"

"The diamonds. He never had them."

"What do you mean? But James said — I mean, you said — I thought that's what happened, that he took them and framed you. That's why he made you plead guilty. That's what happened. What else could have happened?"

"James was misinformed, like Kennedy. That's why I told you to drop it."

"No, you told me to drop it because the reason you're in prison is because Kennedy threatened Mom and me, and that's why you took the blame. But that doesn't answer the question that's caused all the problems in the first place. Where are those goddamn diamonds?"

Peter looked at the guard then leaned forward. "What about the rest of Kennedy's group? Where are they?"

"Either arrested or scattered. Stanley and Ryan are still out there. Probably took off."

Peter nodded slowly and breathed in, resigned. "I have the diamonds," he said under his breath.

Erin blinked a couple of times before she could speak. "That's impossible. You were arrested and searched in the building. I thought that police detective took them."

"He did."

"Then — "

"I took them back."

"I — uh — w — " she stuttered, then finally managed to form a word. "How?"

"Tommy."

"I don't — Tommy?"

"The one and only. The best pickpocket I know."

"I don't understand."

"You know how good he is at not being seen? Well, he overheard someone at Messina's talking about setting me up. Tommy told me, and I was going to can the whole thing, but then I came up with a better idea. Or so I thought. I decided to beat Kennedy at his own game. I figured when they arrested me and found I had nothing on me, I might go to prison, but it wouldn't be long before I got out. Then we'd have all the diamonds, and we could retire." Erin tried to respond but couldn't think of anything to say. "So I had Tommy hang around, and when he saw the detective, he went in and took them back."

Erin shook her head. "So what went wrong? Why not hand the diamonds in for a lesser sentence?"

"I wasn't lying when I said Kennedy threatened me. I had to keep them a secret and plead guilty because if I suddenly brought the diamonds out, then he would know that I had double-crossed him, and we'd all be dead. I don't know what Kennedy thought happened to them, but he didn't suspect me."

"So where are they now?"

"I told Tommy to hide them. Ask him, he'll tell you where to find them. Erin." He reached forward and put his hand over hers. "You could take Mom and the diamonds and go somewhere else and lead a good life."

Erin ripped her hand away from him. "Not a chance, asshole. Why do you always have to be thinking of Mom and me?"

"Erin, come on. We have to face the facts. It's not like you can go handing them over to the FBI, can you? They'd ask too many questions."

"I can as it happens. I have a confidential contact at the FBI."

"You have a contact?" Peter didn't look convinced.

"Yes, I do. I can get them handed in anonymously." Tears filled her eyes. "We're going to be a family again."

It didn't take Erin long to find Tommy. He was always hanging around, doing his best to follow Peter's instructions to look after her and Jodie.

"Tommy, stop skulking around out there, it's freezing," she called from the front porch. "Come say hi to my mom and warm up by the fire."

"Uh. You think that's okay?"

Erin laughed. "Of course it is. Oh, and I also just baked a batch of cookies if you're interested."

"Oh … okay," he said with the sideways grin that reminded Erin how young he really was.

She could see he wanted to sprint for the house, but

he walked casually, as if he had all the time and confidence in the world. But when he entered the house and felt the heat from the fire, he parked himself in front of it with his legs crossed.

Jodie sat knitting in the corner and watched him without speaking until he was settled. "I don't know that we've properly met, Tommy."

He jumped up and went to shake her hand. "Hello Mrs. Hart. It's nice to meet you. I've heard a lot of wonderful things about you."

"You've got lovely manners for such a young man. You are welcome in my house any time."

Erin brought out a plate of cookies and a glass of milk. By the size of Tommy's eyes, she imagined he never got treats at home much, if at all. He was long overdue. Having to grow up so quickly, it was nice he had the chance to just be a kid.

She sat down next to him on the floor, leaning against the couch as he scarfed down his snack.

"Thish ish delishiosh," he said with his mouth full.

"Thank you. Chocolate chip are my favorite. I hadn't made them since I was a girl."

"Could I have some more, please?" he asked after swallowing.

"Absolutely. Why don't you come with me to the kitchen and we can put a bunch together for you to take with you. Maybe you could share some with your mom."

"Maybe."

"I have a feeling you'll finish them before you get home."

He put a hand over his face to hide a smile.

In the kitchen, Erin got a ziplock bag, placing a pile of cookies carefully inside. "I visited Peter. Told him that Kennedy was dead."

"Yeah?" Tommy stepped from one foot to the other. "What'd he say?"

"He told me about the work you did with him. The rocks? He said you took them from the police officer and hid them."

Tommy's cheeks went pink. "Yeah. He wouldn't let me tell. Said Kennedy would hurt you."

"You did the right thing. Kennedy would have been mad if he found out Peter had taken them. But Kennedy's dead now. Peter said it's safe to bring them out. It's safe to get Peter out of prison now."

"You sure it's safe?"

"Absolutely. I wouldn't ask you if it weren't."

Tommy jumped where he stood and then ran out the back door. Erin watched as he bolted across the yard and dove at the unkept garden in the corner, against the fence. He pulled at some weeds before she got to him and pulled him back.

"Is this where you hid them?"

"Yup."

"Well, hang on, it's freezing, and the ground is too hard to dig with your hands. You're going to hurt yourself. I've got a shovel we can use."

Her heart was pounding when she brought the shovel back. Tommy snatched it out of her hands and started to dig. When they heard a clank, Tommy dropped back to the ground and pulled handfuls of dirt out of the way until he finally uncovered a small box. He brushed the dirt off it and held it out to her. A genuine treasure.

She took it carefully, afraid to believe that it was real. The day she had hoped for for so long. She lifted the lid to expose a dark purple bag with black string, then quickly closed it again, looking around the yard. It really did feel too good to be true. She took a moment to steady her breath, but Tommy was getting agitated.

"Aren't you going to take them out?"

"Be patient. This is a big deal." She lifted the lid again, then took the bag out and dropped the box on the ground. She could feel the contents of the pouch as she held it in her fingers. A cold wind swept through the yard, cooling the sweat that had appeared on her forehead. Erin turned to look in the kitchen window. Her mom couldn't know about this.

"Open it." Tommy said leaning toward her to have a look.

"Haven't you already had a look?"

"No way. Peter told me not to. I think he thought I might be tempted to swipe one."

"Was he right?"

Tommy shrugged. "Guess I was afraid he was right, so I did what he asked."

"You tempted now?" She smirked.

"No way. Not even a little. That bag is going to get Peter out of prison. That's better than diamonds."

"You know, for a criminal, you're a good guy. All right. Wish me luck."

Tommy held out his crossed fingers, close to the bag.

Erin pulled the bag open and looked inside. Even with the cloudy sky, the diamond sparkled.

Tommy whistled.

"Thanks for keeping them safe."

Tommy shrugged. "It was nothin."

"Not nothing." She reached an arm out and pulled him into a hug.

____

Chapter 33

____

ERIN STOOD by the Ferris wheel, blowing on her hands. She had on a warmer jacket this time, but there was a light snow falling from the bitter gray sky. She stomped over the thin layer that had gathered on the ground while she waited. When she looked up again, she spotted Nick by his stroll. She was surprised to realize she could recognize it.

They met each other, unsure and awkward. At least that's how she felt. Nick looked like he was trying to keep a smile off his face as she reached out to shake his hand.

She didn't linger in the shake, instead, slamming her hands into the safety of her pockets. "Thanks for coming. I know you had to fly from New York, but you're the only person I know I can trust."

That touched Nick deeper than he expected it to. "You said it was important."

"I have something for you," Erin said, wrapping her fingers around the bulge in her pocket.

"So you said," Nick replied, watching her face for any hints. She hadn't said anything other than it was important that he come alone. He told himself it was curiosity that brought him there, but when he saw her, he realized he hadn't gotten over her … at all.

She looked around before pulling out the velvet bag and handing it to him. "I hope you'll know what to do with it and maybe keep the Harts out of it."

His eyes widened as he ran his thumb along the bumps of the bag. "This isn't what I think it is?"

"See for yourself."

He slipped the bag open and looked inside. "I don't understand. Where did these come from?"

"That depends."

"On?"

"Do you want to have to keep a secret, or would you rather not know?"

"Oh-ho, no. I definitely need to know about this."

The warmth and ease of his response was enough to lower her guard, and she slipped her arm through his. "Then let's take a walk."

They strolled around the pier as Erin recounted what her brother had told her and Tommy's part in securing and protecting the riches.

"Tommy. He seems to somehow find himself the hero in this story once again. Maybe I should try harder to get him a job."

"You want to get Tommy a job?"

"He asked me to put in a good word for him at the FBI."

Erin laughed. "I don't know that I could see Tommy working for the FBI."

"He'd be a great undercover agent." Nick stopped and turned to her. "You know, for a second, I wondered if you stole another bag full of diamonds to take the place of the ones that were lost."

"I would be offended by the suggestion, but it's actually not a bad idea."

Nick laughed in amusement, then he shook his head. "I'll say they came from an anonymous source connected to Kennedy."

"Thanks."

"I'm really glad you called."

"I wouldn't have if I had another choice. I didn't want to bother you."

"No, it's not a bother. I'm glad you called. I uh … I actually miss you and your crazy antics."

"Antics?"

"It's as good a word as any."

"For a seventy-year-old, maybe."

"What can I say? I'm mature for my age."

She bumped him on the shoulder as they walked along. "How's the Yenko?"

"You mean the inanimate object that is my car?"

Erin turned to him in mock horror. "If my brother heard you say such a thing."

"Yeah, well, mine's probably rolling in his grave, but yeah, if you're going to be like that then I can confirm she's fine. How are things at home?"

"Good. Even better now. Mom's settled in and doing well."

"Get your chimney sorted out?"

"I did. I thought I told you to stay out of it."

"I don't know what you're talking about."

"Oh, so that guy who contacted me and said you asked him to get in touch, then he charged me next to nothing, that wasn't you?"

"Nope." He kept his eyes forward and grinned.

"Uh-huh. Well, my mom and I are now nice and toasty warm, and with the diamonds going back to their owners, I expect Peter will come home to sit by the fire soon."

"He'll still serve time for breaking and entering."

"I know, but he's served some time already, and even if he has to spend more time, it won't be anywhere close to the sentence he's serving now."

"That's true. And how about you? How are *you* doing?"

"I haven't broken the law since I last saw you, if that's what you're asking."

"That's not what I'm asking."

"Oh, well, I've decided to finish college."

Nick stopped and pulled her around briskly. "Really?" Then he got ahold of himself and let go of her. "You, uh … Where are you going to school?"

"Here in Chicago. Online as much as I can. Mom still needs me around."

"That's good. I'm glad you've made that decision."

"I was thinking of doing a few extra courses on the side."

"What area?"

"Forensic accounting. Thought it might be interesting."

"That is interesting." Nick skimmed his hand down her arm and took her hand. "I'd really like to hear more about it. You hungry? I know this great restaurant."

"Not Italian, I hope."

"Uh, you don't like Italian?"

"I'm just thinking of my encounter at Messina's."

"This isn't Messina's. They've closed down. But it is the same cook. She's an amazing woman. You'll love her. And she makes the best gnocchi."

"I love gnocchi."

"I knew you'd have good taste."

"I do have one stipulation."

"What's that?"

"I don't want to have to change just to walk into a restaurant."

"No, you're perfect just how you are."

"You really think this is a good idea?"

"What, going out to dinner with a guy you like?"

"Who said I like you?"

"It's your body language. Have I ever told you I've been trained in reading body language?"

"For the FBI?"

"Yup."

"Now I'm going to be self-conscious."

"Don't worry about it. I already know everything I need to know."

"But wait. Don't we still have the same issues we had before?"

"Tonight, can we just be two regular people?"

"I'd like that."

He reached a hand around the back of her head and pulled her in for a kiss. It was short and sweet and sent warmth through Erin's body. Being regular felt pretty good.

THE END

Enjoy the book?

Book reviews are the most powerful tool I have as an author to grow my readership. If I had the sway of a New York publisher, perhaps it would be easier to gain attention, but a simple reader review is way better than what any top publisher can offer…

Readers like yourself are what make the biggest difference to an author, and if you've enjoyed this book and wouldn't mind spending a few minutes leaving a review, it would help me out immensely.

About the Author

V F Streets is the author of the Vigilante Justice Series. You can find her on www.pgturners.com or feel free to contact her by email at vfstreets@pgturners.com. Otherwise you can connect with her here -

Acknowledgments

None of my books are published without the help of many. Whether it's encouragement from friends and family, or the editorial skill of my editor, Jenni. Thanks also to Dane from ebooklaunch for making great covers. And thanks to everyone who reads my books. Without you, there would be no point.